Two Brothers

The novels of Stanley Middleton

A Short Answer
Harris's Requiem
A Serious Woman
The Just Exchange
Two's Company
Him They Compelled
Terms of Reference
The Golden Evening
Wages of Virtue
Apple of the Eye
Brazen Prison
Cold Gradations
A Man Made of Smoke
Holiday
Distractions
Still Waters
Ends and Means

Two Brothers

STANLEY MIDDLETON

HUTCHINSON OF LONDON

Hutchinson & Co. (Publishers) Ltd
3 Fitzroy Square, London W1P 6JD

London Melbourne Sydney Auckland
Wellington Johannesburg and agencies
throughout the world

First published 1978
© Stanley Middleton 1978

Set in Intertype Plantin

Printed in Great Britain by The Anchor Press Ltd
and bound by Wm Brendon & Son Ltd
both of Tiptree, Essex

British Library Cataloguing in Publication Data

Middleton, Stanley
    Two brothers.
    I. Title
    823'.9'1F   PR6063.I25T/

        ISBN 0 09 134860 9

To my sister,
Edith

I

The young woman, without haste, made her way up the hill from the market place. She glanced at her watch, checked it with the church clock and decided that she had six minutes in which to do her two-minute journey. The walls of blue industrial brick on either side prevented her seeing anything but the deserted road, the church above to the left, and opposite, exactly to her right now, a Victorian hall, rather ramshackle like a seedy, secular chapel, its front disfigured with ill-assorted fascia boards: W. G. Hopkins, Importer; F. Terry, Wholesale Yarn; B. and H. E. Fearn, Printers.

She turned round to face downhill.

Evening sunshine flushed the sky. Smoky clouds scudded across white, but beyond, behind the Dutch gables of the shops round the market place, all must have broken to produce these spectacular splashes of gold. She stood on tiptoe to peer over the wall; below were the river, narrow but fast now, a railway line, and a clarity of factory sprawl, red-brick and haphazard. Satisfied that she'd wasted an observant minute, she turned below the open iron gates into Church Street, passed a new bungalow, long and white-faced, until she reached the house she wanted.

Up six narrow steps into a path darkly hedged by philadelphus, forsythia, guelder rose and out to a yard paved with the blue bricks of the street wall.

She knocked nervously.

The house, of butter-coloured stone and pantiled, stood at an angle of thirty degrees to the road so that she had no idea whether this door, at the narrow end of the place, counted as front or back.

She searched for a bell, failed, knocked again, waited.

The church clock struck seven, the time of her appointment. No answer. The yard shone wet from a recent shower as wind thrashed about in the front garden. A few feet from the back of the house the wall of the churchyard towered, in old stone, but newly, roughly pointed up. A row of five agapanthus in tubs fronted a small rockery.

She hammered the door again, this time with the knocker, frightening herself.

Footsteps in the street halted, climbed the steps, clumped between the shrubs. A man appeared, looked her over, pushed fingers through long grey hair.

'Mr Weldon?' she asked.

'You could say so.' Immediately he held out at arm's length his right hand with thumb and fingers spread presumably to stop her talking. He was a big man, with a large head on wide shoulders; an enormous expensive overcoat flapped loose from narrow trousers. 'Not the one you want.'

She stood uncertainly.

'You need the man who lives here, don't you?' His voice matched his size, seemed made for bawling across huge spaces.

'Mr Francis Weldon,' she ventured. 'I was supposed to come at seven.'

'And isn't he in?' He tried the knob, battered the knocker, thumped the woodwork. 'Rum. You'd arranged to meet him, you say? You're sure you've not got the date wrong?' She shook her head, annoyed at the vigour of the catechism. The man dipped his hand into the large water-butt, then shook it dry in a spatter of drops on the unopened door. He dragged out a white, ironed handkerchief to complete the work. 'I'm his brother.' Another tattoo. 'He's not in. Now that's not like him. Meticulous.' He laughed at his word. 'Did you fix it by letter?'

He stared down at her.

She began her explanation, not daunted, at a neat attention, her raincoat smart in evening light. Her name was Judith

Powis; she was a student at the Polytechnic and was writing a thesis, well, an extended essay on Francis Weldon's poems. He stuck a hand out, and they shook there on the yard, comically, as the light dipped theatrically and the west wind swooped again. As she stared at her squashed and gloved hand, the man disappeared into space behind the house, reappeared as suddenly.

'We'll go inside,' he said, unlocking. 'I'm Jack Weldon. John James.'

They went through a scullery which smelt of soap, and into a living room, plainly furnished. Two armchairs at either side of an electric fire, four Windsor chairs at a dining table pushed against the wall, bookcases, one Victorian, glassed and leaded, two open. Jack switched on the fire, invited her to sit down.

'It's damp,' he said. 'Always is in these stone places. I won't draw the curtain. He might see the lights wherever he is and come running back.'

Unbuttoning his overcoat completely, he sat down opposite her. His face was broadly decorated by side-whiskers which sprang outwards like grey wings, but his wrists and ankles, she noticed, were slim for so big a man.

'Now, then, Miss Powis . . .'

'Mrs,' she said.

He looked at her unringed fourth finger, twisted his face hugely, like plasticine, with only the eyebrows and fence of whisker unmoved.

'Let's start again. You want to know about my brother, Mrs Powis. That's it, isn't it? Go on, then. Ask me.'

She nervously opened the blue cardboard envelope she carried, fiddled with two or three sheets of paper which she extracted and laid on her lap together with a copy of Francis's last volume, *Words of Ice*, in its dove-grey and white dust-cover. There seemed nothing to say. She cleared her throat and kept silent. Jack Weldon stood, reached for a book, slapped it open on his knee.

'*Who's Who*,' he said, licking his fingers to turn over. ' "Weldon, Francis Jacob. Poet, teacher, born Beechnall, 22 September 1928, younger son of Jacob and Mary Ann Weldon." You've consulted this?' he asked aggressively.

'No, I haven't actually.'

'Not interested in facts?'

She opened her book, turned it, held out the back page. He pulled glasses from the upper pocket of his coat, donned them, peered, laughed with approval at the account of the poet's birth date and place, his four books of poetry.

'How did you get interested in Frank?' Unabashed.

'Dr Byrne, one of the tutors, suggested it.'

'Had you read any poem of my brother's before that?'

'Yes, I had.'

'What?'

' "Forest Fires". "The Call". We did "Safe-keeping" at school. Those are from his first book.' The last sentence fell apologetic.

'You're a reader, are you? You read books?'

'When I have time.'

He laughed again, slapped the insides of his thighs vigorously as if applauding her, then explained in a burst that he had been passing in the street when he'd heard her knocking. At her finale, he'd come up the steps; he was inquisitive, and he wanted a word with his brother, anyway. He snapped his spectacles back into his coat, finger-combed the mane of hair, wrestled again to produce this time a tin of cheroots, offered it to her, and on her refusal asked permission to smoke.

He seemed all energy, unable to light the cigar without rolling, without twisting the chair into creaks. His brown shoes, his three-piece suit were of excellent quality.

'You were born here?' Judith Powis asked. 'And your brother?'

Jack Weldon, cigar opulently alight, pointed with his thumb over his shoulder.

'At Factory House. Our father was chief cashier.'

He enunciated a few sentences, how he used to lie in bed and hear the eight o'clock shift coming in to work, hobnailed boots, shouts, the cling of bicycle bells. As he spoke he picked up from the hearth a sea-washed, rounded boulder, grey with white veins, to balance, weigh in his left hand. When he finished the reminiscence he lifted the stone to his face, pretended to bite into it.

'A batch.'

'I beg your pardon.'

'A little loaf. My mother used to make them on Tuesdays and Fridays. She had the dough rising in the pancheon,' he looked round, leaped breathily, pulled out a four-legged stool from a corner, 'on that. Front of the fire. I don't suppose you know what a pancheon is.'

She explained coolly in exchange that she kept one to make wine. He slapped the top of the stool.

'Local work,' he said. 'Unpolished, except by use. Or bums.'

'How old is it?'

'No idea. Any age. Be my grandmother's, I expect, so let's say nineteen hundred.'

She consulted her notes as he manhandled the stool, lifting it one-handed by a leg above his head.

'Did you have any idea, when you were young, that your brother would be a poet?'

'Solid,' he said, the stool at arm's length now. 'Made out of solid blocks.' He frowned, bit his lip over her question. 'Wouldn't say so. How do you recognize what anybody's going to be? Look at me, now. What do you reckon I am? Now?' She seemed taken aback. 'Go on. Guess.'

'Do you live locally?'

'I do.'

'Are you the headmaster of a junior school?'

'Why do you say that?'

'You remind me of a man who came to the Poly to talk to

us about joining a union. That's what he was. He wasn't so big, really. It's the voice. He rumbled like you.'

'Did he rumble you?' They laughed, she uncertainly. Stool and stone stood contiguous. 'I'm what's called a business man.' She did not answer. 'Why don't you come round asking me questions?' He gestured at her paper. She stared guiltily down. At her silence he laughed again, drew on his cigar, released a lungful of fog. 'I'll tell you. Frank's in the top twenty poets in the country, isn't he? I'm not in the top twenty business men in this town, beg its pardon, city.'

He seemed somehow satisfied with this, added further bravura to his smoke-blowing, well back in his chair, shoulders violently squared. Relaxing, he leaned forward.

'Our Frank was clever at school.' For the first time she made a note. 'But so were other boys. So was I, for that matter. And I'm no poet.'

'You were brought up in the same place, though?'

Again the screwing-up of his face, one side drawn smooth, the other a map of contortion.

'I'm six years older. So that doesn't apply so much. Well, you understand that, don't you?' He looked affronted. 'He was twelve when my mother died. I was at work making my way, getting ready for the army.' Lips pursed, he considered a picture on the far wall. From where she sat light on the glass blotted it out. Catching her glance he said, 'Frank's wife's dad.' Incomprehension noted, he continued. 'Painted that. Up in the woods, somewhere. A parson.' He rose, dashed for an ashtray from the top of a bookcase, ground his cigar savagely out, holding out the ruin for her inspection. 'Now you're going to write down some tommy-rot about being affected by his mother's death. Well, aren't you? So was I. But I was beginning to be a man.'

'You mentioned it,' she said.

'I did.'

'You think that was the most, the most important thing that?'

'God knows. You ask him. Not that he'll know, any more than I do. I'll tell you this. The thing about our Frank's poetry is the surprise. I don't mean seeing his name on a book. I'm used to that. *Over Jordan* by Francis Weldon.' He named the first collection. 'It's what's in them. Take that thing "I know Winnie Greensmith", about how every time he puts the kettle on he remembers this woman. And how he didn't know her very well. His little obsession.' She had not read the poem, shook her head. Jack did not notice, fighting words, hands clasped, skin rasping. 'I knew her. I went out with her a time or two. I was pally with the man she married. I still see her about. We just move now, don't talk. But I couldn't have come up with the like of that in a million years.'

'Why not?'

'She's as ordinary as muck. But he's turned himself inside out. He has, you know. I've sat and read that over and over again.'

'It's not because you know the name and the real person?'

'She's not been called that for thirty years. She's Mrs Palmer. Grown-up family.'

He laughed, loudly.

'Summat out of nowt, eh? More than I can.' He leaned back so that the chair seemed in danger of disintegration. 'I wonder where's he got to.'

She consulted her papers.

'Does he live here on his own?' she asked.

He picked up *Who's Who* from the floor between his feet by thumb and little finger, before rustling the pages over, an inept lay-reader. Out flourished the glasses. He'd found the place without them, so it seemed part of the act.

' "M",' he began, 'that is, married, "1955 Louise May Armstrong (dcsd)," that is, deceased, dead, "one s," son.' He closed the volume, returned it to the shelf, spent a minute there with his back to her. 'It's all in the book.'

'I didn't know. There's a poem about visiting a hospital.'

'There is.'

13

They sat as the fan inside the electric fire ticked, dully animating mock coal.

'You know your brother's poems very well,' she asserted.

'You could say so.' Pensive then galvanized. 'Because I'm in business, you take it I don't read. I went to the grammar school, we called it "secondary" then, like Frank. We were encouraged to read books. I'd say I've as many in my house as he has. It isn't so, these days. Our Cissie's girl, that's my sister, went to the university, took a B.Sc (Economics), was a lecturer at some college or other until she started a family, never read a damn thing bar magazines and papers. And she's an educated woman. A product of the modern system. That's why I asked you if you did any reading.'

'I see.'

'What do you see?' he asked, surprising her.

'You've a respect for literature,' she said, primly.

'In hard-back books.'

'And your brother produces them.'

Jack settled again, as if her sally had pleased him, her quick opposition sedated him.

'Produce?' he said, slapping his chest, with slow, hollow thumps. 'Produce? That sounds more like me. A manufacturer. He does them in ones.' The last word was aggressively Midland. 'Wans'. 'Is that your copy?' he pointed.

'No. It's from the library.'

'Buy your own. Get him to sign it for you.'

Up again, an overweight jack-in-the-box.

'I don't know where he's got to. Unless he's up at my place waiting for me.'

'He's forgotten about this appointment?'

'Looks like it. Though he's not usually . . .' He peered dynamically out of the window.

'I expect he gets a great lot of people . . .'

'Not enough to forget. I suggest you walk up to my house. I'll leave him a note. Like to catch him out. Don't often get the chance.'

'Is this very old?'

'No idea. It's made from local stone. There are quarries round about, mostly worked out now. I'd think, oh, early nineteenth century, but I'm only guessing. It might be earlier. I don't know why he lives here. No proper damp course. It's two little cottages run together. Wouldn't suit me. You think it's romantic, don't you?'

'Has he lived here long?'

'No, he hasn't. When he was married they had a bungalow, in the fields, up by the aerodrome. He still owns it, lets it out. Bought this cheap. Did it up a bit.' He came back into the middle of the room. 'I s'll have to kick you out now. You can come up with me if you like; it's not five minutes' walk away. But you please yourself.'

She thanked him, waited outside where the evening wrecked itself more mildly now, but bright after the darkened house.

Jack Weldon led the way.

2

'This hill is a bridge,' he explained, as they reached the main road, 'over the river and the railway. They dug part of the graveyard out to get through.'

'Did anybody object?' Judith asked.

'No idea. I expect they did. This is a great place for complaints, but they give up. Authority knocked all the heart out of 'em in the Luddite risings. Now they talk about independence and standing up for rights, but that's all they will do. Talk.'

'It's as bad as that, is it?'

'Not for me. I'm an employer.' They made great pace, but Jack Weldon did not keep a straight course. He impressed his personality not only on the pavement, but across his companion's path, with lunges, arm-swings, veering. He offered information about trivia as if she had to be kept amused.

'You've lived here all your life?'

'What makes you think that? No. I served abroad in the army. I set myself up first in Leicester, lived there again, still have a factory there.'

'Is that much different?'

'You wouldn't think so. I wouldn't.'

He ushered her into a private drive off the main road, through shrubs and silver birches up another taller hillock beyond the one where the church stood. 'The happy homestead.'

As they reached the flattened ground at the summit in front of a substantial house, a shower of rain cut down on them, brightening the paving-stones of the area. Weldon swore, laughed, turned his collar up.

'Inside sharp.' They mounted steps, passed through a heavy door with stained glass into an imposing, long hall, bright with wall lamps. 'Anybody at home?'

'You've been long enough,' a woman said, then shut her mouth as she saw the visitor. 'Frank's here.'

'He shouldn't be.'

Jack introduced his wife to Judith, who had her business explained for her. Mrs Weldon, a tall, slim woman, beautifully sober in denim, nodded sympathetically, as her husband pushed off to roust his brother out.

'You can talk to him here, if you wish.' She spoke very quietly, clearly, with a southern accent. She smiled, perhaps at a loss, as they faced each other.

'Here's the truant.' Jack and another.

Francis Weldon was as tall as Jack, taller perhaps, for he stooped slightly, but thin. His face was red, and his slightly prominent eyes, palely blue. The hair was cut short and flattened, narrowing the head, and his face shaven closely shone, on the high cheek-bones, up to the ears. He offered a hand.

'I'm a fool,' he said.

'That's no way to start,' his brother warned. 'This lady's writing an essay about you.'

' "I am two fools, I know," ' she said.

'Eh?' Jack.

'Donne. John Donne.

> I am two fools, I know
> For loving, and for saying so
> In whining poetry,

Francis said.

'I'm a reader.' Judith grinned at Jack, who advanced on her.

'You're a cheeky little bugger, I know that.' He made a

17

formal introduction, and his wife showed the girl, the brother-in-law into a huge drawing room. The windows, framed massively with fluted columns of wood, looked out west, over a broken brightness of sky, darkening houses, a humped church in the distance, a pit headstock two miles off.

Francis remained standing. He was dressed neatly, shabbily, in clerical grey; his trousers though correctly creased bagged slightly at the knees, and hung high from the worn polished shoes. Hands and wrists protruding from the cloth of the sleeves, with no intervention of shirt, were thin, red, strong, awkward. The effect was one of sheepish obstinacy. Whereas John Weldon wallowed in energy, his brother occupied a shiny suit as badly tied sticks keep a scarecrow's jacket wide.

'Sit down,' he said. He had the depth of voice, but no force. He began as she picked a chair on his apologies which he delivered with formality, but rather quickly, handling complex sentences without hesitation. He shook his head, more fiercely than she expected as soon as she demurred and settling opposite, crooked one leg over the other, heaving it upwards with the red hands.

He answered her questions with a polite fluency, not bored, not suggesting he'd been through this before, but diffidently as if it did not matter to him. The blue eyes concentrated on her scribbling pencil.

Yes, he'd begun as a boy. There must be pieces surviving somewhere. He'd not been particularly good, but he'd never stopped. What impressed him now was the nature and size of his mistakes. He had written at the university. They might keep copies of the student magazines in the library; he offered her the dates of his residence. The first poem published nationally was, he thought, in *The Listener*.

So on, quickly, in spurts, for twenty minutes, when he leaned back, escaping from her.

'That will have to do for the present.' He closed his eyes; his hair glowed almost white.

'I'd like to ask you about some specific poems.' Judith felt aggrieved; he'd failed the appointment and now here he backed out before she was anywhere close to anything useful.

'You've a background. Go and read the poems carefully. Then come and ask me questions about them.'

'Are you sure you don't mind?' With sarcasm.

'Ah-ha.' A thin finger pointed at her. A sword flick, fast. He withdrew the digital rebuke, smiled. 'I liked you,' he said, 'for that Donne.' She obediently packed her folder. 'You've seen now that I'm a human being, not a name in a book. That will do.'

'Are people surprised that you're a poet?'

'Can any good thing come out of Nazareth?' He observed her puzzlement. 'I was sent to Sunday school in my youth. My father wanted quiet afternoons.'

'Are you a religious man?'

'Not as you mean it.'

'How do you know what I mean?'

'I don't go to church very often. I don't know whether I believe in a God who has any sort of personality or even consciousness. I don't think there's Providence. Or after-life. That's what you meant.' He spoke without heat, but she felt herself checked.

He nursed his leg again, mildly silent, a grey man.

'What do you mean by "religious", then?' She wouldn't let him get away with it.

'I'm amazed, baffled beyond bearing by the complexity of matter.'

'I don't understand you.'

He rose unfolding himself, stood camel-fashion right foot left of left. 'That's right.' He towered. 'There is no satisfactory explanation. Or no simple one. Science is godlike, isn't it? Sometimes?'

'That would make you a line of verse.'

Francis Weldon considered the sentence, or drifted away. When consciousness of her returned, he apologized for his lapse earlier in the evening. Oddly, she did not feel discomfort with him, only that he had accustomed himself to solitude so that its habits died hard.

'Have you a favourite poem?' she asked.

He shook his head, displeased.

'I wanted to know what I should especially read.'

'You don't need me. Not now. A poem is shared between me, a maker, and you, a reader. Without an audience it doesn't mean anything.'

'And if I don't understand it?'

'It doesn't mean anything.'

Now she joined him standing, but he made no attempt to move from the room. He waited, appeared to be listening.

'Jack would be pleased to catch me out,' he said, after a time.

'Why?'

'He likes to think I'm inefficient. That's not altogether untrue.'

'Are you rivals?' she asked. The blue eyes stared, hardening. His face seemed thinner, reddish wax. He shrugged, childishly.

'He's six years older than I am. And better off.'

'You don't mean that.'

'Sometimes. I can't answer for myself easily. I'm not consistent. Jack works harder than I do. Well, longer hours.'

'He was very careful to let me know he read books.'

'That surprised you?'

'It did. It shouldn't, I suppose.'

The door was pushed open after a peremptory knock.

'Haven't you sat down yet?' Jack Weldon. 'Good God, I'd ha' thought you'd finished. I just came in to say I'll give you a lift home. Somebody in the family has to do right by you.'

Francis searched his pockets, ferreted out, tore off the corner of an envelope and jotted down a phone number.

'That's where I teach. You can leave a message.'

'She can leave it here.'

'I don't want to bother either of you.' Judith.

'There's nothing you'd like better. Especially him.'

Jack invited her to stay for a drink, but she refused. He bustled out to fetch the car. Mrs Weldon joined them, making social noises, until Francis tugged at his sleeves, made for the front door.

'I shall see you, then. Good night.' He was gone.

'Is your brother-in-law nervous? Shy?' Judith felt discomfort at his rapid disappearance.

'He can't or won't get small matters, etiquette, right. Perhaps you said something that's set him thinking, or he's disconcerted himself.'

'I asked him if he and your husband were rivals.'

'What did he say?'

'He didn't seem . . . he wasn't definite.'

'I see.' Mrs Weldon smiled, a handsome woman. 'Jack's long enough, but they'll be chatting outside. Or my husband will. He enjoys laying the law down.'

'He seems forceful.'

'Does he?'

About Mrs Weldon's question there was a diffidence such as Judith had read into Francis's replies, a warning not to encroach further. Polite. Unformidable.

'How did you find little brother, then?' Jack driving her back.

'He'd say a thing or two about himself, but I really wanted him to talk about his poems. He wouldn't. He ordered me home to read them.'

'Frank's not the ordering sort. Not like me.' They moved smoothly away from traffic lights in the Daimler Sovereign. 'I liked the army.'

'He didn't?'

'I wouldn't say that. He did national service. I did a full house in the war. He'd resent authority, in some ways.'

'Because he's a poet?'

'Shouldn't think so. Nobody likes being pushed around. Frank would stand quietly aside. I got myself promoted so I could do my share of the pushing.' His deep voice vibrated like the engine, smoothly powerful. At the next hold-up, he dropped his left hand to her thigh.

'That's mine,' she said.

'So I'd noticed.' He removed it to release the handbrake. 'I'm a lecher, as well.'

'Why do you tell me?'

'So you understand where you are. Women like to hear such things anyway.'

'Does your wife approve?' She felt stimulated into antagonism.

'She knows, certainly. She knows. I don't like to think how she feels about it. That means she doesn't. Approve.' He chuckled, irrationally, not displeased. 'I've not sorted her out to my satisfaction yet.'

'How does she like a poet for a brother-in-law?'

'He introduced me to her.'

'I see.'

'I doubt it.' But he drove silently now, until he began on an anecdote from his youth, when he'd delivered a parcel to a house in the area they were passing through. He'd knocked on a back door, had been shouted in, to find a man soaping himself in a tin bath in the scullery. Unembarrassed, the bather had stood up, searched in the trousers slung across the mangle for money. 'I asked him if he always called "Come in", and what he would have done if I'd have been a woman. "I know what I'd do," the chap said, "and you'd either be flat on your back or scorching it up the street".'

She nodded, did not laugh, issued a direction or two for the end of the journey. As the car stood outside her house, Weldon asked,

'What's your husband's job?'

'Works in a bank.'

'Children?'

'No. Why do you want to know all this?'

'I like the look of you.'

'I'm flattered. Thanks for the ride.' She knew how to get out, but paused on the pavement.

'I shall see you again.' She kept quiet. 'I'll make sure of that.'

'Thanks for the lift.' She raised a hand, marched smartly indoors.

At home, his wife read by the fire, much at ease.

'Good deed for the day,' he said, swinging in with his steaming cup.

'Did she think so?'

'I think people like that girl should learn that poets have brothers. Yes. And that they, the brothers, are no better than they should be.'

His wife turned a page.

'Are you listening to me?' he asked.

'No. Shut up.'

'Have I done something I shouldn't?' he asked in a deliberate leaden voice.

'I don't want to talk. To anybody. Especially not to you. I'd like to be allowed to read.'

Weldon stumbled forward, switched on the television, volume blaring. His wife, closing the book, left the room.

3

Francis Weldon, bag over his shoulder, jumped from the bus at the end of his lane, and, sauntering, marked a light in the kitchen window of his home. It had not been dark when he left this morning, he decided. As soon as he crossed the yard he smelled frying bacon.

His sister-in-law, on the watch, opened the back door.

'It's not burglars.' She looked serious. 'I came across to leave a message from that girl, Judith Powis. She's read *Over Jordan*; she wants to talk. You'd nothing in your fridge, so I thought I'd make bacon sandwiches for us.'

'Is Jack away?'

'In Leicester. Then London.'

Francis cleared his back, changed his shabby jacket for a ragged sports coat.

'I nearly didn't come home,' he said. 'I've a night class.'

'Bacon sandwiches are delicious cold.'

'Why're you doing this?' he demanded. 'Is there anything wrong at Wentworth?'

The electric kettle began to mutter. She took bacon from under the grill, laid it between the slices she'd already cut, quartered them.

'Take and eat,' she said. He opened his eyes at that. 'Tea in a moment.' She busied herself with her own share. 'The girl wanted to come tonight, but I told her you were out. We provisionally arranged for Thursday. Will that do?' Now Kathleen mashed, cosied the pot, mounted it on the wooden stand. 'We'll have milk in a jug. For once. Go on, read your newspaper.'

Kathleen Weldon towered over the table. She moved without effort, imperturbable, like a hired woman, a deaf servant. Her serious face was beautiful, but guarded, eyeing space a yard away from him. When she moved round the table, she took care not to touch him.

He was content to feed, but though he played with his newspaper he read only headlines, and at random. Kathleen opened a packet of chocolate biscuits.

'Luxury,' he said. 'What's up?'

'I never do anything for you.'

'No! Why should you?'

She blushed, darkly red, sat straight-backed in her chair. Twenty-five years ago, he had loved her, or so he'd thought. They had taught for three months in the same school, before she'd moved to the far side of the city on promotion. He'd chased her by letter, in person, until she'd come home with him, accompanied him to concerts though insisting on paying for herself. She enjoyed his company, pulled his leg, suggested outings, read and said nothing about his verse, but when he had proposed marriage, she'd shied away, out of character, awkwardly, as if he suggested an obscenity.

'I don't want to talk about it, even.'

'But I love . . .'

'You only think you do.'

They stood sheltering from the chill in Derbyshire, he remembered, she in a bright-red coat, marvellously dyed the week before, with a fur-trimmed hood. Her nose was pink-tipped; her eyes watered; fog hung cold over valleys where the grass was frosted still, stiff and uncouth. He shivered. He had determined to ask his question this day, had tossed the night, and now, mounting this hill, had stopped her with a hand on her arm and blurted his proposal out.

'Don't say any more.'

'I shall.'

'I'm not thinking of getting married to you or anyone else.' She did not appear put out, even smiled slightly, but stared away into a gap in the hedge, down the slope, fog-hung and icy-damp. 'This is a volcanic sill,' she continued, in the same voice. 'Did you know that?'

'I'm serious.'

'No.' She turned courteously to move uphill, but he snatched at her. She stopped, with an expression of assured patience, comic in the cold.

'I love you, Kathleen. Will you marry me?'

'No, I shan't.' Her voice was icy as the air. 'I like you, Frank. But I've no intention of getting married yet.'

'I can wait.'

'That wouldn't be sensible. I can't promise you anything. If I wanted to be married I think I'd know.' She spoke flatly, logically, with cruelty. This time he let her go, saw the mud on her boots, the swinging coat. The cold squeezed tears into his eyes as she went on, without hurry, her head down, hood-hidden. She turned, but continued walking uphill, backwards.

'Don't stop here all day,' she shouted. 'You'll catch your death.'

Now Francis Weldon folded his newspaper, reached out for the teapot.

'I don't understand you,' he said.

'You never did.'

'Why have you come across?'

'If you're going to take it like that, I shan't do you any more kindnesses.'

'You don't do me any now.'

He swilled his tea, went upstairs to wash and change. On his return, she'd cleared the table, dealt with the pots and, sitting by the fire, read his newspaper.

'I'm off now to my class.'

'It's not quarter to six. You don't start until seven-fifteen.'

'I shall work in the Central Library.'

'Just stay and talk to me for a few minutes.'

He laid his raincoat and scarf across a chair back, sat himself down.

'I've been to see Cissie today,' Kathleen began. 'She's not very well.'

'In what way?'

'She was very quiet. I couldn't get anything out of her. She was odd, withdrawn.'

'How long is it since you spoke to her last?'

'Two, three weeks.'

'You've phoned her? In that time?'

'No.'

'Then why should she start spilling her troubles to you?'

Kathleen did not appear moved by the sharp sentences, opened her eyes wider, nodded, conducted or swashbuckled with the rolled newspaper.

'There's something seriously wrong with her.'

'Did she say so?'

'She hardly uttered a word. Since Emma left home, she's not settled to it, hasn't accepted it.' He made no answer. 'I think she should call a doctor.' Now she looked straight in his face. 'After all, she's your sister.'

'What's Jack say?'

'I haven't seen him. It was only this afternoon. She didn't seem, well, sane.'

'Is that why you got my tea?'

'Don't be stupid. You know it is not.' Though angered, she kept her voice quietly steady, as she stared at him. He thought she'd point the newspaper next. 'Will you go and look at her? When you can. I know you can't tonight.'

'I'll see.'

'She's ill. She really is ill.'

He donned scarf, overcoat, thanking her cordially for the meal, asking her politely to lock up. Troubled, he left the house. On the street, he imagined Cissie quiet in her home, not answering Kathleen, stone-faced, with compressed mouth. The oldest of the Weldon children, Cecilia had looked after her father, until at the age of thirty she'd married Eric Hooper, a local printer, a man just younger than herself who had been in Jack's class at grammar school. They'd settled in a respectable avenue, produced one daughter on whom both doted, if straight-faced, and kept apart from the brothers. Her husband, a decent man, worked hard, made no insatiate demands, though that could not be said of her father, who acted more violently crabby with age, but whom she visited every weekday afternoon. Now that Emma had married, become a mother, moved to Worcester, now that her father had died, Cissie lived her own life, rarely contacting the rest of her family, and noncommittal when she did.

Francis Weldon did not think there was much wrong with his sister, but troubled himself that he took so little pains with her. On the death of his wife, Cissie had made her effort, but had been rebuffed. There was no comfort about her; a desire for order and a suspicion that you were about to inaugurate chaos made her careful, gimlet-eyed. This was necessary with her father, who'd shred his newspaper to see if he could tear steadily in parallel, or pee in the coal-scuttle because he could not bother to traipse upwards, but it did not suit Frank, who hated to be watched, and expected women to talk. Cis had called in the early evening, at inconvenience to herself, he recognized, so that it was easy for him to be out, or on the point of leaving. If he'd ordered her not to come, she would not have minded, he fancied, but he was not certain.

Certainly Kathleen would not get much change out of her sister-in-law. Both were inhibited; each embarrassed, annoyed the other. They'd silently sip tea they'd allowed to grow cold. It would make for an uncomfortable half-hour, but nothing else. Why Kathleen had said 'seriously wrong' he could not imagine. Anger at his own lack of interest? Out of her own incapacity or weakness? Some appeal for help on her own behalf?

Upstairs on the bus amongst the smokers, muzak playing and canned voices advising him to save his ticket because Woolworth's would reimburse him for it if he spent more

28

than five pounds, he forgot the women, considered Yeats and old age, about which he'd talk, he supposed. Outside the library, in bowler hat and smart topcoat, he met his brother-in-law, Eric Hooper, on the way to an evening conference. When Frank inquired after Cissie, Hooper eased his hard hat up from his forehead.

'Not ever so bright.'

'That's what Kathleen said. She called in.'

'I shouldn't pay too much attention to her, if I was you.' A worm turning. 'She'll say anything.'

'That's not the case.' The schoolmaster.

'She's a mischief-maker. Apart from having her hands full with your Jack.'

'I'm asking about Cis. What's wrong with her?'

'Run down. Debility. She doesn't eat enough. She's not been right since our Emma went to Worcester.'

Another two men in black topcoats raised hats to Hooper, inquired where he'd managed to park, sauntered on, asking over their shoulders if he was coming.

'I'll have to be off.' Eric was not sorry for the interruption.

'Shall I go and see her?'

'You know what she's like. But please yourself. I expect you will.'

Francis marched straight across the road to a telephone kiosk.

'You sound just like our Jack,' his sister said. 'I could have sworn it was him.'

'Is that good or bad?'

'He liked the army. Barking at people.'

Not too serious. She sounded bright, argumentative.

'How are you then?'

'Is that why you've rung me up?'

'Yes. I've seen Kathleen. She thought you were off colour. And I ran into Eric. He said . . .'

'He said. He said. The Association of Master Printers. Whisky swillers.'

'He's in the dog-house, is he? Come on, what's wrong with you?'

'Nothing I can do much about. My age. Emma's gone. No energy. Aches and pains.'

'I see. It's mental, is it?'

'Mental? You're about as tactful as our dad. Any road, what did milady Kathleen have to say for herself?'

He explained, bacon sandwich, inert face, fears.

'She's a lot to put up with at home,' Cis pronounced. 'I don't like her. As you know. I'm glad you didn't marry her. I thought you would. She had her pick.'

Cecilia did not like Jack. When the elder brother had started work in Leicester he'd lodged with relatives, but appeared at home on Sundays, sometimes even cycling. He was huge at that age, but without fat, a raw-boned youth with his jacket tight across his shoulder blades, his boots thick-soled. Francis looked forward to the visits, and sat, his new grammar school socks and tie bright, his blazer up on a coat-hanger, to listen to tales of the wide world, where men slapped pound notes on dogs or horses, bought roomsful of furniture on the nod, where women did unmentionable tricks, he did not exactly understand the winks or leers, for these red-faced, wallet-bulgers from Leicester town.

Sunday dinner had its ritual.

Cissie walked to the beer-off for a bottle of ale for her father, on this the only day he drank other than water. Once, sometimes twice, a month, the old man went to chapel; on the remaining Sundays he walked into the park, where he slashed at bushes across the paths with a walking-stick. The choice did not, oddly, depend on the weather, and whatever the itinerary, the family must be at table, chewing a first hot mouthful at twelve-forty-five.

This morning Jack asked his sister to provide him with a bottle, slapped manly silver by the kitchen sink where she shelled peas.

'No,' she said. 'He won't like it.'

'He can bloody well lump it, then.'

'We'll have none of that talk here.'

Francis trembled, blushed, agog, ears flapping. But Cecilia had given in at the sight of the large half-crown.

They sat down to the table exactly on time; the father, smirking his pleasure, unscrewed his bottle and poured, concentrating on flow and froth. Jack did likewise. Cecilia clashed as she served the last plateful, her own. Father Jacob swallowed, wiped his moustache, piled his first forkful, mouthed it in. The others started, in relief, happy.

'What's that?' Jacob demanded, pointing, unemphatic.

'Beer,' Jack answered.

'Who gave you permission to drink beer at my table?' Mild still, inquiring.

'I paid for it myself.'

'You paid for it yourself, did you?'

'And yours incidentally.'

Jacob paused; he had laid down his knife and fork. His hands were flat along the table, thumbs out along the edge.

'Did you fetch his ale, Cissie?'

'Yes, Dad.'

'Without my permission?'

'You weren't here. You were on your walk.'

'How old is he?'

'Seventeen.' The girl, hands in lap, seemed crumpled from her shoulders. She did not look up as she spoke.

'Is that the age to be swilling intoxicants?' The old man seemed to draw the scene out, heighten the dialogue. Only Francis, keenest spectator, continued to eat. 'I asked you a question, my girl.'

'No.' Her voice strangled itself.

'Then go and pour it down the sink.'

She rose, miserably slow, leaned over Jack's place, hand out, trembling. He snatched the glass to his lips, took a swig, held on.

'No, she don't.'

'She don't; she don't. There's your secondary school education for you. She don't. You with your matriculation exemption. Do as you're told, Cecilia.'

She moved, hesitating, unable to reach the glass in her brother's hand. Pushing her chair back, she shuffled towards the culprit, but he, laughing, shifted the beer so that it was on the other side of the table by Francis's plate. Jacob grabbed out, fast, but not sharp enough. His hand and Jack's knocked, overturned the tumbler together, on Frank's dinner, in a great brown spreading stain across the starched cloth.

'You clumsy sod.' Jacob towered, face blood-mottled, shaking in rage. 'You clumsy, whore-bound oaf. Get out of my bloody house and sight.' Not a step.

'He hasn't had his dinner, Father.' Cissie spoke. She did not raise her voice, but her courage was obvious.

'Nor will he get his bloody dinner in my bloody house.'

'He's got to go back to Leicester this afternoon.'

'The clumsy, interfering, boozing bogger will go back hungry, then, until he learns his manners. D'you hear me? Are you deaf?'

Jack, pale, smiled almost cheerfully.

'Bogger?' he asked. 'Chief clerk of Thompson and Dunne? Bogger?'

Jacob, shaking, knocked back his chair, made towards his son, who standing, powerfully, taller than his father, picked up his plate and dashed it at the old man. It hit the waistcoat, gold chain, Sunday watch, and gravy dripped greasily dark, mashed potatoes splodged. The plate fell unharmed to the carpet, rolled a yard, wobbled, spun safe, lay flat. Six feet separated two men. Jacob stared at the midriff mess, paralytic with ferocious surprise. Jack seemed almost at ease. Confrontation blazed, froze endless, until Cissie said:

'Come on in the scullery, I'll clean you up.'

Francis got down from his chair, face beetroot, eyes prickling, but walked steadily round the table to retrieve the plate, to deliver it in the sink. The men did not stir. As he returned he saw Cissie touch her father's arm, lead him away. He passed, not eighteen inches from Jack, but ignored him, lumbering off like a sacrificial ox. They could hear the girl tut-tutting as she dabbed, before she instructed her father to go and get changed; they counted the footsteps on the stairs.

Jack stood embarrassed and awkward as Cissie returned with a bowl of water, dish-rags, the roller-towel.

'You go round the carpet,' she ordered Frank, 'and see if there are any bits. I'll clear the table. Wipe them up, clean, now.'

'I'm going,' Jack said. 'I know when I'm not welcome.'

'You shouldn't have thrown that plate. You might have broke it.'

'Broken.'

At the correction she began to cry, but persevered at her work, clearing, dabbing, finally bustling the cloth up and away to the scullery.

'You know what he's like,' she said, face down to the marked polish of the table.

'And he knows now what I'm like.'

'He's your dad, Jack, when all's said and done. That's no example, is it?' She gestured secretively towards Francis on his knees, and the boy stared wickedly straight into her eyes.

'I'm not his slave,' Jack said. 'Not his, nor anybody's.'

'He's entitled to respect in his own house.' She scurried from the room again. 'I spent all morning cooking that dinner. Now nobody's going to eat a mouthful.'

'You tell that to him, not me. He started.'

'You knew there'd be trouble.'

'And there'll be more. As much as he likes and any time he likes.'

Francis, task complete, looked up to see one tear standing on his brother's cheek. Cissie snuffled; Jack stood big and awkward, brutal.

'You go on, our Jack. Get your things and out the back way. I can't stand no more.'

'I'm sorry, then.'

'You are not. You delight in it. And what's that child going to think, seeing his father defied? That's a brother's example for you.'

Jack moved leisurely, felt in his trousers pocket, extracted a sixpence which he presented to the boy.

'You look after her, Frank, there's a good lad.'

He left. In no time a new cloth was laid, and before a re-clothed father jam roly-poly steamed in white sauce. Francis's helping was huge. Jacob talked, in the fast, not very intelligible gabble of his everyday conversation. Volume and clarity came only with anger and swear words. He was not put out, ate heartily, did not mention the incident, but unusually helped Cissie to wash the dishes instead of retiring immediately to the parlour fire.

The suit appeared, no worse, next Sunday; three Sabbaths later Jack also, but without beer. Cissie was adamant.

'I want you here. Our Frank does. Your dad does, if you did but know it. But we're not out looking for trouble.'

It was not until years later that Francis understood that she sided with her father because she had no option. She worked under his eye at the office, and more so at home. From this time on, she recognized that her old man was afraid of his eldest son, thus the long hesitation before he had pointed at the beer. If Jack had kept his eyes down, she claimed, instead of flourishing the bottle, daring him, nothing would have been said. But from this time, she disliked Jack. He was no ally. He made bad worse.

Now, approaching sixty, she had much the same severity of face as on that day thirty-seven years before. Francis sat down in her front room; she received visitors before a gas fire, made them face the window.

'I've been thinking about that telephone call of yours,' she said.

34

'Go on.'

'You're like the rest of them, a mischief-maker.' He waited for her, but she did not hurry herself. 'You and that Kathleen. Still, there might be some excuse for her. Our Jack leads her a pretty dance.'

'You've been listening to Eric.'

'He's my husband.'

'Now, steady. Is there anything wrong with you? That's what I want to hear.'

'Because Kathleen says there is?'

'I'm not staying all night. You can tell me to mind my own business, and I'll go. But I'd like to think before I did that you understood the question I was asking you, and you didn't cover your answer up with irrelevant verbiage.' Francis spoke rather slowly in a flat voice, but straight into her face. Cecilia shrugged, a sad movement.

'I'm a bit run down.' He waited. 'Anaemic.'

'You've seen the doctor?'

'Yes. And I've been to hospital. They're treating me. They've started. ' She jerked. 'Our Emma's pregnant again.'

'Is that bad?'

'The first one's not twelve months yet. People will talk.'

'That bothers you?' he asked.

'You know it does. You know what they are round here. They'll say she's like a rabbit.'

'Does it honestly worry you, Cis?'

'I know it shouldn't. I should be pleased she's so healthy. But she's educated, Frank, a B.Sc. She should know how to go on.'

'Perhaps she does. It's maybe what she wants.'

The woebegone face, the tight-scraped hair touched him as it angered.

'You think I'm daft, don't you?'

He grinned, began to describe his interview in a television studio. She settled her face to listen. This was better.

4

Jack banged his brother's door, ushered Judith forward.

'Mrs Powis, for words of wisdom.'

'You're early.' Francis, glancing at his watch.

'Mr Weldon picked me up. I'm sorry if I'm disturbing you.'

'You weren't here at all last time. This'll make up for it.' Jack in heavy joviality. 'When you've finished with him, love, walk along the road and I'll take you back.'

Francis gloomily indicated a chair.

'Picked you up? Where did he do that? On the way?'

'He knew I was coming. I rang his house. He left a message at the Poly that he'd be round to Sandon Road.'

'Why should he do that?'

She flushed, hastily turned the folder over.

'Your question shows you think you know the answer.'

'And are you interested in my brother?'

'Not really.'

'Is he interested in you?'

'You think so, obviously.'

He composed himself to answer questions. She fiddled in her folder, her face flushed, fingers thumbs. When she finally drew out the sheets, she was still flustered.

'I want to ask you about one or two poems.' She spoke harshly, even aggressively. 'This one first. "Veteran".' She held the book out.

'I remember it.'

'That's your brother, isn't it? He's the one who fought at Arnhem. He's the one you met in the street and said good morning and you remembered all he'd gone through.

But in their day greeted
Dragon death, in youth, gave
Him as good, shook off his
Handshake, managed a good day.'

The repetition of the verse steadied her as it made her voice tremble.

'No. It's not.' He felt sorry, would have liked to agree. 'But, oddly enough, Jack told me how he'd met a paratrooper on the street, a very quiet chap, wouldn't say boo to a goose now. Jack wasn't at Arnhem. He was out East, then, I think. I put myself in his place. Like Wordsworth and the Highland Lass.'

'I see.' She examined the text. 'Did Jack say anything about fear, and exploding pain, and shrapnel?'

'No. I provided that.' He smiled. 'I don't remember what he did say, to tell you the truth. But it would be something like, "I met Ken Peach this morning. Nervous sort of bloke. He was badly wounded at Arnhem," and then he'd go on with stuff about the man's job or his relatives or his hobbies. I thought about one who'd feared death, and I provided the rest, the polite exchange, the failure to mention battle.'

'You won't give your brother much credit, will you?'

'That's a silly thing to say. He's been complaining, has he?' She blushed. 'Don't worry. You can make your own poem out of that.'

She recovered after a while, asked accustomed questions, fell easily into the discussion about his persona, whether the 'I' of his poems was himself. Francis soon was bored, but did his best, and twice corrected her interpretation of a verse.

'You think I haven't read this carefully enough?' she said.

'Yes. Perhaps. And then I think I haven't done it properly.'

'You don't believe that.'

'No.'

Carefully, she was not dashed, she took him through two other poems, made notes, asked for explanations, but dropped her pencil when he refused to comment on the quality of his work.

'It's the best I can do. I didn't dodge, or cheat. At least I hope not.'

'Do you feel more strongly than other people?'

'How can I judge? I feel strongly, certainly. But, no, I can't speak for other people. Not even my brother.'

'Why did you say that?'

'To pull your leg.'

She accepted his offer of tea, nursed the cup primly.

'I don't feel altogether comfortable with you,' she said. 'Well, I'm not sure that I'm learning anything.' He asked her to elucidate. 'You won't say anything about the background of a poem, how you came to write it.'

'That's literary chit-chat.'

'But interesting.'

'As my poems aren't? Oh, dear. I don't want you there making easy generalities. "He hated, envied his brother." I did now and again, like every other man.' She held her cup to her face, giving nothing away, while he recalled Kathleen.

Twenty-five years ago they had met by arrangement in a teashop, where they ate triangles of toast and sweet jam while they arranged, as usual, the evening's entertainment. Kathleen wore a smart blue coat, with grey fur at cuff and collar, and a cossack cap in astrakhan. For the first quarter of an hour they did not talk freely, as though the gap between the present Thursday and the last Saturday was too jagged to be bridged without blood. They looked away from each other, a handsome couple, shoved out snippets of information like moves in a chess game, affected bogus interest in other people.

When they had nearly finished eating and Francis was pouring his third small cup, she said:

'I want to walk round with you when we've finished.'

'Anywhere particular?'

'No. Just to walk.'

He remembered exactly how she looked, pert and unmoved, making the unusual request as she dabbed her lips, brushed crumbs from her fingers. They strolled from the city centre, up towards the castle, through a cutting called 'The Ravine' and down into the park, where Victorian grandees had built their mansions. Leaves burned gold but thick still on the elms, the limes, and all was quiet behind brick walls and the stained glass windows of commercial success's domestic grandeur.

He took her hand. She was not keen on public demonstrations of affection, but it was so quiet here they might well have strolled in a wood.

'I have to tell you something,' she said.

They stood face to face. He tried to kiss her but she drew back.

'Go on, then.' He stooped, picked up a yellow lime leaf which he twiddled between thumb and forefinger.

'I don't know how to put this. Not really. Your brother has asked me to marry him.'

'What did you say?'

'I said I would.'

It was as if he'd been struck, not with a club or fist, but by some debilitating disease that emptied his legs of power, dried him, dispersed his breath, soaked his eyes with tears. He staggered, feeling for the bole of the tree behind him, feet awkward among roots cracking the pavement. Leaning on the trunk, he could neither shift nor speak, weakened, in a stretch of pain. He could not see properly, but heard himself moan. Later, he imagined a man drilled with a killing bullet would bear his last seconds thus.

Neither spoke.

Had he tried, his voice would have burst into a gabble, a sobbing incoherence. When his strength did not return, while he still swayed, he pushed himself straighter on the roughness of the bark behind him, and stepped out. He was surprised that he could walk. His legs did not collapse. Bone existed. He stepped diagonally past her, moved down the street.

Four or five yards on he became aware that he was dragging his feet and that he moaned at each step. It seemed natural. He did not mind. For five, ten paces he groaned, slouching forward. His hand reaching to wipe tears from his face found his cheeks dry. Bowels wrenched, he dragged to a halt, heaved in a huge mouthful of air, sagged on in the dust.

He had almost reached the end of the avenue, downhill, when he realized that Kathleen was walking behind him. He stopped, without turning, perhaps encouraging her to speak; any word bettered this agony.

'I'm sorry,' she said. 'I had to tell you.'

'When did he propose?' Each word grunted separately. 'Last Sunday.'

'That's why you wouldn't go out with me?' The triviality loomed in importance. 'You'd arranged it beforehand.' She agreed, nodding, and with a monosyllable. 'You weren't open with me.' Again one sound from her, 'No.' He pushed on again, without speed, but she would not catch up, walk alongside.

Every step was painful, not in itself, not even physically, in that it underlined his living, his personality, his consciousness when he needed an anodyne, an oblivion.

As they reached the castle entrance, he turned left up Standard Hill, where she followed. He forced himself to turn, to choke an instruction out.

'Go home,' he said.

'Will you be all right?'

His contempt spilt into tears; his mouth, hard a moment ago, trembled with violence as he limped off, hiding his face. She watched him.

Now, twenty-five years later, bitterness seethed. He did not forget. It was bearable, as he sat facing this girl, Judith Powis, he'd show no sign to her, though he knew with the onset of age, weakness, it would break him again. He would not forget. He preserved its acid power. She sat with her eyes wide open, papers on her knee. He smiled across at her.

'Your brother said you wanted to marry his wife.'

'That's so.' He did not like it, but he could answer.

'You haven't written any poems about that?'

'I don't publish my defeats.' Smooth, ironical. 'Not overtly. Nor too often.'

'But it will be there somewhere?'

'Have you noticed it?'

'I thought I had.' She spoke, hesitatingly.

'Then you've got something to write about.'

'You won't mind?'

'I shan't ever see it, shall I?' You smooth-faced, neat-bummed, little prying bitch with your scribbled insignificances, I shan't read my shame with a red tick in the margin, good point; and you'll be so chuffed with your insight, you teacher's pet, that you'll drink a glass of gin or two to your scholarship and insight, and let your husband up you for your intelligence.

He had got home that evening without difficulty; tragedy does not interfere with bus schedules, and his father had noticed nothing. Jack did not return from Leicester until Saturday night, about ten. He'd had a drink or two, but this did not hide his discomfort. Francis groped round his head for a first sentence, not delivered until Jacob had retired belching and grumbling.

'Kathleen has told me,' Francis began.

'Uh.' Jack produced a whisky bottle from his bags, poured, proffered.

'On Thursday.' Silence. 'You've seen her since then?'

'She rang me up.' He sipped. 'I'm sorry, Frank.'

'What's that mean?'

His brother, legs apart, stood huge, hogged the fire.

'I know how you feel, how you must feel.' He nodded, gestured with his glass. 'All's fair, they say. Love and war. I wish it hadn't been you.'

Two or three glasses of whisky and Francis would have fallen in comradeship on his brother's neck. As it was, he sat glum, hands clasped, eyes glowering at the carpet.

'You won't hold it against me, will you?' No answer. 'Or her?' Frank looked at the wall, at a bookcase, blank-eyed. 'I haven't told my dad yet.' The uncertainty trembled; a big man sowed the wind.

Frank dragged himself back.

'Where will you live?' he asked.

'I shall buy a house here, somewhere. I've been looking round.'

'Since Sunday?'

'No. Kept my eyes open. I shall be working here most of the time. Well, from next year, if all goes well.'

He could afford a house. He had a car, for business. Frank thought he was getting on when he'd bought a second-hand bike.

'We don't know when the wedding will be. You'll come, won't you?'

'No.'

'Why not? It's no use holding it against us.'

'No.'

'Please yourself then. You're as bad as our Cis. I told her. She said, "That's our Frank's girl." '

A bitter gush of triumph at that, but it died, sank. He hated his brother's smug face, the hands clasped behind him, monarch of all he surveyed.

'Good night,' Francis said.

'Are you going to bed then? Won't you have a drink with me?' Jack waved the whisky bottle, helplessly, pointlessly. 'Show there's no ill-feeling.'

'No, thank you.' Educated voice. 'Good night.'

A good exit, but he'd lain struggling awake. She'd preferred Jack to him. He'd never compared himself with his brother. They'd never aimed at the same goals. Francis had, without consideration, judged himself superior in that he'd outclimbed his brother on the educational ladder, but Kathleen, spry, beautiful, sharp as a blade, had decided the other way. His degree, his culture, his literary ambition scored lowly against money, house, motor car. What of his appearance? He'd seen his brother as big, rough, uncouth, energetic but crude. Kathleen had no qualms. She knew which man she wanted. Frank hated her more virulently. She had been trained to recognize quality, and had failed to do so. The pale, beautiful face sabred his brain into agony. She, she.

For three weeks he had lived in blind misery.

He had just managed his job, had found relief in ordering and instructing, but let his mind slow down, then the pain burnt. He slept fitfully; dreams banged his head, and when he woke it was to a gross anticipation of disaster. Physically he seemed affected, listless, aching, aged. He could not read nor listen to music. When he wrote he scratched down clusters of flat clichés, his screaming pain reduced to platitude. He could not concentrate on his father's brand-new television screen; desperately he gulped down whisky at night.

Twenty-five years, his success, his own marriage, the death of Louise had not smoothed the scar. He hated this young woman on its account.

'Is that all?' he demanded, when she'd finished her tea.

'There's one thing I'd like to ask you to do,' she said. 'You might be angry.' She waited, in vain, for his comment. He folded his arms in mock exasperation, grinning so that she disliked him, reading into his expression a contempt for the essay she meant seriously. He did not budge, gave no help. 'Would you write me a poem about my, my,' she paused, having the word ready, 'inquisition?'

That surprised him.

'Not a bad idea.'

'Will you, then?' She looked eagerly young.

'We'll see.'

She gave him a hand with the few pots while he inquired about her husband, her plans. They were not even considering a family, their first priority was a house with garden. She explained her worries about the possibility of unemployment once she'd finished her course, claiming that though she did well in college examinations, there was no certainty of work in the locality.

'You wouldn't leave your husband? Temporarily?'

'Not really. He'd mind if I did.'

'He couldn't look after himself?'

'Yes. He's as good a cook as I am. And very good with his hands. But he wouldn't want us to live apart.'

'You wouldn't mind.'

'I would.'

He saw her to the street gate. She walked handsomely, so that he stood, half-hidden, watching her, in the direction of his brother's house.

5

Judith and her husband sat with Jack Weldon in the restaurant of the Mansfield Club.

They looked uncomfortable in glad rags, apprehensive at the coloured marble of the pillars, the substantial mahogany doors, furniture, surrounds, the heavy, starched table-linen, the silverware, the silent, swooping waiters. Their host, on the contrary, appeared slightly crumpled, but much at ease. The young woman on the downstairs bar knew his name, as did the head waiter here and the flying Italian; the proprietor, in by chance, had waved a hand, called him, 'Jack'. Now, after excellent soup, he was explaining himself.

'I have to make up to your wife for that unsociable brother of mine. His idea of a good meal is a cheese sandwich with pickles. And this is the place where I do some of my best thinking. There's no rush.' The Italian's feet hardly touched the floor as he dabbed and served with volatile obsequiousness. 'I can think about what I'm doing. So I come in once or twice every week. Kathleen's no time for meals out. And she gets worse. So I come in on my own. Always meet somebody, if I want to. And now and again, I'll bring company in, like you.' Their faces were tense, peaky, like urchins at the school treat.

Judith, in fact, enjoyed herself. She recognized the formality of Jack Weldon's talk; this was an occasion and his speech must be made appropriate, stilted, above average, perhaps even ironical of itself and yet with a large ingredient of truth. He needed to play the host, and advertise himself in a place where they could be overawed. She admitted that he was succeeding; affluence polished these doors, shone this weighty silver cutlery. Spirits sharpened every word; the air was meaty with cash.

'Doesn't Francis come here, then?' she asked.

'He's been. He's been.'

'Was he impressed?'

'He doesn't give that impr . . . didn't seem to be. But he wouldn't miss much. No, that isn't right either. There's a lot of the obvious he doesn't see. But he's on to his concerns. He'd note anything he could use.'

'How would he know what was useful, and what not?'

'Your wife's intelligent,' he said to Alan Powis, who grinned.

'He's realized,' she answered for him.

'He wrote a poem about knives and forks. He was a blind man weighing his table implements and because they were heavy and he could feel the embossed handles he prepared himself for a finer diet than if they'd been plastic in a café. And yet he was a poor, not rich, chap, not used to luxury.'

'I don't know it, at all.'

'Perhaps it hasn't . . . yes, it has. In the *New Statesman*. He showed it to me. Months after I'd brought him in here. Suggested everybody was ruined. By materialism, though he didn't say that.' Jack chewed on a hearty mouthful, encouraged them with his finger to taste the burgundy. 'Give me this,' he balanced his knife across his palm, 'I expect something worth eating. Surprised me he thought so. Pulled his leg about it. It ended something like, "The poor are never hungry nowadays." You bloody Conservative, I told him. You're worse than I am.'

They laughed, obediently. He pressed them to admit they liked it here; they acquiesced. Expansive, he leaned back, explained that by calling in at lunchtime he had done himself a power of good, by chance. The anecdote rambled, exchange of ideas, two phone calls in the afternoon, Bob's your uncle, a bit to be made, given a year or two. It sounded pathetically like boasting to Judith, chest-beating.

'Francis wouldn't come in here on his own?' she asked. 'He's not a member.'

'Don't you think clubs like this ought to take in distinguished people such as your brother even if they aren't rich enough to pay the fees?'

'He could afford the subscription. It's not so high as all that. He prefers it outside.'

He spoke without emphasis as a chef, white hat, blue flames, prepared them *crêpes suzette* on a trolley. They watched; the deep voice sounded. The conjuring over, they turned to eat.

'Good?' Jack inquired.

They made noises of approval, satiety.

' "The poor are never hungry nowadays." Does that remind you of anything?' They offered no answers. ' "The poor ye have always with you." The Bible. Jesus and Judas Iscariot. I told him. And do you know what he said? "Jesus could be wrong. Even when he exaggerated." "Our dad wouldn't have liked you saying that," I said. "He's another who was wrong as often as right." '

Jack switched his head to act the two speakers. When he spoke his brother's lines he sat up straighter, pursed his lips, a vinegary pedant. The performance was comical, a caricature, but not without its truth. He reduced the bluffness of his own speech, as if he were a disciple, ardent to learn, snubbed by Frank's hen-like stare, his thin gruel of instruction. When the meal was done, he led them to the downstairs bar, suggesting liqueurs.

'We shall ruin you,' Judith chided.

'Expenses.'

'Why do you do it?' She knew.

A couple forged up to the bar, dressed to kill. The woman stood draped with elaborate shawls over the plainest of gowns. She was pretty, with tinted hair, stiff as a bonnet. Both greeted Jack who looked them over at length. Neither resented the scrutiny, seemed to expect it; the man signalled Weldon aside, whispered with long-faced importance. Jack scratched the chest of his waistcoat, raking noisy swathes, neglecting the woman who moved a stool, perched on it, smiling at the Powises. Alan mentioned the weather, Judith summer drought; both began on gardens. The look on the woman's face was fixed, a shop assistant's attention, all teeth.

'Well, it doesn't rain in here,' she said. They sat, taken aback.

'This is the last place,' Judith answered. The woman simpered into her gin, then started.

'My God.' She blushed under her make-up, leaned back to rest her hand in the middle of her companion's back, gesturing. He followed her becking, towards a group at the door.

' 's a free country.' Rudely. He turned away. She, jittery now, breathily described the Livingstone's daisies which had done so well for her in the heat.

The other party, three people had crossed the room, made talkatively for an upstairs bar.

'Thank God.' She blew breath out as they cleared the place, but offered no other information. Garden flowers were an inadequate tonic, so they looked with fervid interest at their glasses. Jack Weldon and the man were still hard at it, beating each other in low voices; too solid, substantial these citizens for infantile confabulation, with black, formidable backs. 'That was a close shave,' she said, fell silent.

Judith talked about buying a print, but caught no one's interest. Alan peevishly evaded her eyes, shrugged. The conversation between the men concluded, abruptly.

'You won't want to stop, then?' To the woman.

'What do you think?'

'You're a bloody nuisance.'

He winked at Judith, a fat, strong man with false teeth, who drained his drink. His companion gathered her shawls, without haste, smiling still, pensive and concerned only with appearance. The pair left, shoulder to shoulder.

'Drama?' Judith asked.

'You could say so.' Jack collected glasses, reordered without permission. The girl in the bar seemed in on the secret. Before she had completed the service, a man blocked the upstairs doorway, frowned. Judith recognized him as one of the party who had passed through, though in years, build, attitude he was indistinguishable from the one who'd just left, middle-aged, paunchy but strong, a scowler. He stared round the room, made a murmur of dissatisfied satisfaction.

' 'Evening, Mark,' Jack called. A dyspeptic jerk of the head in his direction, a word.

' 'Evenin'.'

'They've gone.' Did he laugh?

'I can see.'

The doorway seemed suddenly light as he left, then darkened as the panelled wood silently swung inwards.

'The wronged husband.' Jack picked up the drinks. The barmaid conspiratorially arranged her face. 'Interesting.' He occupied a chair, Hunnish in a Roman villa. 'Joyce,' he sketched the shawls in the air, 'left him no more than a week ago. Marcus Wells, light engineering. Three kids, still at school. But the interesting thing is,' he lay back in his chair, thrusting belly and genitals upwards, handling his thighs, 'our friend wasn't the concerned party.' He paused on his last word, mischief puckering his big face, reached out for his drink.

'Go on,' said Judith. 'Don't keep us in suspense.'

'Chap in here,' again the hand movements, as if they needed help with the identification, 'business associate of mine, do a lot together these days. Nothing to do with this ta-ta. Brought Joyce in here, for a meal, because he spoke to her on the phone. Wanted Sparkes, man she's run off with, but he's in Brussels, talked to her, felt sorry, said he'd take her out.'

'Was that wise?' Judith in cock-sparrow ignorance.

'Bloody stupid. If you've just eloped, you don't flaunt

49

round with somebody else. Or do you?' This violently at Alan. Jack scratched his head deep as ploughing. 'But there you are. And the first sod she runs into is her husband.' He laughed, hurling sound in gobbets to the ceiling. The bar-girl smiled. If one only saw him, Judith thought, without the noise, one would think he was having a fit, or crucified with asthma. 'Christ knows what he'd think. It can't be much over a week.'

'Did he, was it expected?' Alan floundering.

'Don't think so. Marcus isn't the wife-swopping sort, is he, Sue?' The girl froze, polishing a glass, looked alert intelligent, unmoving, unanswering. 'I'd think he'd be shaken. Not that I'd leave home for Joyce, I'll tell you.'

'She must have been unhappy.' Judith.

Jack eyed her as if she spoke Greek.

'Every bugger's unhappy, aren't they? We can't get our own way, and we don't like it. And there's only one answer to that in my book. Money.'

'That doesn't . . .' Judith began.

'No. It helps. That's the top and bottom. I can come in here, and keep warm, and have people to talk to and things to look at. All bought.'

'Wouldn't you get much the same in a pub?' Alan.

'Sure. Not so comfortable, but, yes, you could.' He changed tack. 'I've seen men fighting in here. They shove 'em out into the street. I laid one on a man in this room. A lot younger than me, but it stopped his yapping. Didn't hit his face; no need. Shoulder-joint. That was enough.'

They fell silent.

'Funny thing. Nobody noticed, or appeared to. And yet on the housing estates, in this city, there are men, and women, setting about each other every night of the week. It's their way of settling scores.'

'People of your age?' Judith asked with intent.

'Well. Mostly youngsters. But the old brigade lash out with their fists. It's expected. Drunken tantrum, you say. And they don't fetch the police unless it gets either too serious or too public.'

'You approve, do you?'

'I don't do one thing or the other. It's the way of these people. Would you say it was worse than the law courts? It's their way. And sometimes such tag-rag make money, and then they come in here. And they'll brawl here as they do on the street corners.'

'Like you.' Judith.

'You should watch your wife.' The voice rumbled below the stare. 'No. Mine was deliberate, calculated; and worked out as I expected.'

The door opened again; Marcus Wells, glum and hangdog, framed himself. Jack grinned his delight. The man waddled across.

'Who was that in here, with Joyce?' Phlegmy voice; face red with broken veins, jowled. The question wasn't rude, but lacked a refining introduction, a stance, a hint of obligation.

'You know damn well who it was.'

'Walter Wilkinson.'

Nobody budged; a tableau of un-breathing. Jack relaxed first, slapped the table.

'Sit down, Mark. What'll you have? Go on, man. Get the weight off your feet. Gin, is it? Straight? Neat gin for Mr Wells, Sue. Sit down, man, for Christ's sake.' He edged a chair suitably with his foot. Wells obeyed as Jack shot up to the bar. 'Get this down you. Mrs and Mr Powis. Friends of my brother.'

Wells saw them with bloodshot eyes. Though he had picked up his glass he did not lift it to his lips. The hand trembled; the gin was safely lowered untasted. As if to comfort himself, to reassure the world, he went through his pockets, producing from the first he'd touched a case of cigars. These he offered round, and on Alan's refusal, and with Judith's permission he and Jack lighted up.

'That's better,' Jack said. It was. A richness of aroma,

suitable to the décor. Judith smelt Christmas, smiled her pleasure.

'What's bloody Wilko . . . ?' Wells huffed, snuffed the sentence out. His eyes were like a cow's on a butcher's floor.

'Sparkes is in Brussels.'

Wells's face sagged at the name, but he sucked his cigar.

'And what's he,' hand-movement, 'doing then? Wilkinson?' He drained his gin, stood rapidly up, dazed, thanked them, said, 'It's a bastard,' knocked a chair over making for the door. Jack restored order to the furniture.

'What'll happen now?' Judith.

Jack shook his head. Hopeless. Hopeless.

'Is he, Mr Wells, upset?'

'There are three kids to be looked after. Mightn't be a bad thing, a housekeeper. Specially if they're always rowing. Never got on with my kids. Too busy for them, and they knew it. Both away from home. Frederick's just qualified as a solicitor, lives in Oxford. Helen's still at university, but got married. Didn't tell us. Last summer. Finished her degree, spliced some young lecturer. We haven't seen the man, so we've nothing against him that we know.'

'What's she doing now?' Alan asked.

'Qualifying as a history teacher. I couldn't understand her. Sent us a letter on the day of the wedding. Her mother hasn't recovered. Doesn't say much. Just holds it against me.'

'You'd think she'd want the trimmings?' Judith. 'It might have been the man.'

'Kitto. From Cornwall. I can't fathom it. Helen was friendly with her mother. Like sisters; used to make things together, go on shopping expeditions, picnics. Then she started to mention this man, Harold, and Kathleen said it was her final year, hoped she wasn't throwing her chances away. They had a bit of a bust-up. I supported Kathleen, though she said I didn't. That was at Christmas. Bloody awful holiday. She just turned up at Easter for two days. Revising. Could do it better back at college. Got an upper second so she wasn't wasting her time. Then got married.'

'And she's not been to see you?'

'Yes. She came up to collect things in August. Pleasant enough. Off-hand. No idea what she's done to her mother, no more idea than flying in the bloody air. Baffles me. I catch the blame, of course. I'm responsible. I'm the criminal.' He spat the words out with bravado. 'I got hold of her. I asked her about presents. "Buy us what you like," she says. "What the bloody hell d'you want?" I asked. "You should know," she says.'

Weldon relapsed into a huge silence, hand across his mouth.

'Why won't she bring her husband home?' Judith asked.

'She couldn't that summer. He was lecturing in America, or researching. That's why they got married in such a hurry. Didn't tell us, because they thought we'd try to stop it, or postpone it.'

'But they could come up from London. At weekends.'

'They could, but they won't. She's making a thing of it, now.'

'And you never hear from the husband?'

'No. She showed us the wedding photographs. He looked presentable. There's no bloody sense in it.'

'You gave them a present?'

'I did not. Kathleen sent them a cheque.'

'And you,' Judith leaned forward, 'didn't agree with that?'

Jack pulled melancholy, comic faces.

'Agree? She's money of her own to do as she likes with. I wanted to make a bit of a splash for the girl. Top hats and Rolls-Royces, honeymoon in Greece or India. I'd have coughed up. I'd have complained in here, but that's only a way of boasting. That girl's not the faintest inkling what I think about her.'

'You've never told her?'

'Of course I've never told her. She'd ha' been frightened out of her wits if I'd tried. But she could have given me the chance.'

'If I were you,' Judith said, 'I'd write and say that you and her mother were coming down to see her to discuss presents.'

'Kathleen wouldn't.'

'Go yourself, then.'

'You talk like her mother. How we've got ourselves in this state I don't know. But Kathleen's not reasonable, nowhere near it. Nor me.'

He fell to silence, brooding on his cigar, sending wreathed smoke upwards. Suddenly he pulled himself together, jerked a hand at Alan, asked,

'What do you think, then?'

'Do as Judy says. Go down and see her. You should make the first move.'

Jack sighed, stood, rolling his shoulders.

'Come on, you two. Time I got you home.'

He did not, however, dismiss them straight away, but drove them down to the river where they sat in half-darkness on the embankment watching the play of light on the oily water. There Weldon boasted a little, spoke about his own share of a prosperous club they could see floodlit on the far side, complained about the difficulty of replacing a machine in his Leicester factory, a place which cost him trouble for next to nothing in profit, described a brush with a union, an inconclusive affair, with everybody boxing clever.

'You're socialists, aren't you?' he finished.

'If anything.' Alan, startled.

'You'll change. If there's half a chance. If there's not fighting in the streets.'

'What makes you think . . . ?'

'I know I'd bloody well fight, streets or anywhere else, for what I wanted if I was pushed far enough.'

'Aren't you one of the pushers?' Judith asked him, but he laughed, began another industrial anecdote, turned his car, delivered them home, where the Powises sat enjoyably until midnight making neither head nor tail of the man.

6

Jack Weldon met his wife in the hall, said he'd eaten. Immediately, she'd swung round to return to her own devices, having demonstrated token care.

'I've made my mind up,' he said, stopping her, wrestling his overcoat off. 'About Helen.'

'Yes?' She turned, without pleasure.

'If Helen won't come to see us, we'll go and see her. What about Saturday? Is that all right with you?'

'You go. I shan't.'

'That's not sensible, now, is it? We should make the first move if we want a reconciliation.'

'We? You.'

He hung his coat in the cloakroom, returned rubbing his hands vigorously. She had not moved, not changed her expression.

'Aren't you bothered, then?' His voice was aggressive, but strangled.

'You say some silly things.' He thought she'd walk away. 'They don't want to see us. I don't know why. You don't. So let's leave it alone.'

'You can leave things too long. They've taken the hump, or you have. We should go, and give 'em a wedding present.'

'They've already had one.'

'That was from you.'

'You think I'm unstable, that I'm making a fuss for nothing. Perhaps you're right. But if we went, I should have the talking to do. I should make the apologies. You'd be there with your cheque book, as if that was the answer to everything. Well, I'm telling you now that it isn't. I am not prepared to visit them to make soothing noises. For whatever reason they didn't see fit to invite us to their wedding. That's their look-out, and they must take the consequences. If they turn up, I shall be friendly enough, I shan't bar the door, but I'm damned if I see why I should chase down there. . . .' She broke off as if she'd observed some interesting happening above her head, staring so strongly obliquely upwards that he followed her eyes. Nothing. The long cross-landing upstairs.

'Now, look here, Kathleen . . .'

'I'm looking.'

'We can't let it go like this.' Pacifically. 'She's our daughter.' His wife considered the statements, then turned to leave. 'I'm talking to you.' She affected mock humility, hands clasped, eyes lowered. 'I'm sorry,' he said. 'But we ought to do something.'

'You do it,' she said briskly. 'Ring them up, arrange to see them.'

'I'd like you to . . .'

'No. I've told you. I'm not coming.'

'Why?'

'We don't need to go over this a hundred times, do we? Helen has done something I don't approve of, for which there's no excuse. I'm not making a great hoo-ha about it, but at the same time I'm not begging to be taken back into favour.'

'Why didn't she invite us to the wedding?'

'She thought we wouldn't approve. Unless she's ashamed of us.'

'Is that likely?'

'Yes, it is. I know in your eyes she can do no wrong, but she doesn't see us as any great shakes. You've got money, but you shout and drink, throw your weight round. Harold disapproves perhaps.'

'What are his parents, then?'

'His father's a GP. So's his only brother.'

'How do you know that?' he asked, near anger.

'Oh, for God's sake. She came over, didn't she, in August? I asked her a few questions. As you should have done.'

'You didn't tell me the answers.'

'Did you ask?'

Jack shuffled uncomfortably to his right, ramming fists into trousers' pockets.

'Did they attend the wedding? His relatives?'

'I don't think so. I'm not sure, but . . .'

'So it's nothing to do with us?'

'I don't know. I don't care much. But we shall find out in Helen's good time.'

'Next Saturday. I shall ask one or two things.'

'You do.'

Kathleen waited as if to be dismissed. Her husband lumbered about the hall, uncomfortably, but neither suggested that they should sit somewhere together.

'There's more in it than meets the eye,' he began. She did not alter her expression at the cliché. 'One thing I don't like.' He paused for an unforthcoming interruption. 'Your attitude. You're not acting right.'

'I shan't quarrel with you.'

'I can see you're annoyed. So am I. They were fools. But you shouldn't take it out of them just because you're, well, dissatisfied with yourself. You never write.'

'Nor do you.'

'I work. It's your job to do these family chores. You've the time.'

'But no inclination.'

'That's because there's something wrong with you.'

'Such as what?'

'I'm not looking for trouble. I don't want more rows here as well as there. But you're like an iceberg, a bloody, miserable iceberg. Nothing suits you. Nothing's right. You're like a wet week. What's got at you?'

'What, indeed?'

'You've got a comfortable home, all the money you want. I do my best for you.' She raised her eyebrows. 'You can pull your faces, but if you think I enjoy coming home and barely hearing a word out of you . . .'

'You're not to blame?'

'I'm not saying that. I'm what I am. But I do the best for you I can. I'm not perfect. But, by God, compared with you, I'm . . .'

'Well?'

'What's the use? We'll rave and bawl, and in two days we'll be back where we were. It isn't worth the energy.'

She did not answer, sniffed, waited for him. He did not immediately leave, but hung about helplessly, expecting something to happen, some soothing gesture, word, look from her. He clumped away unwillingly. As soon as she heard the door of his study close she put on a coat, went out on to the patio, where she stood blinded in the darkness. Up here, behind the trees, she was cut off, in an almost rural solitude, but she walked to the far end where she could see now the houses on the main road, and, beyond, lines of lamps on the far side of the valley, the roads of the new estate, farm land less than ten years ago. The siren of a police car hooted, approaching, was silent. Another, close, howled. A third screamed on the road below, and momentarily she saw the flash of its turning blue light.

Kathleen listened.

She'd no wish to quarrel with her husband, nor to establish rapport. She wanted to be left alone, to drift, to exclude herself from every thing, body, to be cold, untouched, unfeeling. It did not matter to her whether Helen appeared or not; problems would gnaw, action be required. She needed solitude. Leave me alone. The appeal itself demanded too much energy. She shrank inside her coat, listening.

The police cars were circling like mechanical, angry wasps. Or mad boys at some game. Soon she knew the front door would open as Jack, he couldn't resist, would push out to see what the row was. She moved sideways, to cover, out of any area he could light, pulled at her collar, waited distant and uninterested.

Francis Weldon, walking the streets, stopped in the welter of sirens. The tumbling in his head, an inconsequential farrago of repetitions, neat havers, self-advertisement, obscenities, modest poses barely covering arrogance, a half-phrase of verse, 'a candled Christmas Eve', stilled itself to concentrate on noise battering between houses. A patrol car braked, leapt left, not thirty yards away. He turned back, uncertain, made his mind up, followed, half ashamed. He remembered his father's judgement on a neighbour: 'She'd turn out to watch the dust-cart.' So would he, now.

As he edged round the corner he could see two white cars along the road under a street-lamp. Already people opened doors, pottered in shirt-sleeves to the front garden gates. The staple fare of television served on your own pavements.

He slowed down, crossed the road, fortuitously on the spot.

Another car braked hard. Two policemen dashed out, into a garden. From some distance there was a shout, then silence round the one policeman, the three vehicles. A pedestrian with a dog joined Francis.

'Bit of excitement, eh?' No, he did not know what was happening; they must be after somebody. Francis Weldon put his head back to stare at the dim stars. From behind one of the houses there was noise, a commotion, nothing much. They waited. Two policemen frogmarched a prisoner; all were hatless. When they reached the first car they shoved their man on to the side of the car, face down, his arms spreadeagled on the roof. They pinned him, hands flat, in a second. A third stood behind, searched the body, violently patting, again, up, down. They turned the figure, frisking the front. 'No.' Police voice. Handcuffs clapped on. Now there was a cheerful handing back and donning of caps. The prisoner, a young Negro, slimly leaned curved against the car, like a boxer over ropes. The policemen did not hurry themselves, dusted jackets, chatted jovially. 'In.' They bundled the man inside, took without haste to their cars; two drove off leisurely enough.

'I wonder what he's been up to?' Francis's neighbour. 'Must have thought he was armed, to search him like that. Unless it's routine procedure nowadays. Shouldn't be surprised.'

Frank replied with grunted assent, crushed, uncertain.

'It's a bogger, isn't it? Men wi' guns. Don't seem like our country. Well, come on, Bessie, or we s'll never get us walk in.'

While Francis retraced his way, he found himself trembling, as if he were implicated. The street hummed alive still, with knots of people, running children, lights from open doors, uncurtained windows in straight-edged shapes over gardens, fences, privet. He was pleased to reach the main road, felt he had escaped from some polluting contact, straightened his shoulders. A woman waited some yards ahead, headscarfed. He recognized Kathleen.

'Thought it was you,' she said. 'What was all that?'

He described what he had seen, grudgingly, in shame. She walked alongside.

'Are you going out?'

'Just a walk,' she said. 'I heard the noise. I thought I'd look.'

'Isn't Jack at home?'

She did not answer, and they turned together into his street. He invited her in, as she obviously expected it. She turned on his fire, dragged the curtains harshly along their runners, then flinging the scarf, scarlet silk, across the table, walked about the room, touching objects, opening books, lifting the lid of a biscuit box, allowing it to clang shut.

'Whisky? Tea?' he asked.

'Both.'

As they sat drinking he described the arrest of the Negro. Kathleen did not listen carefully, fiddled violently with her handkerchief, dragging it taut; not until she had given an account of her quarrel with Jack did she calm herself.

'I'm unreasonable, aren't I? About Helen?' she asked.

Francis uglified his face in thought.

'You think so, don't you?' she pressed. 'You might as well out with it.'

'Who are you getting at?'

'What do you mean?'

'Is it Helen? Or is it Jack?'

'It's no use trying to affect him. He's like a stone wall.'

Oddly she did not now seem much disturbed, crossed her legs, stretched them, lifted her face towards the ceiling. The fine features in full light were pale, in pride. He wondered how much she had changed in twenty-five years, in the twenty years since she had thrown herself sexually at him for no good reason he could think of. He did not bother to get up, go across to her. On occasions like this he suspected she hardly knew he was in the room.

'You're taking it out of yourself,' he said.

'Trust you to try and be clever.'

'I don't suppose Helen cares much. She'll be busy, and happy. Has she written to you?'

'A thank-you letter. For my present. Have you heard from David?'

The mention of his son did not hurt, seemed no more lethal than the glare from a sullen child.

'No, he's not been near.'

'Has Dave,' she seemed to haul her words into sentences, 'ever said anything to you about your poems?'

' "Congratulations." ' He felt sorry for her. 'When a new book's come out. I sign one for him.'

'Does he read it?'

'I expect so. I've always imagined so. He doesn't comment.'

He did not ask why she inquired. He had emptied cup and glass, and now waited on her.

'Jack's been talking about your writing, since that Powis girl started. Is she any good?'

He shook his head.

She made a small noise of dismay or disappointment.

'Jack sees her,' she said. 'Takes her out. Has taken her out. And her husband.'

Kathleen was smiling now, but rocking her head, downwards stiffly and smoothly towards the right shoulder. 'I think she's more interested in you.'

'Good for her.' He'd stop that rot.

'You and I don't live in the same world.'

'In what way?' Cold words, hard as dominoes.

'Nothing bothers you that I can see. Or nothing to do with us. Not even David. You float about. Nothing's ever got anything to do with you. If anybody asked me who I knew least among my acquaintances, I'd have to say you. Your son leaves home. You do nothing, don't even speak about it. If you're pushed, you'll act, but that's as likely to be heartless and silly. I send you to see Cissie, and all you do is upset her. And I bet you don't realize you've done so. Do you?'

He shrugged.

'I'd like to talk to you sometimes, but you're not all there. You don't listen; you don't understand; you don't even go through the motions. You've changed, Frank.'

'There's something wrong with you, not me,' he said.

'It's easy enough to say that. To accuse me. Because you don't want to talk.'

Now Kathleen sat tight in her chair. He refilled her glass.

'Do you bother what people say to you?'

'Sometimes. Depends.'

He put his own drink on the table, took her in his arms.

'Don't start that,' she said, 'for God's sake.'

When he kissed her, she did not struggle. He tasted the whisky on her lips.

'Stop,' she said. 'Stop it.'

She pushed him away, but he held her, long enough to establish physical superiority. Twenty years ago she'd run to him, distressed, furious and battered by her husband's confessions of infidelity. Then she'd needed her own back, turned to her brother-in-law, flung herself at him, degrading herself to level scores with her husband. And Frank? He, wild, aghast, terrified at her, had sunk into her, seeing himself as she saw him, an idol, a golden calf, provided but never itself, an ineffability, a second best. His excitement had skidded intensely through the life outside their few copulations; at this period his own son David had been conceived by Louise, his wife. She had known nothing of her husband's aberration, his two-month madness, had lain ignorant in her bed at home and waited for him.

When Kathleen had called a halt out of the blue, he had been dashed flat for the second time. She sprawled on a grey-blanketed bed in an attic at Wentworth as he dressed hurriedly, shuffling into his trousers in front of a dressing-table that had stood in his father's bedroom at Factory House. He could not lie patiently after their bout; he must be up, dressed, tie on, in case Jack came home. Kathleen lay across the bed, sulkily, her vest rucked up from the long nakedness of her legs. They had charged at sex, and it had failed them.

He looked ridiculous, adjusting his braces, tying his shoes. Soon he'd be peering in the mirror, combing order into his tangled hair, apologetically looking back at her, ashamed and proud of her pubic crop. Harmless and useless as a pet rabbit. Little man. She scrambled from the bed, dragged on panties, slipped her frock over, buttoned it, adjusted the belt. Shoving her feet into her shoes she made for her own bedroom to straighten face, coiffure. Soon he'd come tapping at her door, to sit like an infant on a roundabout, bemused, or wanting her praise, dismissed to brew tea.

63

Today he went straight downstairs. She heard the footsteps pass her door, and was angered.

On her arrival in the kitchen he poured.

'I thought I heard Jack,' he said, lamely.

'At three o'clock on a Saturday afternoon?'

'You never know.'

'You don't.'

She did not finish her cup, put a coat on, said she was going into the garden. Her children were out for the afternoon with her cleaning woman. At the cost of a few shillings to their mother, Freddie and Helen would be fussed by weekending grown-ups, carriaged round the park, stuffed with carbohydrate, dazzled with telly, dizzied with ride-a-cock horse, and, faces wiped roughly clean with flannel and scented soap, delivered home fractious if near exhaustion.

He had completed the washing of the cups.

Outside in the garden, she bent vigorously, shaking earth from an uprooted plant.

'I'll telephone,' he said. 'Or call.'

'No. I don't want you to.'

'Why not?'

'Today's the end. That's enough. I've made my mind up.'

'When?'

'In there. This afternoon.'

It had seemed ridiculous, in gusty sunshine, to stand exchanging these short sentences. Kathleen directed her attention to her red-rubber gloves, the white roots, the earth rather than to him.

'Doesn't it mean anything?' Francis asked. 'What we've . . .'

'No. Not really.' She lobbed an unwanted clump into the barrow. 'I don't think it does. Anyway, it's finished now.'

'Kathleen.'

'I'm not going to argue. I don't want to spoil what little time I get in the garden. But you think about it. Go back home to Louise. You'll see that's best.'

He had tried to argue, but it was difficult to be eloquent in a

wind, to a woman who pulled, grunted, trudged off, threat-
ened him with her husband. He surrendered, and for six
months they hardly met, did not speak.

Now, twenty years on, he had still no idea why she had
ditched him. He feared, the thought festering still, that he'd
been unsuccessful in a fixed trial period. Or she'd seen sense.
If Jack had found out, how would he have moved? Com-
pliant? Doubtful. But on whom would he have worked out
his malice? Francis could not answer. There would have been
a rough-house, but its form, its time and place, were mysteries.
The poems, blood-lettings, scribbled in and out of the period
he had not published, were locked away from Louise, from
himself.

> Who walks with white ferocity through the long grass?
> My brother's wife.
> Her breasts have blubbered me to a child,
> Clubbed manhood, cut my vigour back to a wild
> Shriek in shrunk loins.

Senseless, wit-battered appeals that shamed him, described
his shame exactly, in a school exercise book, Name, Form.
He looked at the poems, crossed out words, squinted in
detachment at his alterations, but made no attempt to publish,
and did not even keep typed copies. He sat amazed at himself.

> Nevertheless, fine lady, I draw
> No veil, prefer
> Your secrecy, my own unguarded, frenzied
> Cleaving to, of her.

Today, with her mouth puckered in, she appeared middle-
aged, needing glasses to read the paper.

'I'm going,' she muttered.

'I should.'

Startled, her face stricken, she gaped. Recovering, she
answered mildly:

'If that's what you think.'

'I don't know what I think with you,' he said.

Now she touched him, but gently, almost business-like, as if testing the cloth of his jacket. They stood so for some minutes, only her hand moving. Outside a police siren sounded off again.

7

Cecilia telephoned Francis at his school.

He was fetched from his classroom to take the call in a closet off the entrance hall. His sister had claimed it was of importance.

'Well, what is it?'

He made no attempt to hide his annoyance, though he expected some demonstration of instability from his sister. Contempt might souse sense into her.

'It's our dad's grave, Frank.'

'What about it?'

She began her convolutions. The infrequent Sunday visit. Yesterday. It was nice. Took a bus, Eric busy at work. Bought flowers; nice chrysanthemums, all yellow and russet. He sighed his impatience at the rigmarole noisily into his mouthpiece. There followed the trip, the conductor, inflated fares, the mud on the paths, her difficulty in getting bearings, a new extension, a wall she'd never seen before.

'When I got to your dad's grave, the headstone, you should have seen the headstone.'

He waited, peering through the foyer into the forecourt with its grass and beige flagstones, the silver birches. Two girls practised skipping; he wondered why.

'Are you listening, our Frank?'

'Yes. Get on with it, will you?' He laughed at his exasperation.

'It was cracked right across. The headstone. Right across.'

'How had that happened?'

'How do I know? Perhaps they'd caught it with a machine.

It looked as if it had been hit with a sledgehammer. Or perhaps it was vandals.'

'Did you not inquire?'

'Inquire? Where? There wasn't anybody about.'

'The superintendent's office.'

'I don't know where that is. I thought you could ring them up, and report it, and ask them what they're going to do about it.'

He chided her. This happened yesterday. Why hadn't she moved before?

'I was upset. Eric said they wouldn't do anything, or couldn't. They weren't responsible. But I said our Frank'll talk to them. I mean, it's their job.'

'Have you told Jack?'

'He wouldn't bother. If I thought he'd go up cemetery, I might think he'd done it.'

'That's not well said.' He ribbed Cissie for her good.

'What about when he was dying, then? What did our Jack say?'

The old man had died four years ago, at the age of eighty-three. He'd lived on his own since his daughter's marriage five years before his retirement, and she had called in on him every afternoon excepting Saturday and Sunday for nearly a quarter of a century. He'd been allowed to keep the factory house, as no one else wanted it, and he collected his dinner from the canteen, under tin covers, slammed down without grace, for he was unpopular with kitchen staff as with everyone else. On Saturday he bought fish and chips, and on Sunday descended hungrily on his daughter and her husband. Since Cissie's departure his stove had been used for nothing more complicated than boiling water and grilling toast.

During the last winter of his life he visibly ailed, so that Eric fetched him about in the car, and a woman from the canteen marched over with his midday meal. Thus one noon she had found him lying on the ground, and the factory nurse had despatched him to hospital, where he coughed through day and night on to the nerves of staff and patients. A week later, to the surprise of his family, the doctors reported that he was dying.

At this moment Jack, who had not visited the ward, chided by his sister had said, 'The silly old sod can snuff it without my help.'

Cissie, in tears, had flung out of her brother's house and round to appeal to Francis. He refused to intervene.

'You know why it is, Cis, and if he feels like that, there's nothing I can do.'

'You can talk to him.'

Some half-dozen years previously Jacob had rung the bell at Wentworth, lunged into the hall behind Kathleen, and there with a hoarse, mad shout had exposed himself.

Kathleen spoke sharply to him, then locked herself away in the back. She had not been afraid, she said, merely careful that Helen, who was helping her mother in the kitchen, should not come out to find her grandfather making a fool of himself. She'd listened, and apparently the old man after stalking round very briefly had cleared off. She'd seen him walking down the drive, trilby in place, raincoat buttoned.

Kathleen reported to Jack, who jumped in anger, swore he'd sort the dirty sod out.

'He's senile,' she said. 'It's no use making a fuss.'

'What would our Helen have thought if she'd have let him in?'

'He might not have done anything with her about.'

Jack cursed, insisting he'd get down to that factory house. Kathleen argued, agreed finally as long as Francis accompanied him. All the way there, the older brother puffed, grunted, took his anger out on walls and paving slabs.

Jacob let them in, retired at once to his window chair in front of a one-bar fire. A forty-watt bulb shone from a holder on the mantelpiece. Jack rudely switched on all the lights in the room, banged down on a chair-arm, motioned Frank to the settee.

'Kathleen told me about this afternoon,' he began, hectoring.

His father pulled in his lips, sucked gums. He rarely put his dentures in. These days he looked frail and furtive; he never shaved cleanly, and the skin of his scalp stretched as thin as the few hairs brushed across it. His eyes were pale, rheumy, red-rimmed, though his cheeks had a bloom still. Fingernails were dirty; the twisted hands grotesque. His suit hung loosely on him, made to round a prosperous paunch, but slack now, sagging, food-stained. He would not look at his sons, pressed the scraggy neck into the rumpling collar, dribbled.

'Do you hear what I say?' Jack asked.

'What's she been telling you?' Tissue paper and comb voice; phlegm-strung.

'You know bloody well, you dirty bogger.'

'That's no way to speak to your father.' Jacob made an effort, appealed with a look to Francis for support.

'Flashing your tool in front of women. Nobody'd want to see that sixty years ago when it was some use, never mind now.'

Jacob mumbled, a humming sound.

'You are not to go round to that house again unless you're invited. Is that understood?' The old man shrugged, with a childish bravado. 'Do you understand? You're not welcome.'

The father glanced quickly, from one son to the other, then shrank into himself.

'I didn't mean anything. I didn't know what came over me.'

At the whining tone, Francis remembered his father in his prime, at the office, issuing orders, straight-backed and stout, to be reckoned with, and yet with a voice that was too high-pitched, too breathy for the solidity of the prosperous body. Gutless girth. Jack was on the rampage, enjoying himself, vulgarly dressing his parent down.

'You'll end up in prison, and serve you bloody well right. And I shall do nothing for you. Get it out to pee with; otherwise leave it alone.'

Francis felt distaste for his brother's words, but recognized that they burst from a real hurt. Jack held property, respected ownership; one of his most precious chattels, his wife, had been spoilt, as though one had trampled across a flower border, been sick on a freshly raked drive, muddied a fine carpet. He would not hold it long against his father; soon he'd be calmer, revoke his sentence, but for the moment his anger goaded.

Again Jacob murmured in apology, but his son blundered on.

Now the old man presented them with his face. It was drawn, gaunt, skull-shaped. Tears rolled from the squinting eyes, glistening, still as glycerine, on the lined cheeks. He made no attempt to hide his weeping; Francis wondered if he knew what he was doing. He leaned forward, laid a hand on his brother's leg. Jack stopped, saw the old man. A spasm of contempt twisted his face, but he did not resume his monologue. Francis unwrapped a folded handkerchief, bunched it, passed it to his father. Jacob mopped, and closing his eyes leaned back in his chair like one desperately weary.

'Come on, Jack,' Francis ordered. Jack rose. 'You'll be all right, Dad?' Jacob nodded, like a mandarin. 'Come on, then.'

'Remember what I say to you,' Jack growled.

Outside as they walked down a yard and then on to the main factory gate, Jack rumbled discontent.

'He's past it. Not fit to be let about. Should be locked up somewhere. And he puts it on. To get bloody sympathy.'

'I don't think so.'

'You're as bad as he is. He's always been self-willed. A bullying bastard. Now he's adding the bloody cry-baby to it.'

They walked together. Francis did not answer. He knew

that before his brother had blasted through two more complaints, the man would be ashamed of himself, wanting but not daring to ask for his brother's forgiveness.

'I'll just go in here.'

Jack barged into a beer-off where he bought a packet of cheroots. He smiled at the woman behind the counter, and she responded. After he'd pocketed his change, the woman talked on, her face alight, lively to attract, hands fluttering. Now Jack's face was humorous, manly, of a man of the world, matching the well-cut suit, the large manicured hands. And back in the factory house? A snivelling husk switching the lights off, who'd already forgotten his trouble.

Jack had visited the hospital, bent gentle at the death-bed, the best of them all. Jacob had opened his eyes, they seemed bright again, and taken his older son's hand.

'We've had some good times,' he said. 'Between us.'

The others felt excluded, as perhaps they were, but Francis scented exhilaration as he took the brunt of Cissy's complaining. Jack and the old man were birds of a feather, big boys, not frightened of power, not without cruelty, predators; they'd known how to enjoy the good times.

'You'd think he was the favourite.' Cissie.

'He was.'

'After all that rowing?'

The father's property was exactly divided between the three of them, according to the will. Cecilia nursed resentment; she'd wasted her life ministering to his whims. She let her brothers know.

'You're not short,' Jack spoke bluntly. 'And you've got your third.' Cecilia soured her features. 'Our Frank's the one who needs it. He's had the bad luck.'

Francis had used the inheritance to buy and reshape the stone cottage. He let the bungalow where he had lived with Louise to a colliery official, and then had found that David, his son, seventeen now, would not join him. He argued, but without force. He'd used the windfall recklessly in that he

72

did not himself wish to move, thought only to take David, who'd left school, out of the house of his mother's death.

> Ghosts will not sweep across this muddy town.
> We go; she stays. Our heads shudder in bone.
> This open exodus precludes her moon-light flit.

But David, counter clerk at the National Westminster Bank, suited and sober by day, jeaned and footloose at night, took digs, volunteered for a spell in London, made minimal contacts with his father, refused offers of posts from the buoyant uncle. He was satisfied.

'Are you all right for money?' his father asked.

'I work in a bank.'

Francis had been delighted to see his son enter the local library one evening. He did not carry books, so perhaps he made eyes at one of the assistants. Any girls he walked round were good-looking. Perhaps reconciliation would come before the death-bed. Neither worried the other; one tormented himself.

This evening Francis Weldon closed his notebook. He'd been working all day at school on a poem, between composition and drama and 'O'-level exercises, and now he'd made out a draft, put it down plainly and shut the book. He would not look at it again until he'd slept; he could almost forget it, now it was on paper out of his system. He washed, inspected his shirt-collar, changed because it was crumpled, brushed his hair this way, that, fetched out his best tweed jacket. He was to receive Judith Powis.

He'd been surprised to have a letter from her, asking for an interview. She listed possible dates, insisted he said nothing to his brother. Her essay was not yet complete, but she had done the preliminary work, had delivered a praised lecturette to fellow students, had organized a poetry reading which he was to attend, and felt confident enough to take her tutor on in argument. What she now wanted he could not determine.

Perhaps her adventure with literary criticism had been so successful that she had to prolong the experience.

She turned up, pretty in a navy jumper, red jacket and trousers, a matching, dark hat, like a fruit bowl on the back of her head. Before she removed the headgear she pulled out a huge, black-beaded hat pin. He'd seen nobody do that since his mother's day. Immediately his mind trembled, curdled with the first wild current of poetry, so that he re-remembered her action, the long pull, the placing of pin and hat together, the patting at hair, then the expression of bright readiness. He was not a child again, but he noted with a child's vigorous freshness. He'd talk ordinarily enough in a moment, but he marked a credit on the slate.

She followed his eyes.

'My hair's long enough now to pin into,' she said, flatly.

'Uh.' He didn't need her interference. His mind, warmed, had become blank, not receptive; it had already received. Not yet time for writing; sitting still. He'd learn later when he worked on it whether his rickety fruit-machine had spun up with a straight run of luck, though he'd need to hammer and kick the paint to score his three bananas. Now, nothing. Or orange blank, warm stability, the moment for breathing.

She smiled at him in the silence, attractive, knowing it.

'I've got a personal question to ask you,' she said. He feigned interest. 'It's about your brother. He's offered Alan, my husband, y'know, a job, and I wanted to see what . . . You hear such things about business these days. Is he . . . ?'

'What sort of job?'

'It seemed part administrative, part public relations.'

'Living and partly living? Not selling? Which firm?'

'The transport company. Welcar Road Haulage.'

'That's a moderately new venture. Yes, it's doing well, I hear. His partner's out of action, man he started with. Stroke. Early forties.'

'Is that why Jack wants . . . ?'

'I expect so.'

Judith looked even more delicious as she frowned.

'He's getting on quite well in the bank. It's boring, but steady.'

'I know,' Francis said. 'That's what my son works at.'

'He's passed his exams. He'll probably end up as a manager, he thinks. It's responsible work.' Her sentence she delivered aggressively, but not loud. She flushed by the cheek-bones. 'If he goes in with Jack, will he be out of work in a year or two? You say this other man's had a stroke. Was it the worry? I don't want Alan killing himself.'

'If he's a worrier, he'll have plenty on his mind as a bank manager.'

'This man?' She pressed, lips parted, fresh as a starlet.

'Name of Carlin. Ran a smallish haulage firm, did well, started to expand. As far as I remember, he wanted to take over somebody else, hadn't the money, got Jack in.'

'And he had the money?'

'Yes, or knew where to get it. They went into it together. Four years ago. They're both colossal workers. The thing's never looked back. But Jim Carlin's ill.'

'He won't ... ?'

'I believe he's getting better, but he'll have to go steadier. I'd have thought they'd have put an accountant in to manage the thing temporarily, but Jack's not altogether keen on accountants. "They can add up," he says. "They can't multiply." '

Francis listened to his own voice which spoke assurance. He in no way felt this certainty; he made up excellent sentences, but he could not vouch for their truth. He remembered the amalgamation in that Kathleeen had been frantic with anxiety, answering the phone, working herself madly, unpaid. It was the time he had published his last collection, *Words of Ice*, a success. His picture had appeared in the Sundays; his volume became a Poetry Book Society choice. He had talked banalities through a television interview; the whole world had seen it. *Kaleidoscope* dealt with, read, judged with encomia, rejoiced over his verses. His pupils, wide-eyed, searched for his secret, one bought a copy, asked him to sign the title-page. Colleagues combined suspicion with joviality; the area education officer congratulated him. He had become somebody.

His brother, working seventeen hours a day, had grumbled, then dragged Kathleen round to Francis.

'Now, then, cebloodylebrity, will you take this woman to the theatre for me?' He flashed tickets; they watched London elegants act *Godot*. Francis doubted the wisdom of choice, but Kathleen was taken up with the play. She'd not seen much of him since the death of Louise a year before, when she'd made overtures which he'd ignored, out of lassitude. Now she seemed excited, drinking gin in the interval with the élan of a schoolgirl, willing to gush into criticism, voice it about the bar. This was a new figure, and he did not understand. She drove him back to his bungalow, and over coffee had given him her account of the 'Welcar' amalgamation. The jargon rattled perfectly; the obstacles and their surmounting were beautifully described, the large cast introduced and kept alive in his mind. Kathleen proved herself that night a remarkable woman, clear-headed, forceful, and when the fifteen-year-old David had come down out of curiosity, she was tender, without sentimentality, ironically loving. She captivated the ungracious boy as she had his father.

'Is it straight back to bed?' Francis asked, David now out of the way.

'Yes. But the kids will be crashing round after midnight.' Frederick was back from the university for the weekend, and a friend's twenty-first. Helen was out at a school dance.

'And Jack?'

'In bed. Just. If he's home. He may not be.'

'Is he worried by all this?'

'Yes. He must be. There have been so many snags. But

he's stimulated. He likes danger. He doesn't think to himself that if this goes awry he'll lose everything.'

'Will he?'

'Yes, he will. We shall be penniless. He knows that. He likes it. It's not gambling, though. It's deliberate choice, coming down this way or that. He's suited. Nothing will stop him. Or that's how he feels.'

'Is that so?' He saw the point of her illogicalities.

'There are a thousand things that can go wrong. I'm terrified. In nightmares you're in some ludicrous situation that's shredding you. I feel exactly so in broad daylight.'

'What do you do about it?'

'Work. Take his phone calls accurately, write messages. Exact time; exact words. Like reports. It amuses him, because he thinks there's no need, but if it comes to grief, it won't be through me. I'll see to that.'

'Does he read your reports?'

'Yes. And I file them. It's all I can do, except go mad. And I prefer it.' She laughed. 'Until this started I'd nothing to do with his work, except for saying things about the furniture he had in stock. Those shops'll be sold off if this goes through. I shall be sorry. I think I understood what a decent settee looks like.' She laughed, without amusement. Her hair was marginally untidy; dark patches underlined her eyes; she seemed thin, hungrily colourless.

'How do the kids take it?' he asked, after another long paragraph of her report. She talked, easily, rationally, not gabbling, but compulsively, driven to explanation, unwilling to check herself. Francis saw this as a desperate summary made for a third party in the hope that it would, if carefully constructed, logically ordered, present in the end, as if by magic, the deliverance, the way-out, the all-clear.

'They don't notice. Helly's got "A" levels and boy friends. They're a bloody worrying nuisance, but they've no idea what we're up to, thank God.'

'Why thank Him?'

'I wonder what they'd think if all the money vanished? Vindictive. Furious. They don't know how hard Jack drives himself.'

'Are you sure? Young people are not so blind as . . .'

'That's how it seems. May be me. Up my wall. I can't pinpoint . . . Oh, God.'

When she left he watched her make her way to the car; she walked thin as a matchstick, her coat blown about her. In spite of his intentions they did not meet again for some time, and by then the deal was through, though she still put time in at the office. The first year brought strokes of luck, and by the second the business expanded, made big profits above huge expenditure, set the two men on top of the world. Jack wanted to buy his wife a house in the country; she refused. He reported her obstinacy to Francis.

'Do you know what she says? "We've tempted Providence far enough."'

The men laughed together but Francis had shivered, understood.

Judith Powis listened, head on one side, eyes seriously wide. Presumably she knew something of this saga, for Jack would have 'filled her in'. He enjoyed his own exploits.

'What sort of employer is he?' she asked Francis.

'Reaps where he does not sow. An austere man.' Ignorance pouted on her lips. 'Authorised Version. He gets his money's worth.'

'If Alan didn't do well, he'd sack him.'

'He would. He'd make it clear. There'd be a probationary period. He'd have to work longer hours than he does now. Annual audit all the year round.'

'There's been,' she spoke coyly, 'no mention of pay.'

'There should be.' He felt shame laying down the law. 'Work out by the hour what your husband gets now, and then tot up. He'll have to go in again on Saturday.'

'We realize that.'

'Is there a pension scheme? Car? Help with the mortgage?'

'You're warning me off?' she asked.

'I can't. I don't know your husband. I wouldn't have the job, because I think in terms of security. I want my bolt-hole. I teach in my school with a steady cheque in the bank every twentieth of the month, so that I can write what I like.'

'You can't live on your poetry?'

'I couldn't die and be buried on it.'

'Doesn't that make your work, well, timid?'

'Did you find it so?'

'No.' She had blushed, moved uncomfortably in her chair. Timid? He could have rushed her into his arms; Jack would have moved. He expected no rebuff. Women need men who want women. Give. 'But if one is careful,' she glanced up to note his reception of the euphemism, 'in one way, one is in another. I mean Jack's poetry . . .' She crumbled.

'Has he written any?'

'Not that I know. He likes action. He doesn't hesitate.'

'Has he made a pass at you?' Francis asked, sharp-sour.

'And offered me a job. I was flattered.'

'Did you tell Alan?'

She flushed again. Her skin seemed abruptly reflective of her living; herself; an extension of her emotive quickness. Her body thought.

'No. Hinted. Your brother likes danger, you say?'

Now she waited for him to reply, got nothing.

'Have you ever seen him frightened?'

8

Francis Weldon, ten years old, sat alone at the breakfast table.

In the kitchen his sister blacked his shoes; at his elementary school they strapped those whose footwear was not up to standard. The headmaster stood at the entrance, pouncing on the late, the chewing, those with unparted hair, those he disliked, the smiling.

Cecilia knew this, called out to her brother to get a move on, brought the frying pan in to issue scorched sausages.

'Whose plate's that?'

'Our Jack's. He came home last night.'

'Is he badly?'

'No, he isn't.' The pan clanged back on the gas stove. 'It's twenty-five to nine. Hurry yourself.'

He did so, began his run to school, ten minutes, forgot his brother until lunch time.

His father was in, unusually early. Jack, Cissie reported, lay in bed. She had made a covered tray, and Jacob nodded approval. They told the boy nothing. At tea Jack was down, apparently normal, asking about school, whether he'd been punished, what he was learning. Again the father approved. Frank could make nothing of it.

A fortnight later he learnt on the way home, from a classmate, what had happened.

Jack had taken a job in Leicester, had been sent by his father to lodge with distant relatives, a Mr and Mrs Wilcox, Uncle Leslie and Aunt Lena, a young couple who rented a terrace house not far from the office. Les was a quiet chap who worked on the railway; Lena lively assertive, stayed at home with a two-year-old girl, Rose, provided huge dinners, was pleased with Jack's company in the evenings when her husband was on shifts. Now and then she'd leave him in with a warning to listen for Rosie, while she called on a neighbour, to borrow or return an ounce of this, a few tablespoons of that, to stay for gossip. She was never out for much above an hour, and as soon as she'd taken her coat off she'd run upstairs to look at the child.

She made use of her young lodger thus; he was afraid of her, with her perfume, the cleft of her breasts as she bent, the loud voice, the squawks of laughter. She was sex, woman. He touched her purple or green directoire knickers as they hung on the clothes horse. But she gave him no encouragement. Big as he was, she made it clear he was a kid. Sometimes she asked him if he washed his ears or told him to change his socks. He wondered in the small back bedroom what she and Leslie were up to in the front, but he heard nothing. Once he heard crying from the child's place, the sound of footsteps, of talk, and he looked round his door, along the passage. Lena, in bare feet, wore an outdoor coat over her nightgown. She murmured, swayed with the child she held, under the shadeless, brand-new electric light at the top of the stairs. Les thumped about in the kitchen. Nothing was said next morning; she'd missed Jack's inquisitive head at the crack.

He heard quarrelsome words now and then, Lena loud but Les grumbling, whining. He would have been surprised if he had not, but as he now attended a night-school class in accounts once a week, and worked washing-up in a pie restaurant for three more, he saw little of the couple except at occasional meals. Lena was a good, slapdash cook, and both men left the table satisfied. A quiet house, he'd judged it, with Les outside in his shed, at the bench, or two streets away on his allotment.

That morning he'd woken to hear Rose screaming; again he was not surprised. Lena had breakfast on the way before she fetched the child down. The mother might bawl back for silence, but often she did not exert herself so far. Rosie would get attention when the mother was ready, and not before. Jack looked at his clock, a present from Cissie. Eight-ten. He leaped from bed.

Half past seven was rising time. Then he'd slip on his trousers and shirt, and sluice down in the kitchen, at the only tap in the house, with a ladling-tin or two full of hot water from the boiler. Five feet away Lena would fry his bacon and eggs, singing wireless, dance hall, favourites. She loved Henry Hall. By eight-fifteen he'd be out of the house, and on the way to the office, unlocked at eight-twenty-five by his immediate superior, a twenty-year-old with whom Jack discussed women.

He bundled clothes on. It was possible to make it on time, unwashed, fasting. He shaved each night before he went to bed, not quite of necessity. He knotted his tie, donned his jacket, the last rite before he left. Rose shouted still, but not violently. She could occupy herself during short periods of neglect.

Downstairs, darkness with blinds drawn still.

He snatched on the light, in a silence. Lena sprawled face down on the hearthrug, her head smashed, the bulldog-headed coal-hammer by her side. Her hair was dense – matted with dark blood, but the horror lay in the sag in her skull, which dipped as if it were paper. Her hands were wide, fingers bent, but otherwise she lay decently, comfortably, frock-ends neat over stockings, slippers in place. Only the obscene, caved, bloodied head. He did not touch her. Rosie let rip upstairs. The *Mercury* dropped through the front letter-box.

Back from his wife, in a chair over the table, Les hunched. At his feet was a galvanized tin bath he must have fetched in from the yard. He had slit his throat and both wrists with a cut-throat razor, but if his intention was to bleed to death into the bath he had failed. His flannel shirt was black with blood, the tablecloth, with gobbets like skin, soft icicles, the floor dry puddled. He lay over the table in the filth, his hair lively still, parted.

The boy screamed. The sound was dragged with involuntary violence from his maw, through his gullet, reverberating in his frozen face. He rushed to the parlour, dragged at the bolts, top and bottom, turned the key, tumbled out into the street, where trams clashed and shuddered, and the people he passed each morning raised eyebrows at his wild running. He did not know how he crossed the roads; he cannoned into a man on a bicycle, left him sprawling.

At the police station he could not speak, crouped, gibbered without breath. The station sergeant steadied a lad as big as himself, coat wet with drizzle, face polished with tears mouthing madness. Within five minutes he'd recovered. Men were on their way. Rosie had been accounted for. His office had been telephoned.

He did not go back that morning.

After the first thorough questioning, he was surprised to find Mr Drury, his employer, had taken time to come to the station. Jack had not been sick. He ate bread and butter. His father, they said, had offered to take the train over to Leicester. Did he not want that? No. Then when they had finished with him, they'd see he went back home. A doctor looked him up and down; they examined his jacket, shirt, shoes. He knew this as sensible, but it frightened him. Perhaps they suspected.

A well-spoken man with a moustache catechized him, for the third time now. What had he heard? Nothing. He'd gone to bed soon after ten-thirty. Lena had been up reading a magazine. Les had called in on a neighbour, she'd said, about some Christmas Club business. Lena had been singing, an old thing. 'Dancing with my shadow / Feeling kinda blue / I'm dancing with my shadow / And making believe it's you.' Something like that. She loved sentiment. 'Somewhere in a corner / Nothing else to do.' She offered him cocoa, but he'd eaten at the pie shop. She often sang. Broken love. 'I'm dancing with tears in my eyes / 'Cos the girl in my arms isn't you.' They were men's songs Swooning men. Henry Hall's men.

The police collected stipulated belongings, drove him to the station. He could hardly believe as he sat on the Beechnall train that he'd seen murder that morning: the world occupied itself, cheerful, insouciant, rowdy. His father insisted he went straight up to bed, where he was given bread and milk in a basin. Francis, away at a junior choir practice, was not told of his brother's arrival until next morning.

Jack stayed only for one day. A colleague found him a room in Leicester. Drury took an interest, offered him a new post. The police thanked him for his speed. He appeared, conducted himself with admirable calm, at the inquest. Rose was taken to live with an aunt in Etruria.

Gossips quizzed him, instructed, elucidated, improvised, theorized.

Lena, it appeared, had become friendly with an insurance agent three streets away. Everybody knew; Jack did not. He remembered no remonstration from the husband. But then he had not heard one killing thud from the hammer. Had she turned away from her husband? Crouched terrified? He could not imagine it. Lena would face him out, weapon or not. When had he gone in the yard to the coalhouse? She had not screamed; possibly she did not believe her husband had the cruel heart to strike her; he hardly looked capable of lifting the hammer. But he had struck, from behind, cracking the skull, bone splitting, shattering. And then.

The quiet man had ventured again into the yard to fetch in the bathtub. He had rolled his sleeves, taken off his wrist watch, put it in safety on the table, before dragging the razor in a great slash across his throat. Which first? Wrists or jugular? In a silence. Blood pumping loose, he'd died dumb, murderous.

Jack spoke to his brother about the incident only once or twice.

The first time, Frank was on leave from national service, Jack had been dismissive, callous, 'I've seen worse.' A day or two later he'd called the younger aside, poked out a finger, said, 'I shan't trust anybody again. Les was as quiet as a mouse.'

'But he must have been roused . . .'

'He was. Even so, I'd have said he couldn't knock the skin off a rice pudding. That was a violent blow with a big hammer. She must have knelt and let him do it. That wasn't like her either. She was alive.'

'I see.' He didn't. He was embarrassed by his brother's confidences.

'If I'd have come in an hour later, it might not have happened.'

'Did she deserve it?'

'Don't talk like a cunt. Does anybody deserve having her skull smashed in? And I'll tell you another thing. He went out to fetch that bath, and then, before he killed himself, he came upstairs to look at Rosie.'

'Did he think of killing her?'

'I don't know what he thought. That bath hung on the back of the coalhouse door; it wasn't used for washing; it was old. They found his footprints in the bedroom, mud and slack by the baby's bed.'

'Why did he go?'

Two brothers – men of the world, ex-soldier and temporary squaddy – troubled themselves with a railwayman, wife slugged dead, on his way upstairs. Did he speak? To himself? Groan, shudder, curse, switch lights on even? Did he, intent on death, stumble or crouch, walk straight? Pale-faced, hands clawing the wall for support? Mind a tumult, or in final calm?

They did not know.

A few yards away a boy had slept through the end of two decent people, and had recovered. Frank, his brother had walked that stair, up and down, for thirty years.

9

Francis showed Judith Powis through the door.

He mentioned nothing of the murder, nor even his poem about it, unpublished, shut away in a hard-covered exercise book. She thanked him, attractively attitudinizing. He wondered what advice she'd give her husband.

He sat down, picked up a book, read a series of sentences he'd marked. 'I was born under a black sun. I wasn't born, I was crushed out.' 'She's the ghost in the weed garden.' 'She's the occidental sun.' His eye wandered. He could make poetry out of these disguises, these muted calls from hell, but he would not do so. Or not yet. Not until his own anxiety dumbed itself.

His back ached. Tiredness raked his shoulders.

A hammering on his back door. He dropped Laing to the carpet, groaned over. Kathleen. He invited her in.

'Have you seen Jack?' she asked, rock still. He had not. 'Is he out with that Judith Powis?' He explained why he thought not. Then, only, she came in, dragging a headscarf from her hair. 'Pick that book up,' she ordered, but stooped before he did. '*The Divided Self*,' she read. She placed it on the table.

'Sit down.' He fetched her whisky which she did not refuse. 'Now what's up?'

'He's spending a lot of time out. Nights.'

'With Judith, you suspect?'

'I've no reason to think so.' She shook her head vigorously. He explained about the job offered to Alan Powis, slowly, therapeutically. Kathleen sipped.

'I don't like to be left alone in the house,' she said.

'Is that reasonable?'

'It's recent. At one time I didn't care. Something happened.' She shut her mouth. He encouraged her to speak. She writhed in her seat.

In the end it came out. A year or two back in the Christmas holiday, Helen had violent earache. Kathleen rang the emergency doctor, who arrived promptly, a polite Indian with little command of English. He examined, wrote a prescription. Where could she get it made up? A smiling, shrugging incomprehension, and she was left at ten at night with a useless slip of paper, and Helen white, shaken with pain. No sign of Jack, who had been out since eight in the morning. She rang his two offices in the city; nothing.

The situation soured, sore.

She visited an all-night chemist, found it closed without instructions on window or door. She rang the emergency service again, was told to get to a police station. There they were kind, read 'urgent', knocked up a pharmacist, who tousle-haired dispensed tablets from a locked shop a mile out of the town centre. The hour she'd spent seemed endless, but she was back home before eleven. Helen, feverish, dozed. It pleased the mother to see her daughter sip water, swallow the drugs. For the few minutes they sat together Helen was a child again, dependent, but Kathleen feared for her, flinched from shadows in the room.

Her husband had not come back.

She wrote a sharp note, in her anger. He might be out all night; she did not know, but at half past midnight he appeared in her bedroom. She had not been to sleep. Curtly she described her evening, asked where he had been. He answered, she considered, vaguely, mumbling. He'd had to meet this man, that. Certainly he'd been drinking, she could smell the whisky, but he was unaffected, stolid, unconvincing.

She snatched up her dressing-gown, rushed along the corridor to see Helen, who, flushed, slept soundly enough.

Straightening the bedclothes, Kathleen tiptoed. Jack stood in her room still, lifting his face in a question.

'Asleep.'

He put his hand on her flank tentatively. She slipped away.

'Go to bed.'

Jack looked at her, made his way along the corridor. All attention she listened whether he opened Helen's door, but he did not. He made for his room at the back of the house.

Next morning he gave no word of apology and his wife said nothing. Helen was up and about inside a day or two, but Kathleen felt something of the fears she'd experienced when her children were small. They'd run out of the drive on to the main road, they'd burn, maim, cut themselves, be bitten by dogs. Everyday vicissitudes dulled the expectation of these catastrophes; small illnesses, knocks, accidents inoculated against major terror. But, now, on her own, Kathleen looked for disaster. Rationally she could argue herself free; inside, fierce apprehension ruled. Her husband was to blame; or there, as she grew worse, she wronged herself.

As she explained this to her brother-in-law, in flat words, not choice, with an awkwardness of pauses, the story carried no conviction, seemed inflated, an excuse for the intrusion. He sat, not intervening, without a question, staring mildly at her, listening as far as she could judge. Yet there was about him something of her husband's selfishness, or lack of concern. What she expected she did not know, but he should reassure her. She did not want physical contact. She needed from him some sentences, some justification of her mood, some pronouncement that would calm, satisfy, humanize her.

When she received nothing, she drained her whisky and shocked him by asking for more. He passed her glass grudgingly.

'What do you say?' she asked.

'I don't know what you want. Is he still away late?'

'Sometimes.'

'Do you mind?'

She remembered the first time she'd tumbled to his behaviour. Turning out his pockets on washday, she'd found a handkerchief smeared with lipstick. The red-brown smears did not catch her attention, but the scent. She threw it down, retrieved, sniffed.

That night she put the handkerchief on his dressing table. He quietly cleared it away, saying nothing. She challenged.

'I found that handkerchief,' she said.

'Which handkerchief?' Childish.

'The one I left out.'

'Oh.'

He would have gone from the room without a word.

'I left it there,' she said. 'You'd been with some woman.'

Jack did not answer. Brazenly he took a handkerchief from his pocket, flapped it loose as if to rile her.

'Well, have you?'

'I have.' He sounded formidable, bull-strong. 'It'd be useless denying it.'

'And is that all you've got to say?'

'That's all I've got to say. Yes.'

She trembled, sat down. She felt again the weakness, the pang which had cut into her when she'd first found the evidence. Still he dandled the handkerchief in whiteness, its ironed stiffness apparent in a disordered shape. He did not speak, but waited, all of five minutes, at his ease, milording it. At the end he stuffed the handkerchief away, got up, went out.

At breakfast she did not open her mouth. When he spoke, she ignored him; if he demanded, she did not move. He poured his own coffee, reached for his eggs and toast. As far as she could tell he was not put out, and he went off to work dumb as a beast. When he returned for his evening meal, she served portions she thought fit, and that was that.

Jack made no overt fuss, but craftily included her in the words he directed at their babies, Frederick and Helen. She rigidly excluded herself again, but felt her obstinacy hurt the children. At the ages of three and one, they did not miss, she was certain, the exchange between father and mother, but she sat uneasily, and when Karen, the nursemaid, chattered softly with Jack, played a game with him and the children, Kathleen seemed exiled. Her anger, strong still, stoked by constant reconsideration, soon disposed of her disquiet.

On the second day, Jack made an overture.

'It's daft not to talk,' he said.

She did not reply, but carefully concealed her reaction. An observer might have concluded that she was stone deaf.

'Oh, well then,' he continued. 'If that's the way you take it.'

On Friday he usually handed her housekeeping money before he left. He was generous, giving her ample to save or spend on herself. This morning he left without the usual slapping down of an elastic-banded wad of notes. She did nothing about the omission. He did not say when he'd return.

She sat at nine-forty-five with her feet up in front of the television screen when he came in.

'Hello, there,' he shouted.

Ordinarily she would have jumped up to inquire what he wanted to eat. Tonight she kept her legs firmly on their stool. He sat down, still wearing his raincoat, gloves in hand.

'Good day?' he asked. 'Have you had a good day?'

Kathleen stared straight into his eyes to make certain he knew she heard him, but kept her mouth shut.

'Look,' he continued, 'how long is this going to last?' Again the pause, the saccharine music of TV. 'You've had a bit of your own back.'

He waited for her. She did not comply. He willed; she resisted passively. 'Are you going to speak?'

She watched the screen without understanding; a girl sang, while behind her a troupe of youths cavorted not very tidily. Terrified, for she did not underestimate her husband, she failed to grasp the sequence of words or events.

Jack stood up and with a rough jerk of one knee knocked her legs from the stool. At the same second he lifted her out of her chair by the arms, shook her. His violence was so great that she felt no pain, neither in her biceps, nor in her head which rattled, loose neck the pivot for its eccentric spinning. In fury he let her go so that she dropped to the floor, her lolling head catching the padded corner of her chair-arm. Pain struck then; dully, at a distance, but she lay unmoving, face, blood fiercely beating.

'Get up.'

He put a toe, gently enough, under her waist. Her eyes clamped fast. 'Get up, I say.' She did nothing. 'Bugger you, then, you stupid bitch.'

She felt the thud of his footsteps in the bone of her head, the closure of the door. When she pushed herself to her feet she tottered, her head thick, legs unsteady. Yet she could not help triumphing; she had sent him from the room, dismissed him. The Jack who spoke quietly, urged reason, she feared; he should bawl and bully, because that was her stereotype. Now that he acted as himself, and would regret it, she could begin to talk. Half crazily, or so she judged, she began to accustom herself to his adultery. What passionate exchanges, or tenderness, he and the other woman demonstrated Kathleen could not imagine; the naked pair in some undusted flat, amongst dregs of coffee or crusted cigar-butts, she could picture easily, but did not allow herself to do so. That was that.

She'd spoken again to her husband, resumed family life, and her anger had flared only once when he'd tried to buy her off with a present, a miniature silhouette of an early nineteenth-century young woman, on a long delicate chain, in gold. It was beautiful; she wanted to cry out her pleasure. The heart-shaped locket engraved with small, entwined hearts, the chain, fine as pack-thread was solid, gossamer – intransient. Taken aback, for she'd no opinion of his taste, she wondered who'd helped him. Her thoughts shook rugged. He'd go to his friends the dealers; they'd advise him, and he'd be prepared to shell out handsomely. But had he intended it for that other woman, had she in fact coveted it, until Kathleen's anger had brought him up sharp? She held it on her hand, turned it, replaced it in its case, put it on the table in front of her.

'Well?' She heard the suppressed energy in his word. He hated to ask for thanks.

'Yes.'

'Don't you like it?'

'I do. Thank you very much.'

She did not allow herself to look at it. It lay in its box, dark. Nothing would have delighted more than to feel its golden lightness, admire the workmanship. She stared instead at the folded-back crossword in a newspaper, angry, pleasuring in her malice, measuring the crouched, huge form of her husband. If he had snatched it up and slung it through the window, or twisted its beauty, ripped it apart, she would not have been surprised, but he knew its monetary value, as she did. Frank might well have admired it, but would have given the impression that the gift was not worth owning, that one diminished oneself by wishing to do so.

'Don't you want it, then?' he growled, great fist ready to snatch back.

'Haven't you given it to me?'

'Yes, I have. But you don't seem very excited.'

'It's beautiful. Yes, I think it is.'

Words like ice, thin, thin as water about to freeze.

That had been the end. The locket she had kept for a month in a drawer before she had worn it. His infidelities went unmentioned, but he walked about chastened, bursting to do her favours, not daring to say so.

Now as she sat with her brother-in-law, dulled into comfort by the whisky, she wanted nothing more. Why she had not poured herself a glassful or two of salvation at home she did not know. Frank watched, disapproving, probably of her, a grey man, unhandsome, not tidy. She saw him as he was.

He'd prefer to be left alone, lonely as he was. Her husband chased out after women, and, pleased with himself, knew he'd enough cash to settle any complications. Frank sat like his old cat, suspicious, ill-tempered, slothful. She explained unconvincingly that she did not mind her husband's absences, and swilling her whisky began to believe her halting dogmatisms.

'Why do you come here, then?'

'I don't know. I have to spit it out to somebody, and you're near.'

'In address? Or law?' Poeticisms. Get hold of life. He lifted the bottle, filled her glass and his own.

'Steady,' she warned. 'We'll both be reeling.'

Helen had been an undergraduate, and yet she'd lain crying with earache, a child, while her mother fretted. Jack's view was adult, spoke sense. Helen was a woman, must make her own way, put her head down to her own pain. That must be that. Frank knew.

'Did you let him know what you felt about this Helen business?'

'At the time. We have a row, and it's over.'

'It's not mentioned again?'

'No. That's Jack. One blow-up, get it out of your system. I bear malice.'

Frank put his head on one side. She waited, but not patiently. Now she had decided he could do nothing for her, she had no time for his play-acting.

'Not sufficient to leave him, though?'

He was talking. She'd missed the beginning. Courteously she asked him to repeat himself. He did so.

'No. I'm in a cleft stick.'

'Economically?' A poet? One of the family.

'Yes. That, I suppose.' She rolled her head. 'Money's shorter these days. Interest rates are high. He's worried; I'm sure he is. Perhaps that's why he acts as he does.'

'But that's not really it?' he asked.

'I don't know. I don't mind somehow. In one sense. But I don't want to leave him or lose him. That's pride. I had him and I'll keep him.'

'Do you think you will?'

'What?'

'Keep him.'

'Shouldn't be surprised. He's not sure what he's after and there are plenty of girls who'll have sex at his price level.'

Frank, saddened by the jargon of hopelessness, waved the whisky bottle. Kathleen stood, mussed his untidy hair, said:

'You'll have me drunk.'

'Isn't that what you want?' He stroked her buttocks.

'No, it isn't.' A strong voice, near shouting. That was the Kathleen he admired, sharp with the wrong answer. With the butt of her hand she banged his head, jolting.

'Go on, then. Outline the case.'

'There is no case. He chases off after money and sex. He's allowed to, as long as he's successful. He's getting on, but women want him. What have I got? Books to read. A house to look after. A few friends to entertain. A piano to play. A brother-in-law who fancies me now because he thinks he loved me once. It's not much, is it?'

'Is it any worse than his?'

'I don't suppose so. Jack works. I'll give him that. And worries. When they started this Welcar thing I had some idea how things were going, because he used me, talked to me. But not now. I'm dropped.'

'Ask him for a job.'

'Do you think I haven't?' She sounded unenthusiastic, voice slurred. 'But he laughs. He'll bring a few papers home for me to sort out. It's a game.'

'Is it because he doesn't want you to know how near disaster he is?'

'You ask some bloody fool questions,' she said. 'No, it's because he doesn't think I've any place in his business. That's

94

all. I'm the little woman looking forward to my first grand-children when Freddy's wife obliges. You didn't expect Louise to write your poetry for you. Did you?'

'She wasn't capable.'

'That's what he thinks. But you never bothered to inquire. Did you ever try her out?'

'I never noticed anything, either in words, conversation that is, or ways of thinking that would have led me to believe that Louise could have put down a line of poetry. She did not think that way.' He spoke slowly, as if addressing a jury.

'She never got the chance. You never encouraged her. You're the poet. She's the cook, the mopper-up. You're all the same.'

'Give us a line of poetry, then.' He leaned back, feet flat, jeering.

'I hate the world of men.' She shouted.

'Iambic trimeter.'

'We're drunk. Or near it,' she said. Certainly she did not speak clearly. 'You'll have to walk back with me. Sober yourself up. Where's my coat?' She flapped her arms, turn-ing. 'He found a murder once. Jack did.'

'I know.'

'When he was a boy. In Leicester. He told me about it. Murder and suicide. Once you've seen it, he said, it didn't seem so strange.' Frank helped her on with her coat. 'He's strange. A stranger, now.' She sat down, helplessly spread her hands. 'Come and kiss me, for Christ's sake.'

He did so. It was enough.

10

Jack Weldon's office struck warm. In an armchair a nearly naked Judith Powis sipped tea from a mug. She could hear Jack thumping along the corridor outside; carpets did nothing to silence him. When he emerged, he pushed towards his desk, poured himself a cup, whistled. He wore thin, narrow braces, string-thin to the breadth of his shoulders, his paunch, the limbs. At a mirror he put on his tie, slowly as if exactitude counted.

'Why don't you get dressed?' he grumbled.

'What's the hurry?' She stroked her legs appreciatively, stretching.

'Are we going out to dinner?' he asked. 'We deserve it.'

'No. Thank you.'

'We've worked hard.' He indicated the piles of letters. They had been here since before eleven, and now the clock showed a quarter to five. Graft, sandwiches from a pub, sex, down to dictation, back to the floor. Pleased with himself, with her, he hummed the opening of Beethoven's violin concerto, a favourite of Kathleen and his brother. She dressed now she'd finished drinking, without hurry. He watched, jacket on, in his right mind. 'I'll take you to the Mansfield.'

'No. Alan's been to Derby. He'll be back about eight. We'll have a meal, then.'

'Suppose he's come home early?'

Now she'd donned her few clothes, she made for the mirror, to let down, brush up her hair. Though he sat close he made no attempt to touch her, and that she liked.

'He's gone to his mother's. They'll go to chapel together, and then he'll get a train. Always the same routine.'

'I didn't know he was religious.'

'He isn't. He does it to please her.'

'She thinks he is, then?' He felt mischievous, god-like. While Alan glazed through a sermon he didn't believe in, his wife committed adultery. He enjoyed that.

'I doubt if she is, either.'

He peered out of the window. To the left skyscrapers towered, greyly. Nearer rectangles of offices, glass-walled but blank now, squatted efficiently functional. On the other side, at the crest of a hill, early Victorian houses, neatly untidy, were outlined by the brightness of late afternoon. Quite close, a stone's throw, a black terrace of dwelling-houses remained, like rotted teeth, with gardens, trees, dividing fences, a brick wall in ramshackle beauty this end. Spring declared itself. Forsythia was nearly done. Hedges budded green. Clumps of yellow he guessed as daffodils. Grass burst lusciously green. Judith went out of the room. He'd been here all day, had done three hours' work before she arrived. He liked the placidity of Sunday, without traffic noise, no lifts whirring, lights out in darkened corridors. By special arrangement with the caretaker he had outside keys, he and David Lassman. He'd had to instruct Judith to arrive exactly at a fixed time, then he could let her in. Good. And Lassman had left at twelve-thirty, his homburg hat black over his smart topcoat.

The anticipation of her arrival, his pleasure in overt power, had solved problems for him. He knew exactly what he'd do tomorrow, the day after. That was decided on, re-examined by nine-thirty. On her appearance, he had the details prepared and double-checked, so that he was ready with the dozen letters he'd dictated, she'd typed, the seven complicated pieces of duplication she'd attended to. She worked well, needed no second instructions, enjoyed him sexually, but did not interrupt business for that. He rubbed his hands, chuffed. Good, good. She returned. He indicated an envelope on her typewriter.

'For services rendered,' he said. She slipped it into her

handbag, and they left. They did not kiss, soberly walked abreast to his car. They had drunk champagne, a half-bottle between them, with the sandwiches. She, he thought, preferred tea, provided a carton of milk, had the kettle ready. Twice they'd had sex, the second time more perfunctorily, but better, more suitably, working off inhibitions without ostentation, with no need to demonstrate anything beyond animal need of an easily satisfied kind. Now he'd drive her within five minutes' walk of her home, and then decide on his own movements. She never invited him in unless Alan were about; she was a cautious, hard bitch, but she suited. As he drove he wondered how he'd fare married to her.

He put her down on a main road. She had been describing Alan's home in Derby, with its copper kettle and old-fashioned iron-stand. Her talk was slow, but he was loth to allow its conclusion, and so, unusually, got out of the car. As they stood on the sunlit pavement together, a sharp wind whipped into them, so that they smiled to see a thin, middle-aged woman wrestling to keep her hat on. A bus drew up twenty yards away, and the woman took a step or two towards it, then scuttled backwards when a man stepped off. She raised her hand to her mouth, childishly indicating chagrin at her error. After a pause, the passenger had time to walk past the spectators, a young woman descended from the bus. She, stout, very pale, stared stupidly round her. Now the other dashed forward, in a panic, it seemed, to put her arm round the girl's waist.

The two moved slowly, leaning on each other, tacking, the older guiding against the pressure of the younger's weight. As they approached, Jack saw that the girl was crying, heard the woman murmur comfort. Both faces were blank; the younger's round, mongoloid behind her glasses. Within a few steps, she seemed to have ceased weeping, stared ahead, rather, gaped, gawped. As they drew alongside, they staggered, a jagged yard out of course, into Jack who steadied them.

'Sorry,' the woman said. 'I'm sorry.'

'Is there anything we can do?' Jack asked.

'No. We're walking home.'

'Is it far? Can I give you a lift?'

'Turton Street.'

Judith succinctly explained where that was.

'Get in,' he said, opening the back door.

'Go in the gentleman's car.'

He waved a farewell to the quizzically smiling Judith, completed the two-minute journey in silence.

'Number thirty-four. That's this one.'

He jumped out to open the kerb-side door. The older woman dragged at her companion's arm; she sat stubborn, prepared for a long ride.

'Come on, Else. We're here.' Sluggish obedience. 'She gets frightened, y'know, on the bus. It frightens her. She's slow. On the uptake. Mentally.' The arm supported the fat waist. 'You've been to see your mam, haven't you, duck?'

'You'll be all right.'

'Oh, ah. We shall now, thanks. Say thank you to the gentleman, Else.' The girl turned her moon-face to him, blankly. 'She's not sure where to get off the bus, and she gets frightened. She might be at the wrong place. She cries in case she has. But she likes goin' on her own. Funny, in't it? Aren't you goin' to thank the gentleman? She can talk if she wants to, you know. Come on, then. Your auntie'll have the tea ready.'

They tottered, yoked, across the pavement.

Jack Weldon glowered at the closed door made flush by hardboard. 'I'll tell our Frank,' he decided. 'Something for him there.'

Once he was home he was surprised to find his sister in the drawing room, glass of sherry untouched by her side, sitting straight-backed as age and figure allowed. Kathleen was smiling, much at her ease, as if she'd scored over Cecilia.

'He's here himself,' she said. 'You ask him.'

Cissie blushed unbecomingly. She looked ill, uncomfortable, sullen, sallow.

'It's none of my business.'

Brother and sister-in-law laughed out loud, cruelly.

'Ask him,' Kathleen insisted. Cissie straightened herself stiffer.

'They're saying . . .' she began, and stopped. No encouragement. 'They're saying that you've lost your money.'

Now she seemed a poor, little thing, without animation.

'Who are "they"?' he asked, making for the whisky bottle.

'Eric heard it down at the club. Several were talking.'

'Such as? Who? Who are the several?' Each question prised apart from the rest.

'I don't know. Lionel Spencer, Stephen Limb. They're usually there. You'd know better than me. He didn't say. Some friends mentioned it in conversation. Seemed to think he'd . . .'

'Some friends,' Kathleen said, with sarcastic emphasis.

'He said he'd not heard. He hadn't. But they all spoke as if it was common knowledge.'

Common. Knowledge. Jack selected a chair, then its position, before he sat himself rather gingerly down, on the lookout for booby-traps. Cecilia showed her alarm, writhing. Kathleen watched, as one observes the discomfiture of enemies.

'Let's get this straight,' Jack began. 'They're saying at the Conservative Club that I'm bankrupt.'

'Not bankrupt.' Cissie grabbed the word, to deny. 'They didn't say that.'

'Why have you come here? Out of curiosity?'

'I wanted to know if it was true. I couldn't ask you over the phone. You never know who's listening.'

'Let's imagine it was so, our Cis.' He spoke with heavy joviality, his accent coarsened, his face screwed into lines. 'What could you do about it?'

'Nothing.' She answered immediately. 'Nothing much.'

'There you are, then.'

'I couldn't give you the money back. That's certain. It depends how bad it was. I could offer you a home. Somewhere to stay.'

'Have you mentioned that to Eric, then?' he demanded. 'No.'

'He wouldn't be pleased.'

A spasm of anger, distress, dislike crossed her face.

'I couldn't do less,' she said. 'You're my kith and kin.'

'Eric wouldn't like the upset to his routine. I take it Hooper Bros is doing all right?'

'You haven't answered my question.'

Kathleen almost laughed. This nervy, thin, twisted woman had come out with a statement that showed her breeding. She was a Weldon, Jacob's daughter. Somewhere along the line there'd be a protest. With the father the objection would be maintained until it was seriously challenged; with Jack until opposition had been kicked to splinters; Frank would have sunk it until it festered out of sight into a verse. Awkward, knobbly customers, the three men. And Cecilia, goaded, had reacted properly. Well done, Weldon.

'No. I haven't.'

Something in his tone made Kathleen catch breath. Had he been hiding this from her? Afraid, until his sister cornered him.

'Listen, our Cis.' Relief. 'You go home and tell Eric not to believe all he hears down at that club. I've done all right this year. I shall make a little bit of profit. And plough some back, if that's what they call it.' He laughed, wagging a finger. 'No need for you to springclean the spare bedroom yet. Now get that glass of sherry down you, woman, and warm yourself up.'

Cecilia obeyed the last instruction but seemed no more cheerful. The lines in her face were cut deep; her mouth-ends turned down; her nose jutted rockily irregular, discoloured. The small eyes flashed no spark, puckered themselves.

'I've made a bob or two today, I reckon, apart from anything else.'

'Well, I'm glad,' Cissie said, aggressively.

'You won't have to put us up?'

'You know it's not that, our Jack.'

Now she settled to a dull account of her health, and Eric's duller commentary on it. She had decided to visit Emma, and explained why she should live in a hotel and not stay in her daughter's home.

'The house is large enough. They've got the money. But I'm not going to impose on them. I invited myself, and I don't suppose she could say no. I told her what I intended to do. She argued, but she soon stopped. She knows when I've made my mind up. I shall go out some days. Take the bus or excursions. I don't know that part of the world at all.'

'And what about Eric?' Jack chaffed her.

'He won't go.'

'Who'll look after him? He'll be getting women in.'

'Have you heard of a freezer? A deep-freezer? I can put plenty in there to keep him and six others like him going.'

To Kathleen there seemed an antagonism between the two, as if they could not leave the opponent alone, goading, probing, prodding. Tonight it was genial, for she guessed Jack was pleased, not at his sister's intervention which he'd attribute to Eric Hooper's spleen, but by his day's work. So he refilled his sister's glass, with a wine she neither appreciated nor wanted, but which she grimaced down because her pride was intact. Her brother still had money, wealth even. Francis had name, fame; John James had substantial assets. She could lift her head, make a nuisance of herself in Worcester, if that was the place, to her daughter.

Kathleen puzzled over her sister-in-law's health.

She seemed lively enough. Thin, but wiry, something like a hen, all pecking energy and eye-stare, she held her own against Jack's robust raillery. A month or two back she seemed, was said to be, ill. Her hands perched awry, twisted and bloodless. She looked older than her years, well into her sixties. As far as one could tell, she had no habitual pleasures; she waited round for life's knocks and then put up with them, grumblingly. She had looked after a quarrelsome, bullying father, a boring dodderer of a husband and had idolized a fecund daughter who did as she liked. What sort of life was that? Kathleen had once made inquiries.

'I do what I have to,' Cissie answered. 'It's what I've always done.'

'But what about enjoying yourself?'

Incomprehension spawned on Cecilia's dumb face. Chance would be a fine thing.

This evening, the three sat triangularly apart until Cissie rose with a bustle.

'I s'll have to be on my way.'

'There's no hurry. The good news'll wait.'

'I'm not sitting here drinking all night with you, whatever you think.'

Jack, smiling, insisted on driving her home.

'I'm giving you the benefit of the doubt,' he said, slapping her backside.

On his return Kathleen had cleared the glasses and was knitting, a ploy that sent him elsewhere. He announced his withdrawal.

'Helen's coming,' Kathleen said. 'She rang.'

'When?'

'Saturday. She's bringing her husband.'

'Iron my Sunday suit, will you? Did she say why?'

'No. She just asked if it would be all right to come. I said I'd be in. There was nothing in your home diary.'

'Anything else?'

'She's thinking of doing an MA, starting next year. Something to do with river trade.'

'Jesus.'

The thick needles flew to their clicking.

'Are you . . . ?' he began.

'Yes, thank you.' Finality there.

'Why don't you go out sometimes?' he asked.

'I go when I want to.'

'You don't sound pleased.'

'What do you think? That your sister can come with her questions, and they won't worry me? What do you think I'm made of? Bloody steel?'

'You knew there was nothing in it.'

'I knew nothing of the kind. For all you tell me we might be down on our last penny piece. I don't see your bank books. You don't show me your company accounts.'

'Look at your own bank statement, woman. That's healthy enough, isn't it?' Her fingers, needles, darted. He watched them wry-mouthed. 'I don't want to bother you with . . .'

'Give me a job,' she said.

'What?'

'Give me a job,' she repeated.

'Scrubbing the office floor?'

'I wouldn't mind that. It would be useful. I hang about here all day.'

'You've the garden.'

'I don't give a damn for gardens. If you concreted it over I'd say nothing.' No knitting. 'I sit here wasting time.'

'Whose fault is that? Mine?' His face reddened, but he kept his voice low. 'I give you money. You can gad about if that's what you want. A cruise. You might meet somebody interesting.'

'What's that mean?'

'What you like. You're supposed to be an educated woman and yet you can't occupy yourself. You've books and stereo. You've friends you can visit. You can go on holiday whenever you like. Nine-tenths of the women in this place would give . . .'

'Nine-tenths?'

'I don't want to pick a quarrel with you, Kathleen.'

'I want to pick one with you, then.'

'I understand that you're bored or frustrated, but that's something you have to cope with. Your time of life . . .'

'That's the excuse, now, is it? My age?' She glared, hands, arms, cheek in rigor. 'You've had some woman today up at the office.'

'Come off it.'

'Not that it makes any difference to what I think of you.'

'What does that mean?' He spoke quietly so that she looked up.

'Mean? What I say. On a personal level, we're done, finished. There's nothing between us. You don't even expect me to cook your meals.'

'Certainly I can afford to eat out.' He poured a drink, waved the bottle in question towards her, but received no answering gesture. 'I don't want a row.'

'Want. Don't want.' Her voice harshened, into a screechier pitch. 'You come home from your women.'

'You've no proof.'

'You've had a woman there today.' Kathleen shouted, eyes hare-bright. 'I'd do your typing for you.'

'There's no need.'

'There is. That's what I'm telling you. I need it. I. Not you. I.'

'I see.'

'You don't see anything. You're blind-selfish.'

'Have you considered,' Jack's voice boomed, almost dignified, reason dispersing madness, 'the effect of the boss's wife in the office? They'd look on you as a spy.'

'Because you're . . .'

'It's useless talking,' he said, sipped his whisky and folded his arms. He would not surrender, not walk out, wait for her to scream anger or reduce herself to tears or sullen quiet. He could not win. He wished he'd some gift ready in his pocket, though that would worsen matters, scrawl his guilt large. Today life pleased him; he'd share his pleasure, were she not incapable.

'I've talked to Frank,' she said, more calmly.

'Uh?' He'd not help out there.

'He said I should face you with it. You and your woman. This Powis girl.'

'You'd have done better,' Jack asked, clear word after word, 'to marry him, wouldn't you?'

'You answer that,' she said. 'Go on. You answer it.'

'He loved you. So you said. Loves you still, for all I know. My first love.' Irony cracked his voice. 'Go and see if you'd do better with him.' No answer, but the resumed, easy flurry of needles. 'Go and live down at the cottage.'

'You wouldn't mind?'

'I shouldn't have to, should I? Mark you, he'd shit his breeches. But if that's what you want, go on, get on with it.'

'What will you do?' she asked.

'Do? Nothing I can, is there? Break his bloody neck? Is that what you want? Fist-fighting? Over you? A bit of bloody skin and grief? Drag you back by the hair? Put my boot up your bum?' He did not enunciate with any violence, though his voice was deep enough to suggest menace, welling from the breadth of his barrel chest. 'I don't understand you, that's for sure.'

'You might try.'

She had signalled the end of the battle. The skirmish was hers in that he'd expressed his disgust with vulgarity, but had controlled the expression. That was victory enough for this night. Her fingers flashed as she kept her eyes down modestly to her work. She did not know whether her accusation was true; did not care. She had galled him and soothed herself. One does not cure irreparable hurt; one, by whatever ridiculous means, learns to live with it. Kathleen had done enough for her self-esteem, sufficient for the day. So she knitted, brilliantly, not caring, not conscious of the flaring anger of a few minutes back. Her hands performed with virtuosity, with the whole of her nervous system concentrated on, controlled by, that efficient speed. She exulted, but did not extend herself, did not even recall that her husband hated the process.

He helped himself to the bottle again.

'Steady.' She smiled as she spoke.

'Why do you bother?'

'You might be sick on the carpets.' She smiled more broadly because he'd leave this room puzzled. After a burst of knitting she raised her head. 'I'll tell you something else. Helen's husband is thinking of putting up for parliament. Some constituency wants to adopt him.' She waited, as he did. 'He'll be standing for Labour.'

'He would be. Or bloody Liberal.'

'Labour. Helen seems very keen.'

'If he got in, he'd have to give his job up, wouldn't he?' She nodded. 'That wouldn't be very sensible.'

'They seem to think so.'

She left it at that, but her husband would not go. He perched uncomfortably, legs wide, as if determined to sit or stare her out.

'Do you want anything to eat?' she asked pacifically.

'I'll get a sandwich before the night's over.'

'Why did you tell me to go to Frank's?' He paid little attention. 'You could have said "to Cissie's". She's offered us a bed.' Silence. 'What have you got against Frank? Are you jealous of him?'

'He's a man.' Jack said it slowly, cleared his glass at a swig.

'And?'

'It's a man you want, isn't it?'

'Don't judge everybody by your own way of going on.'

'No fear of that. Not with you.'

'You don't like Frank, do you? That's about the length and breadth of it.'

'You've never heard me say so. It's what you think. Me

107

jealous of him. But I'm not. He's not my sort isn't our kid, but I don't want him to be. And I'll tell you something else. You be careful with him. He knows how to look after himself. He'd drop you in it without a second thought if it suited him.'

'That's not how I've found him.'

'Have it your own way.'

'You don't like him.' She beaked forward. 'You don't, you know.' She halted the needles for emphasis.

'If you said I don't like our Cissie, I wouldn't argue. Or that nose-dripping husband of hers. You'd be right. But she came and offered us house-room. Christ knows if she meant it. I expect she's sharp enough to see that's the last place I'd want to land up. But even give her credit there, I still don't like her. She's my sister. It makes no difference.'

'Frank's . . . ?' Back at work, she seemed relaxed, interested.

'Yes. He's got something about him. Something I don't want. But I'm pleased to see his photo, his name in the paper. There's somebody there. But with our Cis . . . She's nothing but a few airs and graces. Frank's alive, in a half-dead sort of way.'

'He's making an effort,' she thought, 'to please me. Or not to be dismissed. He doesn't usually talk like this. Perhaps this Judith Powis has given him a new slant.' Kathleen felt neither pang nor thrill at the name; the whole train of thought seemed so unlikely. Jack looked almost gross there, trousers tight across his paunch, legs wide, genitals full.

'Shall I tell you something?' She'd reward him.

'Go on, then.'

'It frightened me when Cissie said that. I don't like shocks.'

'Did you think it was true?'

'I'd no idea. You never say anything. Would you tell me if you lost your money?'

'I'd tell you.'

'You wouldn't, you know. You'd be too ashamed.'

'I'd be that, all right. But if I went bust, I'd be a different man. I'd be screaming.'

'How likely is it?'

He stared at her long enough. The question cut deep; slashed her doubts across his hide. The room was solid, with a decorated ceiling, plaster cornices, two seascapes with heavy gold frames, a huge settee, three strong armchairs, velvet curtains, deep Axminster carpets, a dark sideboard, a cabinet with silver, a cabinet with jade, books, a tapestry screen, an arm-wide bunch of milk-white tulips. The air held warmth; the chandelier glittered golden; no draughts fretted; the antique clock on the mantelpiece ticked discreetly, accurately on. Money had bought this house, furnished it in comfort and luxury. How likely? Jack looked with affection at his wife, saw in her her former beauty. Mistress of this, of other rooms, and dependent on him. He stretched proud as he sat.

'At present . . .' he spoke slowly, 'not at all. Do you fancy another house?'

'What do you mean?'

'Outside the city. Trees.'

'We have trees now.' Her knitting was down, in her pleasure. 'We came here when I married you.'

'That's no reason for not moving.' Voice deep, masterly. 'You could start looking tomorrow.'

'You shouldn't put ideas into my head.'

'I don't like Sunday evening.' He prowled about the room, searching, restless, a bull amongst unbreakables. 'The morning's great. But it's dull now. Stinks of cabbage.'

'In here? It does not,' she said.

Her husband laughed, a glass paperweight dwarfed in his hand.

11

Helen arrived on Friday with her husband.

She showed no embarrassment, and once her mother had mentioned the possibility of a new house became almost garrulous. This place stood ugly, built round; its size and grounds were right, but if one could afford to keep a large house one might as well have it in a decent area. Kathleen pointed out that the move was no certainty, but this did not discourage daughter.

'If you want to flit, you go. Make Daddy do something about it. He's doing well enough, isn't he?'

'It'll cost a great deal of money.'

'What's money for? He'll spend it if you don't.'

'What will Harold think when you speak of your father like that?'

Whatever he thought, he said little. A tall man, slightly balding at the crown, he sat in relaxation, mildly amused, handsome in a thin way. He talked for five minutes about enclosures, but without condescension, peered round the walls at Kathleen's pictures and books, was playfully rebuked by his wife for so doing. He dressed well, seemed sure of his status, but without self-assertion or superiority. Kathleen looked forward to his meeting with her husband.

Jack appeared before six, and was down at quarter to seven, shaven and groomed for dinner. Helen had already broached the topic of new houses.

'That's up to your mother,' he said curtly.

'Don't you want a move?'

'I've told you. If it'll please your mother.'

Helen heeded no warnings, gushed on. Jack answered without rancour, but unamused, a shade grim or dour. He asked Harold Kitto if he'd been in the district before, and listened to the courteous answer. Prompt at five to seven, Francis was shown in.

'They're thinking of moving,' Helen said, kisses exchanged. 'Did you know?'

'I wish I hadn't mentioned it.' Kathleen.

'You'll be sorry, won't you?' Helen laughed, arm through her uncle's, treating him as she would not treat her father.

'Yes, I shall. I'm not surprised, but I shall be sad.'

'You can write a poem about it.'

'Yes. That's about all I can.'

Helen seemed childish, Kathleen thought, in a way she was not when she had lived at home. Now the girl must make her mark, sign the occasion with her adult or married status. Before, she'd disappear to her bedroom to live her own life, and at meals or parties appeared soberly, neutrally pleasant. Today her voice seemed higher pitched, her conversation more insistent, her behaviour hectic or hectoring. Mrs H. I. F. Kitto was their equal; let them not forget.

Harold asked a question or two of Frank, making it clear he knew his work. He did not obtrude, but if questioned answered at some length. He observed Helen's febrile exchanges, but without criticism, overt or hidden. Kathleen wondered if he were enjoying himself, asked him.

'Yes. I'm pleased to meet you. It should have happened before.'

'And are we as you expected?'

'Yes. Helen talks about you a great deal. And I've seen plenty of photographs. So I'd a good idea. But, of course, people differ from one's expectations. That's obvious.'

'In what way?'

'That would tell you more about me than about you.'

'That's what she's after.' Jack, sharp, deep.

'Mr Weldon is rather quieter than I imagined.'

'And I'm noisier.'

'No. Less like Helen.'

'Is that bad?' Frank, in mischief.

'Not at all. There are all kinds of good. I'd have been a bit disappointed if my wife had been a mere copy of her mother. In both. I like uniqueness. As long as the other virtues,' he smirked as he hesitated on the noun, 'are there.'

Kathleen remembered the time when she thought this was the way gentlemen should talk, with a polite sheen. It did not please now, could not. She herself wanted singularity from the man, who was her daughter's husband, not a tailor's dummy. Still.

He talked to Frank about King John, and Shakespeare's view of 'commodity'. Very briefly, almost ironically, he outlined for his father-in-law the administration of university funds. His anecdotes were mildly amusing; he knew human folly, but was not slow on arithmetic or short of fact. Once when Helen interrupted to contradict him, about the character of the head of the history department, he immediately stopped his flow and cocked his ear to listen to her.

'He's a fraud, Harold, you know he is. And idle. And inconsistent. Look at the way he treated René Weekes.'

Kitto broke his bread and lifted a piece to his lips, as one at holy communion. Helen showed she had spoken out of her turn, even putting her hand to her mouth, childishly. Kitto did not comment, but nodded, as if his mouth were too full for speech.

'I like scandal,' Kathleen said. 'And these men do.'

The younger people said no more. Would Harold chide his wife when they were alone? Beat her? Not much more than a year ago, Helen had been praising Professor Talbot as a brilliant lecturer. Now. Were these new views borrowed from her husband?

'Don't we hear any more about René Whatshisname, then?' Kathleen persisted.

'Boring,' Helen said.

'Not worth the effort.' Kitto could speak again. 'Like all university politics, it's complicated, and not worth the explanation.'

'You could try us,' Kathleen said.

'Not on my first day here.' He seemed ten feet tall, as he sat gracefully there, smiling at them from his dry, handsome face.

'You've managed to shut 'em both up,' Jack said. 'More than I ever did.'

Frank laughed wispily. The rest concentrated on plates.

At the end of the meal, when Kathleen had cleared the table and they sat down to coffee and liqueurs, Kitto came across to her.

'I hope I wasn't rude,' he said. 'I didn't mean to be.'

'No.' She didn't want his apologies. The others made it obvious they were all attention.

'I don't like Ian Talbot. I don't get on with him. I make a point of not talking in public about him.'

'Are we public?' she said, rudely.

'Within my wide terms of reference, and on this occasion, yes.'

Kathleen looked over at her husband as if to challenge what he made of that. He stared back with hostility or bloated unconcern.

After an evening passed pleasantly, during which Frank described a poetry festival and his cat's mousing expeditions over the churchyard wall, Jack a dog-fight and the Wakes, Helen a dream kitchen, Harold a day at the races and Kathleen a birthday, a child's trip to the seaside, her butcher's wife and the transplanting of a large tree, they retired to bed, staggering politely. Francis sang as he negotiated the drive. 'The farmer rides proudly / To market and fair / And the clerk in the ale-house / Still keeps the great chair.'

Jack, himself humming, appeared in Kathleen's bedroom.

'What do you think of your son-in-law, then?' Anointing her face, she got after him.

'He's used to setting kids right, saying what's wrong with their essays. You can see Helly likes it.'

'And do you?' She was impressed by the sharpness.

'Yes. Smart fellow. Literate. Unlike us.'

'Speak for yourself.'

'When did you last read a book? Be honest.' He slapped the front of a massive wardrobe.

'This afternoon.'

Jack chuckled, swayed off. From the back he looked help-less, at the mercy of a draught. She was pleased, standing there, then mindless, until she had undressed and peered through the curtains to the lines of street lights, the black houses below, the dull bulk of the church, the dark shapes of her garden.

Next morning the two men left together. They'd have lunch out. The women would go to Newthorpe to see a house for sale. Helen shouted shrill. Quite how this had been decided over a long, word-flying breakfast Kathleen, up and down, was not sure. The two men, standing either side of Jack's Daimler, looked brotherly.

In Newthorpe, aubretia and snow-in-summer shone in the gardens; lawns were freshly cut; bright green flecked the hedges and trees. Kathleen had a careful note on the where-abouts of the house, but they drove through the village un-successfully before a dapper clergyman expounded their route. They were to turn left just before they reached the iron-railed churchyard and up past a terrace of three cottages into a lane with a sharp right turn giving the impression of a cul-de-sac from the main road.

'Why the hell does it do that?' Helen demanded, man-handling the wheel.

'There'd be a building there once,' her mother answered.

'I bet that's right.' The historian took over.

Hawthorn hedges enclosed the tarmacadam road, kept in good repair. After a hundred and fifty yards they stopped at a white, brand-new five-barred gate, marked Dickens House.

A concrete drive stretched over the slope of a hill; on the right they made out a copse, black still with winter, but nothing of the house.

'If we drive on up to the brow we'll see the place,' Kathleen said, confidently. They could, did.

An early nineteenth-century block, now painted white, stood on the south slope of the hill, in the lee of the wood. Though they could view only the back, and that partly obscured by outbuildings, it appeared square, and elegant, with a graceful low-pitched roof.

'Nice,' Helen said. 'Jane Austen style. There's a paddock as well as a copse.'

Kathleen caught a flash from the distance.

'That's the road. We ought to see the front from down there.'

'We'll see the front when we drive up. Surely the road will round the house.'

'We aren't driving up.'

'What are we doing here? Picking blackberries?'

'Looking. The sight of the place from a distance might have put me off.'

'Has it?'

'No.'

'Well, then.' Helen spurted words; they'd go in, walk about the rooms when they had furniture in them, talk to the owner.

'No.'

'It doesn't commit you to anything. You scrutinize it, and ask.'

'You waste somebody's time.'

'They want to sell it.' Helen sounded aggrieved. 'They'll be delighted to see a prospective buyer. They're probably glad to talk. You might learn something you won't from the estate agent. Why they're leaving, for one thing. That's important. What it costs to run. What sort of furniture they're getting rid of, the fitments.'

'No.'

'You're hopeless.' Helen laughed at her mother but recognized a warning note. Kathleen explained she knew the three sitting rooms, the five bedrooms, the two bathrooms, the oil-fired central heating, the treble garage. Her daughter asked the price, was told, surprisingly, wondered at the cheapness of Nottinghamshire. 'What do you think?'

'I don't know,' Kathleen answered. 'I'm slow making my mind up.'

'You don't really want to move, do you?'

'I think I do. But I don't want it at enormous cost.'

'It'll be no more expensive to run than your present place.'

They drove back, parked just off the main road along which they walked to catch a glimpse of Dickens House. Along the pavement stretched the deep front gardens of desirable residences, built post-war in the grounds of the older building; a wide gap between two bungalows revealed both the frontage of the old house, and the protecting wood.

'There was a lane from here to the portico,' Kathleen informed her daughter.

'How do you know?'

'The estate agent. And I've seen an aerial photograph.'

'I thought you knew nothing about the ...'

'I'm slow. And unsure.'

A woman, with an elaborate grey coiffure which contrasted with a scruffy anorak paused from her gardening to watch them, to smile when she caught Helen's ready eye.

'Were you looking for something?'

'Dickens House. From this side.'

'You can see it. That's it. But you know that.' A far-back, southern standard voice. Smiles of confusion.

'My mother's thinking of buying it,' Helen said, plainly. The statement impressed.

'I see.' The gardening gloves were removed. 'Would you like to walk through to our back fence? You can see straight over the grounds.'

They thanked her, passed through a highly polished hall, a

brilliant kitchen, along a crazy path past shaven lawns, trellis work, apple trees, a regular patch. Though they were perhaps eighty yards nearer, and were not distracted by the houses on the road, they could see no better.

'I could fetch my husband's binoculars, if that would help.' Kathleen declined the offer, sourly, not wishing to be beholden.

'My mother creeps up on it,' Helen said. 'Nothing will rush her.'

'That's sensible.'

'Is it a good buy?' Helen asked, half in earnest.

'I don't know anything about it. I've never been inside.'

'Would you live there?'

'There are only the two of us. My son is in America and my daughter in London. It would be too big. This house is too large. We're heating rooms for nothing. But we like the district; we have friends; if we see a bungalow we like it's in the wrong place.'

'So it wouldn't suit you?'

'We'd just be helping to keep a building in good order. The rooms are beautiful. Elegant, I'm told, with large windows and elaborate fireplaces. We couldn't afford it. If we could, we wouldn't want to spend our money that way. I'm sorry. That must have sounded rude.'

'Sensible,' Kathleen said.

'Old houses need money spending on them. That's for certain.'

'Who lives there now?' Helen.

'A man called Clark-Williams, a surgeon.' Her mother had answered. 'He's retiring.'

The three stood by the fence. A flurry of gusty breeze rustled the thick grass of the field beyond. This side all was cut, tied down, trained.

'Eighteen-twenty-three.' Kathleen announced.

'Was it called Dickens House then?' Helen asked.

'Shouldn't think so. Doesn't Dickens mean devil? Though

the estate agent said something about Charles staying there once.'

'What would it be? A farmhouse?'

'I don't think so. A gentleman's residence. In a modest way.'

The lady offered them coffee, but Kathleen refused, politely, escaped, bustling a reluctant Helen.

'What's the hurry?' demanded Helen. 'The old biddy was just getting interesting.'

'She knew nothing.'

'You didn't give her time. Even if there wasn't any scandal, she'd have told us about herself.'

'I don't want to hear.'

Helen gently driving uphill out of the village smiled about her. At the crest she drew on to the grass verge with a panorama of ploughed fields, grass, a dusting of green corn.

'It's bigger than you think. There are servants' rooms up in the roof, not heated, left locked. There are outbuildings. It seems ridiculous to take it for two of us. It could house a little nursing home, or a school.' Helen stared blank-faced over the hedge in front of her. 'Your father's never in.'

'He could have an office there.'

'That's the last thing he'd want. If we took it, it would be to pander to my vanity. That doesn't seem a very good reason. I'd have to buy expensive furniture, and hire domestic help. For what? I hardly do any entertaining. Your father meets his business contacts in his club in town.'

'Do you and Daddy get on?' Helen frowned, softening the question.

'That's not easy. We don't have a great deal to do with each other. But we've been married a long time. People do grow away from each other. More often than one imagines.'

'Harold's parents are divorced. When his father retired, he was sixty-five, his mother just upped and left him. She had a job, and some money. Then they divorced by consent. She was fifty-two. She has a little flat – and still goes out to work.'

'And the father?'

'He sold the house with the surgery, bought a bungalow not far off. He'd have done that in any case. He looks after himself.'

'What does Harold say about it?'

'It happened before I knew him. It was sad, at the time. I think he sided with his mother. She was waiting to go. The old man was, oh, dictatorial. Not so noisy as Daddy, but worse. She'd made her mind up. She'd been lucky. One or two legacies.'

'I've nothing.' Kathleen spoke cold as the morning.

'That doesn't mean you'd like to leave him?'

'It means I can't.' The one faced the other. 'It also means I don't ever think about it. Once you know what is or isn't possible, it makes a difference.'

'I'm sorry.'

'There's nothing to be sorry about. There must be thousands in the same trap.'

'It's not fair. He could leave you, if he wanted.'

'He could. But he hasn't, so far.'

'Do you think he will?' Helen's voice was lower, not sharing her confidence with the branches above her head. 'When you talk like that, I . . .'

'I don't know.' Suddenly Kathleen's throat clogged and her eyes gushed tears. It seemed as if a passion leapt from inside her, expanding and expropriating, until her quiet words became incoherent, her control a shudder of sobs. The change struck without intermediate phases; one minute she held an interesting conversation, the next she wept.

Helen did her best; embraced with soothing words. Incongruously hugging one's mother on a roadside did not please. Kathleen pushed herself free, wiped the offending eyes.

'That's not why you're considering moving, is it?' Helen, ordinary.

'Part.'

'You think he'll share with you, have this in common?'

'To tell the truth,' Kathleen spoke gruffly in recovery, 'I don't think thinking's got much to do with it.'

They reached home without trouble, lunched out and Kathleen spent the rest of the afternoon in the garden, interrupted only by her husband to arrange dinner for the four at the Mansfield. She did not mind; her cold collation would come to no harm.

While Kathleen was in the bath, Helen bearded her father. The two men had come home rather pleased with themselves; Jack had showed off his empire, and the son-in-law his intelligence. It suited both. Helen, who had been waiting, asked for a word.

The room into which her father led her had been a junk store in her childhood. Now it had a desk, armchairs, filing cabinets, a cupboard for drinks.

'I've never been in here,' she said. Jack eyed her up and down. 'My mother and I went to Newthorpe this morning to look at Dickens House.'

'So I understand. What do you think?'

'She wouldn't go inside. It was weird. That's really what I want to talk to you about.'

'Go on, then.' He was in no hurry.

'You might say it's none of my business.'

He grimaced, and for the moment lost his vivacity. He seemed grey as old dough, heavy, almost fat, fit to wheeze away the remnant of his life. As he sat flabbily, hands dangling over paunch, she could not look at him. Ugly. Old.

'On our way back,' she said, 'my mother broke down.' Still he did not answer. 'We were standing, just looking at the view on Newthorpe Hill. She isn't happy.' Now Helen left him to it.

Her father moved irritably.

'Well, come on,' he said. 'Get on with your story or whatever it is.'

'Do you think she's happy?'

He slapped the inside of his thighs. She remembered how he'd once frightened her, frowned.

'You don't get on too well. You don't sleep in the same room. I noticed that. You never had this,' she waved her hands, 'in my day. You're out a great deal.'

'She's been complaining, has she?'

'No, she has not.' Helen had flushed. 'That's not fair. But I don't like to see her as, as she was this morning. It wasn't like my mother.' He remained impassive still. 'It made me afraid. I wondered what was going to happen next.' Silence, again, thick silence. 'You're not answering me. You don't say anything.'

'You asked to speak to me.' Voice deep. 'I'm listening. Not interrupting.'

'You're not helping me out, either.'

'That's true enough. You're blaming me, I take it. Go on. Speak your piece.'

'What about my mother? What's wrong with her? Never mind blame. Is she all right? She was talking, natural as could be, and then she sobbed. Somebody's at fault.'

'Yourself?'

'Yes, myself. I know what you're going to say. About our marriage.'

'I wonder. You're our only daughter. She wanted to make a bit of a splash with your wedding. But we aren't even invited. What did that do for her, eh?'

'You don't know the circumstances. I was unsure, nearly out of my mind. What with finals. And I thought you'd disapprove. Because you didn't know anything about it. The college was rotten to me. My tutor kept sending for me, to ask if I really meant it with Dr Kitto. I couldn't stand any more. I wanted to run home. It was a nightmare. But she'd have sent me back and so would you.'

'You didn't give us the chance.'

'I didn't trust you. You, especially. Those old women at

college were bad enough. They talked as if Harold was a criminal, instead of a colleague. Did I need to? Want it?'

'Wouldn't it have been sensible to have come home for a day or two?' Jack spoke evenly.

'Yes. I think so, now. But I'd got enough trouble. Exams. These silly old women. Guilt that I hadn't said anything. I could just keep steady by working myself like hell all day, and spending the evening with Harold.'

'Did he not say anything about . . . ?'

'Coming home? Yes, he did. He wanted me to. I wouldn't. He was surprised, but he didn't press me. I see now he'd no idea how bad I was, what a state. He was busy himself. And I guess uncomfortable. Marrying a student. He likes to do the proper thing. But I was wrong.'

'You were.' No sympathy. Curt agreement.

'She took it badly?'

'What do you think?'

'Yes.'

Her father sat stiffer, more formidable, ready with rebuke or chastisement. Helen hated the quietness, sensing his guilt through her own. She had not rid her ears of Kathleen's lapse that morning.

'What about you?' she began. 'Between the pair of you.'

'We just get along. Just.'

'Do you want to leave her? Or her to leave you?'

'It never concerned me. Does she want that? Is that what she says?'

'No. But if she did?'

'I'd think about it. She'd get her third.'

'That's a cruel answer. Don't you see how she's placed? Cooped up here, with nothing to occupy her. Certain you don't want her. Or anybody else. Don't you see what it's like? You're running around, busy, making money, doing what you enjoy. She's here cooking meals you don't even turn up for.'

He waited, weighing his answer up.

'I expect you're right. But your mother never could occupy herself. And I've neither time nor inclination. She's a reasonable woman, but she blows up every so often, or makes a big demand. Like Dickens House. I don't mind. I give in. My contribution to peace in the world.'

'It isn't a joke.'

'No. But it isn't anything I can set right. If she'd married your uncle Frank, and been in those different circumstances, I don't think she'd have been settled. She nearly did, you know.'

'So I've heard.'

'He wouldn't be any better than I am. I chase about the country and work myself silly, and he comes home at four-thirty every night and stands in his garden looking at his magnolia tree, but neither of us could have saved your mother. She'll whittle herself. But she'll not die. She'll end up like her father, grumbling, but nowhere near the grave at eighty.'

'I'd like to do something. I owe it to her.'

'You talk to her. About the wedding. Invite her down to see you. Give her a problem to sort out. My guess is she's not as bad as she appears. I may be wrong.'

'It was rotten, this morning.'

'Yes. I expect it was.'

'You're not going to do anything?' she asked, pointlessly.

'I've been doing it for twenty-five years, so it's not likely anything I think up will work the oracle now. But I'm open to suggestions.'

They talked for ten minutes more, as friendly equals. Her father sat calmly, did not raise his voice. He chided her again about her wedding, but dully, as if the matter had been settled long ago and elsewhere. The impression he gave was that of listlessness; he wasn't much concerned, nor did he wish to appear so. He evaded nothing, but admitted no fault. When they had finished, he grinned, put a heavy hand on her shoulder, said:

'Make a fuss of her. Even if she does jump down your throat for your pains. I'm a shag-bag.'

'What does that mean, exactly?'

'Helen. You don't expect me to condemn myself out of my own mouth, do you?'

'Would you mind if I talked to Uncle Frank about this?'

'Please yourself.'

For the moment he shrugged his shoulders, in unease, but as soon as they set out for the club, he grew genial. They relished the meal, the jubilant drinks, rubbed shoulders with people glad to see them, later slept well. Helen talked next morning to her mother, apologizing for her behaviour. The older woman watched, unpleasant, then concluded brusquely:

'There's no need to worry about me. I shall be all right.'

'But yesterday?'

'I was tired. I hadn't slept. Don't keep on about it. There's no need.'

Helen felt sympathy for her father, slipped in that evening for half an hour with Francis. He sat in western light by an electric fire with the smartly suited Judith Powis. Introductions were made.

'Mrs Powis helps your father sometimes.'

Neither woman spoke; admiration tangled with dislike as Francis explained Mrs Powis's visit. She had to give an extended commentary on two of his poems to her fellow students, and wanted help.

'Who chose the poems?' Helen asked.

'I did.'

'Because you liked them, or because they'd be easy to talk about?'

'A bit of both.' Judith did not look for trouble. 'I wrote an essay on you uncle's poems, a dissertation. I find them fascinating.'

'Do you ever disagree with him on what they're about?'

That started an exchange on meaning, which Francis, at least, enjoyed. Though Judith called the poet by his first name, she spoke respectfully, as if he'd foraged beyond her. This modesty impressed Helen.

'Do you see any resemblance between Francis and my father?' she asked.

'There's a slight physical likeness. Chin structure. Forehead. You probably don't see it, they're so different in size. Otherwise it's hard to say. I keep thinking to myself that there is somewhere if I could only spot it. I haven't managed yet.'

'When I asked Daddy where Uncle Frank would be, he said, "In the garden, staring at his magnolia." '

'There are worse things . . .' Francis.

'Maybe. But that's not you. It might be a symbol. Might.'

'Is Daddy a good boss?'

'He likes things done right. I do some typing for him. That's what I did before I started this course. I was a secretary. It has to be set out exactly, and no errors. "I'm looking for work," he says, "with your letters. Your typing, not my immortal phrases, is what counts." '

'Does he get angry?'

'He can. You have to try to keep up with him, with his thinking.'

Helen wondered if this smart woman were her father's mistress. She'd overheard his extramarital exploits discussed while she was still at school. Oddly, she'd believed the scandalmongers immediately, needed no persuasion, was not even disgusted. True, the tittle-tattle was admiring. She'd moved away, said nothing, squinted at her father differently. Now, and it was no more than five years back, she wondered if she'd considered what her mother felt or thought. Men in plays or novels or history had mistresses. Her father ate his breakfast egg as he'd always done, was as captious about her behaviour.

'You admire Francis, don't you?' Helen asked. Francis had gone out for glasses.

'Very much.' Judith seemed bright, a-flash with intellectual energy, intent at being ahead. 'But not in the way you think.

Not just for achievement. It's potential. When I talk to him, he seems no different from my husband, or my father, and then you realize that's wrong. He's making out of everyday speech something different.'

'While he's talking? I don't understand you.'

'The common language he uses to buy bread and butter, or convince his pupils or bank manager becomes uncommon in his mind.' Judith smiled. 'You think I'm making this up. It's not schoolgirl imagination, you know.

> He who has pared the claws of eremites,
> Civilized dogs, pacified
> The raving tetragrammaton, unites
> Cliché and password, wide
> And rearing ravines of sense.'

'I don't think that's anything but fine sound,' Helen said. 'I've not much time for incantation.'

'I can't get it out of my head. It's like great music, Haydn or Beethoven.'

Helen was more impressed. About this woman there was something serious. In a fashion, it was provincial, but then it claimed more, knew the great classics, lined admired modernity up with them. At her own university she'd met enthusiasm, but it gushed, was less serious than this. The smart, pretty young woman regarded culture as a prop, a goal, not a mere passing stage to be brilliantly skidded through. As she eyed, not without admiration, Judith's clothes, hair style, fine hands, she wondered how far the reciting of a few lines of verse had misled her.

Frank returned with the sherry.

Now Judith began to talk again, but this time about a visit to her corner shop. She was amusing, with her sharp description of a chair by the counter, round-seated with a pattern of small holes, for favoured customers, usually elderly ladies. But that evening it was occupied by a frail man, in spectacles which against the pallor of his skin and the dead spareness of his hair seemed the only living part of him. He had been served; his shopping bag was by his old-fashioned shoes with polished toe caps but he sat on, his faded brown eyes lifted blindly.

'That's how it is these days,' he said to the shopkeeper who chased after Judith's order.

'That's right, Mr Cattermole.'

'Nobody wants to know you. Nobody wants to hear.'

The energetic dash of the man behind the counter, his red face, quick smile, sharp questions or statements, his ready service contrasted with the whine, the paralytic stillness of the old man. When Cattermole fumbled for the trilby on his knee, donned it, shuffled towards the door, the storekeeper lifted the counter flap to hold the door open.

'How old do you think he is?' he asked Judith.

'Eighty.' Ninety would not have surprised.

'Not surprised you say that.' Goods marshalled, shifted, priced. 'He's sixty-three.'

'Is he ill, then?'

'He's a hairdresser, has a little shop on Hazel Street. Six months ago some youths got in just as he was cashing up for the day, set about him, stole the money, left him unconscious. He wasn't found till next morning. He'd come round a time or two, crawled about the floor, passed out. Blood everywhere.'

'Wasn't there a phone?'

'What would he want a phone for? They thought he'd die. Was in hospital weeks. Concussion, God knows what. It's six months back, and he's only just started to get about a bit again.'

'It's a shame.'

'If I caught them, I'd string them up. All they deserve. He was quite a smart little chap, had his wits about him. Bit of an old woman, but spruce. Now look at him; he might just as well be dead.'

'Did they catch them?'

'No chance. How could they? He didn't remember much. I blame the parents. They've no care nor authority these days.'

Judith spoke sharply, slightly altering her voice for each speaker, until they could easily imagine the opinionated man behind the counter. Francis wondered aloud about parental responsibility.

'I don't think David's much like me,' he said. 'For good or bad.'

'Are you and Daddy like your father?'

'Not really. He hadn't much time for us. Jack worried him more than I did, because he'd kick up louder. Our father wanted his own way, and as long as he got it, apart from snatches of trite advice, that was that. Anyway, Jack and Cissie seemed grown up almost.'

'Didn't he force you to do anything?'

'He sent us to Sunday school. He advised us to do well at day school, and gave us half a crown if we did. But he didn't recommend books. There was no music except on the wireless, and we'd be told more often than not to turn that off. The school did more for us, culturally, than home. Cissie had an admirer who painted pictures, but he died. I used to enjoy his yachts and reflections when I was very small, I remember. They seemed the more telling as he was dead. Cissie never went to grammar school; she doesn't read much outside the paper, and wouldn't thank you for a ticket for anything fancier than *White Horse Inn*.'

'Mummy made us read, and sent us to the library,' Helen said. 'But she hardly opens a book herself these days.'

'My father read to us,' Judith said. 'Dickens, Wells, Sir James Jeans. And his hero is Beethoven. Artists were set apart, for him. It rubbed off a bit. My brother went to university. I wouldn't. I left at sixteen, because I saw how hard he had to work. But my dad keeps Sid's card out on the mantelpiece. S. J. Smailes, MA. They've got the same initials.'

They touched their lips with sherry.

'Does it make your father any happier?' Helen asked.

'It did. But now that he's getting on, and he's not so active, I'm not sure.'

'No.'

They talked of what comforted old age and incapacity. Sadly, because they spoke in blind ignorance, unconvinced of happiness.

'How would you like to die?' Francis muttered, in a dumb break. That scared them. Old age and death touched their elbow. Helen, sharp as her mother, would not allow them to discuss the subject.

Back to politeness, Judith inquired how long Helen was staying.

'We go back tomorrow.'

'I shall miss you,' her uncle said. 'I like to see you here. More so than David.'

'Freddy or Em?'

'They don't count much. You are my favourite.'

'Why's that?' Judith, smiling, matronly, almost aunt herself.

'Physical, purely. A pretty child, as the others weren't. Or more so.'

He laughed it off.

12

Rain pelted hard; puddles shook in the garden.

Kathleen Weldon pressed her nose to the window, in ambivalence. The shrubberies glistened. Sibelius played gloomily from the radio. She made her third mug of instant coffee that morning, cupped it in her hands, feeling the warmth as life, a comforting touch in a dead world.

She had stripped the Kittos' bed, set the automatic washer to work, hoovered the vacated room, but without concentration. She willed the phone to ring; it was silent. Wireless programmes did not attract. Rain splashed down. The forecast promised its continuation. A car turned in, negotiated the drive.

The front door bell pealed. She felt aggrieved.

A personable young man in a belted mac. Handsome, he touched his wavy hair, trimmed sideboards with a well-scrubbed hand.

'Mrs Weldon?' He did not relax. His face was in trouble with itself. 'My name is Protherough. I'm a deputy head at the Edward Curtis Comprehensive School. I'm afraid I have some bad news for you.'

She invited him into the hall where he realigned his belt.

'It's about your brother-in-law. Francis Weldon. He was taken ill at school this morning.'

How did one answer? Sibelius's chordal trivialities echoed distantly.

'They've taken him to hospital. It was a heart attack, we think. School had only just started, or first lesson. We'd had assembly. He was in the staff room, a free period, and had chest pains. There was a nurse in the school fortunately, and she had an ambulance down in no time.'

'Is he alive?'

Her question took him aback. Did blunt truth never appear in classrooms?

'As far as we know. We've not heard anything, of course. We rang his son at the bank, and he's going to the hospital. He asked us to let you know, but said we weren't to telephone, somebody was to come. That's why . . .'

He let the voice trail delicately off. David? Dim, unco-ordinated, unambitious David laying the law down about what they were to do? It seemed impossible. She smiled to herself in her distress. David. Cometh the hour.

'I'll ring up now,' she said. 'Find out.'

Protherough politely asked to stay to hear. He put together humming sentences about his privilege to teach with so distinguished a man, the kudos conferred, famous person, how lucky. She sat him down, put off by his social skills; some white-faced, tongue-tied, cap-wringing urchin or caretaker or junior colleague would have met this case. Francis with his heart fighting, leaping for life, did not need end-of-term, school-magazine banalities.

The hospital took a little sorting out.

In the end, they placed Francis in the intensive care unit. As comfortable as possible. No, not the slightest use visiting. Ring again by all means, certainly, certainly.

She passed the message to Protherough, who was standing reverently. He offered the correct sentences. First, comfort: Francis was not a heavy smoker, not overweight, took exercise. Next, herself. Was there anything he, they could do? Would she be all right? Could he get . . . ? Was there anything he . . . ? This young man did not put a foot wrong, and she wished he'd go, leave her alone. He breathed his way through Francis's achievement. A name that would not be forgotten. He might be dead already. Privilege, again. Opportunity for the children. Then, to her. Was she sure there was nothing? He'd be only too . . . Some sense of repayment. Debt owed by all. In her misery she could not believe her ears. He shook hands, manly firm, breasted the rain, took the drive sedately, in decorum, propriety observed.

She sat down, was surprised to find herself whimpering out loud, small, animal noises, puppy distress. In a hurry, knocking against an armchair, she switched the radio off, stood motionless, blank, a frown of puzzled hopeless ruin printed on her. She must act, in some way, rationally, but could not begin.

Her husband. Jack. Jack.

At the word she was ready. She must ring him, explain. Then Cissie. But she did not know where he was. At this office? In Leicester? On the road. She dialled the local number; a reassuring secretary put her through. She began.

He was gruffer, less forthcoming than she expected, caught out, perhaps, flattened as she was. Sorry for him, she said it was no use visiting the hospital. No, he could see that. There, well. He'd finish what he was about, take perhaps half an hour, an hour, and then he'd come home. No need. He'd come home. They'd have some lunch, if she'd . . . Or out for a bite. They'd ring again. He spoke steadily, sharply now, captain of industry.

She charged about the house, pushing from room to room, before she rang Cissie, unable to find the will to direct her news. When she dialled, she judged Cecilia was out, it was so long before her sister-in-law lifted the receiver. In the ordinary course, Kathleen would have given up, but today she swayed in lethargy, and was answered.

'I was up the garden.' Blowing, almost painfully.

'Isn't it raining?'

'I'd gone in Eric's greenhouse.'

'I'm afraid I have some bad news. It's Frank. He's been taken ill at school.'

There was a pause, and when Cecilia spoke again her voice had altered. Breathless no longer, she sounded drained of life. Her questions were disjointed, not sensible. Once she broke off so that Kathleen could imagine her staring, hen's eye.

Methodically, with prosaic strength, Kathleen instructed her sister-in-law. Cissie could ring her husband and tell him. Otherwise, nothing but waiting. Well, she could get hold of Emma if she wished, but it hardly seemed . . . Tell Eric. When Jack arrived, they'd inquire again from the hospital and immediately pass the message on. Cissie should make herself some coffee, then go on with the lunch, the washing, whatever. Now followed a few authoritative statements about Frank's age, weight, habits, and comfort was deduced. Cissie approached normality. She'd tell Eric; he'd want to know, do what he could. Kathleen remembered the hot smell of his printing works. He'd have his jacket off, in the office.

These final sentences steadied her, as she set about preparing a cold lunch. She worked efficiently, but dragged her pain round with her, never forgetting it, only its course. Soon after midday Jack arrived.

'Heard nothing else?' he asked.

'No.'

'Shall I ring?'

She followed him into the hall. The grandfather clock showed seven past the hour. Her husband was wearing his mac, which he now removed, and hung in the cloakroom. The place was dimmed in rainy light, the stained glass behind the staircase grey and surly. Jack glanced back at her, reprehensively. He clumsily handled the phone book.

'That's the hospital number,' she said. 'On that paper.'

'Uh.' Angry? He picked it up, glared, fiddled for glasses. She did not shift, listening. His voice dropped deep, but he asked the right questions. He knew his rôle. He recradled the phone, turned. 'No change. Intensive care. David's still there. Visiting four till seven. We can go, but it's unlikely they'll let us in.'

'I see. They didn't say . . . ?'

'No. Except he's very ill. We'll drive down. We can always give David a lift.'

'You ring Cissie. Then we'll have lunch.'

Her voice betrayed no fear, steadily without tremor. She stepped out into the kitchen, to carve cold beef. When Jack arrived he had washed, smiled at her, easy, assured, sat down claiming hunger.

'How did Cissie seem?'

'She talked a lot. About some friend of Eric's. She was right enough.' He ate heartily, and was out of the house before one. He'd be back just on four, and they'd try it. Might have to call in the office after that. Depended. They'd eat out, if she could wait. He was himself, in a hurry, energetic, matters weighed up.

He banged in at five to four, called her. She had been ready for an hour, wasting time hatefully with a thriller. People died in the first bloody pages. She read words, did not understand, forced herself again, could not prevent the wandering of her eyes, the twittering of her mind. The rain cleared, but her eyes wetted themselves. She pitched into the print, but ricocheted from sense. What she had needed was some manual task, with a hoe, a cleaner, on a keyboard. She trembled as she stood.

'Not very warm out.'

Jack played with the money in his trousers pocket, nervously, ungainly. His nostrils snarled, black diamonds.

Kathleen enjoyed her husband's driving. Never in a hurry, he judged and acted perfectly. He parked his car in front of a solicitor's office in a space marked private.

'Arranged it. John Jardine. Not at work today.'

The explanation soothed, did not enlighten. They walked down the street, as smoky clouds were combed loose.

'Don't know whether we ought to have brought Cissie?'

'No.' He might have spoken Greek.

'But they won't let us in.'

Jack carried an umbrella, which he flourished. When he

asked instructions at the office, the uniformed man answered respectfully, came out of his cubbyhole to point the way.

Corridors seemed endless, burrowing down. Painted instructions were frequent, clear. They arrived at Annesley Ward. She would have preferred to traipse endlessly, following directions, never making it. Here the passage widened, into a waiting room, with chairs. No Smoking. The window gave on to a roof which bore the peculiarities of a yard, untidy with chimneys or ventilators, hydrangeas in tubs. David rose to meet them.

'How is he?'

David shrugged, crumpled, did not answer. He looked smart, old-fashioned in a suit. She had spoken to him in a whisper.

'Have you been in to see him?' Jack, with bravado.

'Yes. Just for a minute or two. They let me in.'

'How was he?'

'All right.' She could not believe that answer.

'Did he know you?'

'Yes.' David in surprise. 'He seemed doped, sedated, and wired up to some machine. Otherwise he looked normal. As normal as anybody does in bed.' David flagged his difficulties with his arms. 'He looked taken aback as if he didn't know what had hit him.'

Well observed, Kathleen thought. David was a somebody, had something of his dad in him, or that awkward woman, Louise, his mother. She was as ordinary as soap, until you got across her.

'This first, this bit's crucial,' David continued, and they nodded. 'So they said. Some sister. No visitors. No excitement. They let me in. Don't know why. Perhaps they felt sorry for me. Perhaps they thought Dad wanted to see me. Didn't seem likely from what they said, but they did. Nurse on duty all the time.'

'Haven't you been out?' Jack asked, then forcibly. 'Have you been here all the time?'

'I had something to eat. Walked down to the square. Wasn't gone more than half an hour.'

'Did they tell you to stop?'

'No. They just smile when they go past. Otherwise, they don't say anything.'

'Why did you wait?' Kathleen asked distantly.

'He might die.'

That let it out. A talisman. A charm. If I don't leave, he won't pass on. I sit; he does not die. They understood instantly; that's why they were here. When one is helpless, one's reduced to magic.

'What's the action now?' Jack. The boy shrugged. 'Where's the sister?' David explained; Jack said he'd have a word, marched off.

'Where's your dad?' Kathleen, whispering.

'Through the swing doors there to the left. At the end of a short corridor.'

She touched his sleeve, thanked him for his consideration in asking the school not to phone. He nodded absently, acknowledging his due, perhaps. He twitched at his trousers, a small movement with the thumb and finger of the left hand, then described flatly, not fluently, even without interest, the machines by his father's bed.

'Is anybody else in there?'

'No. But there's room for another. Another lot of hardware.' The word jarred, cheapened. 'I wasn't in for more than a minute or two. I don't know why they let me.'

'Was your father glad to see you?'

David considered, stroking his chin almost in caricature.

'Probably. But he looked so baffled. As if he'd lost himself.'

They stood until Jack returned, accompanied to her door by the ward sister.

'No use staying. They'll ring David if there's any change for the worse. She seemed quite hopeful. We'll take you back home, young man.'

The boy nodded, but explained he must thank the nurses. Another ju-ju. He did so, then followed obediently out to the car, ate supper with them, rang before his uncle drove him to his lodgings for another report.

When visitors were finally allowed into the patient, Kathleen was prompt each day at four, leaving as others began to arrive. Francis seemed cheerful enough, if pale, willing to describe his ordeal. His room blazed with flowers; tongue-tied groups of his pupils appeared; shyness and scent. The local newspaper issued a bulletin: 'Poet in Hospital'. Kathleen's phone chattered.

Jack thundered round, immensely relieved. His wife was astounded at first at the effect on the man, for no amount of stentorian bravado covered his concern, his fear, his desolation. He might be the next, certainly; his habits encouraged the belief, but that was as nothing compared with his love for his brother. Our Frank needed looking after, and if God, or chance, had thrashed him, so they were bastards. How to kick back at these entities made the matter tricky, so that Kathleen guessed that underlings or business rivals acted as surrogates, were pitched into, satisfactorily squashed.

In the hospital Jack was circumspect. Nurses and orderlies soon favoured him; he nodded at gratified patients. It refreshed to see him take his brother's hand, jocularly ask how much more time he was going to waste in this dump. But then he became quieter, watchful, as if he couldn't quite make out what was expected of him, or what might happen. He'd start an anecdote, stop in the middle, ear cocked for an interloper. Death. He wanted to do something for his brother, but could not. Heartiness, heart even, does not redden bloodless cheeks. He did not like it.

Frank showed his affection. He seemed older, frailer, than when he walked about, but he and David hit it off in a way Kathleen had not noticed before. They spoke, cheerfully grumpy, in a convention where the son found it a pain in the neck to visit his father, and dad knew it was useless to ask his layabout lad to manage a small errand. It seemed so far out of character that she questioned her nephew.

'He's all right,' the boy said. 'It's when we start arguing we get across each other.'

She praised David to Frank, who wrinkled his eyes.

'Takes a heart attack, eh, to make a man of him.'

Her brother-in-law concentrated hard on his ailment or the hospital routine with her, but when Jack visited and did most of the talking, they seemed to be back forty years in Factory House, recalling old faces, now demolished buildings, eccentrics at every street corner. This bored her, Jack Arlott, Harry Jordan, Prog Roper, George Stacey, Harry Gale, Digger Sheldon. The list spread endless. Bill Bashem, Gaffer Good, Yacker Severn, Chokker Beeston, Knocker Twine, Enoch Knox. They frightened the girls on the main street, survived wars and accidents, thrashed wives, defied bosses, went mad, pouched fabulously towering catches on the cow-field boundary, pitched downstairs, did time, jumped naked into the quarry ponds, preached halfway through dinnertime, died fighting.

The two men lived orally together in a lurid light, between Bulwell stone walls, expecting excitement with every breath. Nobody was ordinary. Blood splashed. Beer glistened. Local teams triumphed. Tram drivers braked heroically. Every conductor had bayoneted Huns or ripped his lungs with gas.

Kathleen saw it as a fantasy, pulled their legs.

Why two grown men needed to wallow in boyhood, she did not know. They improvised, and it was her husband who played the poet, exaggerating, launching further into never-never land. A neighbour head first in delirium tremens in the washtub, legs cycling crazily suggested life, perhaps denied the ordered cleanliness and silence of this place, of drugs, surgeons' fingers, physicians' grave processions. Jack hated illness, backed away from death. Forty years ago he'd long life to live, energy to spare, could spit into the wind and dodge.

Sometimes she spoke about these conversations to Frank. He answered rationally, but he was reluctant to share. Was life wilder she wanted to know.

'More abundant,' Francis said, 'to quote the pulpiteers.'

'It was the depression,' she answered. 'People were poor.'

'We were young.' Primly propped, his mouth thin. 'These are pub stories, but we're enjoying ourselves. We seem more of an age, more like brothers.'

'Cissie doesn't join in.'

'She was with my dad. Indoors. No idea what happened in the dark streets. Though if you ask me, I'd guess there are old folks about who remember my father as an oddity. Beaver Weldon. Must have had a beard at one time.'

Jack came back from the hospital friendly, pleased with his progress as a visitor, glad he spent time interestingly to himself. He mentioned a new venture first to Frank, then to his wife. She listened, surprised and delighted. They held half-hour conversations, a bit taken aback with the development.

'Does Frank ever mention Louise?' she asked one night.

'No. Not to me. Why?'

'I wondered. He went to the hospital a lot with her. When she was dying. I asked Cissie, but she said, "No." '

'How about Dave?'

'I haven't asked. He's got enough to put up with.'

'You used to be down at the General pretty well every day, didn't you?' He meant to praise. 'Was it in the same part as Frank?'

She thought not, though it was only four years ago, they'd built annexes into corners of the hospital, divided wards, boxed in pipes and lifts, re-routed traffic. The chapel looked no different. With a small picture of a pre-Raphaelite Jesus by the door, and a diploma of invitation in italic letters. What did the Pakistanis do? Catholics, for that matter?'

'I couldn't make out our Frank and Lou, you know.' Jack spoke comfortably. 'She was a funny woman. And that cancer killed her so quick. She must have known and said nothing about it.'

'Perhaps they both knew.'

'Ay. I never fathomed the pair of them.'

Louise was pretty, but stiff, never letting on what she wanted. She never made an overt fuss of David, though she'd lost three children in miscarriages. Her bungalow gleamed spotless, a reaction from her mother's untidy, gloomy house, with its rumpled cushions, its undusted surfaces, its huge dark furniture. Her voice spoke small, little girlish and breathless, but she could obstruct. If she did not want to go, she stuck. A school teacher like her husband, they lived their lives in parallel, not asking too much, not overdoing love. In the last months of her life, she had grown more awkward, cantankerous, but Francis knew she'd guarded the secret, biting cancer, then. When she finally consulted the doctor, she was beyond help, and with belly swollen, prim as ever, slipped away from life in a week or two. Frank said nothing, nursed his grief out of the way, silent, face hardened. The fourteen-year-old David seemed noncommittal, demanded no sympathy, light-weight as his mother, as elusive.

'Don't know why he married her.' Jack cleared his throat. 'To tell you the truth, I thought he'd get married again.'

David, since his aunt pressed him, came round for meals once or twice a week. She went down every day to Frank's house, kept it tidy, habitable.

'Your father'll have to come to us,' she said, 'when they discharge him.'

'I don't know if he'll like that,' David hazarded.

'Then he can lump it.' She'd learned the expression from her husband.

Frank improved, slippered his way round the hospital. Early June weather matched April's, with rounded masses of white cloud, shifting fast over blue, and black smudges which dashed rain siling down. Good gardening weather, the wiseacres said, but too cold at night.

'I'll be glad to get home,' he told Kathleen, as they sat hot in the glass corridor where a great snowball tree bobbed in the wind. She explained her plans; he took it quietly. 'How d'you think David's getting on?' he asked.

'At his work, do you mean?'

'Yes. And in himself. He comes to see you, he tells me. I'm glad. He's like his mother. Don't you think so?'

'Neither of you. I never got to know Lou. One way or the other.'

'Tell you why I ask. He seems too satisfied to me. He doesn't ever complain. Not about coming up here. Or anything else.'

'Has he got a girl friend?'

'Oh, he's a bit of a ladies' man.' Pride detected. 'He knows his way about there. But he doesn't grumble. I do. Lou did, in her fashion. Not David.'

'You never call him Dave?'

'His mother didn't like it. I fell in with her.'

'I tell you, Frank, I like him. A lot. He seems sensible in a way that Helen isn't. She's always on the niggle, interfering, prodding somebody. And if you think she's my daughter, and I set higher standards there, well, he's steadier than Emma.'

'She's got our Cis for a mother.' They both laughed, not serious. Hospital encourages such.

'I thought girls would be more reasonable. And they both were at university, but sometimes they go on as if they're cracked. Is David good at his banking?'

'He passes his exams. They seem pleased. As far as I can find out. Doesn't talk about it much. Not even the people at work. He did well enough at his "O" levels. But he made it clear he wasn't staying on. And then he set up his own place. Costs him more to live. Must do. We didn't get on too badly. But I think his mother's death must have shaken him up. Not that he said anything. He's been off a time or two to work in London, and enjoyed it. But when he turns up here, he seems so rational, as if he's come in to inspect the hospital.'

They enjoyed these exchanges, but Kathleen could not call them confidences. Staying on the surface, their conversations mined no truth. This pale man had loved her, she reminded herself, had made love to her, but here, behind glass, hygienically sealed from the shrubs and lawns, from the wind, she barely believed it.

'He's got a look of you sometimes,' she said.

'Mrs Armstrong always said so. Lou's mother. I don't think she meant it as a compliment, either.'

'She didn't approve?'

'Not good enough for her girl. Her father had been Lord Mayor. Don't you forget it.'

Kathleen had attended the wedding, had known Louise slightly. By the time she had met the bride as a relative, been rebuffed by her, she was at her busiest with the family. It was as if her sister-in-law had ferreted out that she was her husband's second choice, and resented it. That was impossible, though plenty of tongues could wag, but Louise's lack of interest was so marked that Kathleen gave up her attempt to close the breach. When, later, she became Frank's mistress, shortly, they mentioned his wife out of a kind of duty, having neither sympathy for her nor pleasure from the deception.

It seemed far enough off, now, dead ground. The snowball tree bounced, and nestled the glass, rich in wind and sun.

'Jack's doing well, isn't he?'

'So he says.'

'I don't know what I'd do if he slipped up.' Francis shook his head, puzzled now, mournful. 'Does he bring Judith Powis home at all?'

'He's mentioned her. They're having an affair.'

'Has he told you so?' Now he sat up startled.

'You ought to know him better than that. What's she like?'

He described her, the bright clothes, the sharp mind, the determination to sort problems out, her intelligent failure to understand the muddle from which his poems oozed. Now he spoke with a directness, adducing minor detail like treasure, not at a loss for a word, skimming at his topic, a lively man.

'Do you know what I'd say?' she asked, voice contralto with delight. 'You've fallen in love with that young woman.'

His pale cheek reddened, deeply.

She laughed, crowing, to see this fifty-year-old blush like a schoolboy. He did not know where to look, clutched his blanket as if he'd rip it in two.

'She's married.'

'Have you met her husband?' She was glad to let him off the hook.

'Tall chap. Nice-looking. Works in a bank. Like David. I've met him once, just by chance.'

'Not good enough for her?' No answer. 'What about Jack then?'

'He's the sort of man she'd admire.'

'Not you?' She spoke warmly, comforting his awkwardness.

'Only on paper. And that's not quite human. As if I'm one of the great and glorious dead.'

He asked again later, with a quiet anxiety, about the relationship between Judith and Jack. She could not reassure him. He could not bear to leave well alone.

'I don't really know. He's not faithful. Sexually. I'd sooner not find out. When I do, I make him writhe, but I'd just as soon know nothing about it.'

'I don't like that.'

'We're both secretive. He'd talk sometimes, but he knows he'd get no change from me.' She'd no idea whether this was the truth, but it sounded interesting, as if she'd a grasp of what they thought and did. It filled in the pauses, made a little sense of this sun-filled intimacy among white beds, an equivalent, friendly discipline.

Kathleen was mischievous enough to mention the conversation to her husband, who now came regularly back for an early evening meal. This was another talisman against disaster; home for salad with the wife, and nothing goes awry in the hospital. Once or twice he had nipped into the ward for ten minutes on his way back: Thursdays and Saturdays were his official days.

'Our Frank's in love with that Judith Powis,' she said.

'Oh, what makes you say that?'

As she described the blush, the stutter, Jack chewed steadily on. He enjoyed his food, reaching abstractedly for slices of brown bread or cake.

'What's she like?' Kathleen demanded.

'Oh, bright. Very quick on the uptake. She's worth thirty of our typists.'

'Would she be good for Frank?'

'Love-making's hardly likely to be in his programme, is it, with his complaint?'

'Love needn't mean sex,' she said, bluntly. 'It isn't always.'

'Somebody's being got at.' But he grinned. 'She thinks he's marvellous, but whether she sees him as a man . . . Might do. I've never thought about it.'

'You like her?'

'Yes, I do.' Then his mouth closed, and they concluded the meal in silence, with neither too uncomfortable, since they knew the inquisition would not be pressed. He yawned, widely, an ugly physical gesture; she worked away at her almost completed crossword square, busy, efficient, self-contained. He advanced no further in confidence.

As he helped her wash up, another recent gesture, he said, 'Is David calling in tonight?'

'Um. Imagine so.'

'Does he know about his dad? Being in love?'

She screwed her mouth in, let him flounder.

13

Francis Weldon died two days before he was due for discharge.

This time, this afternoon, his son telephoned Kathleen; the boy sounded stunned, but said he would make his own way back to her home. She called up her husband, who immediately left his office. When Jack pushed in a quarter of an hour later, David had not yet arrived.

'I don't know anything,' she said. 'I didn't like to bother him.'

Jack staggered flabbily breathless. He dropped into a chair like a deflating balloon. His eyes were grey with moisture; his hands trailed upwards into the air; mouth sagged. He blew violently on to his tea, sucked noisily, bit at his knuckles. David's ring at the doorbell startled them; neither had kept watch through the window.

David seemed calm, sulky-faced.

He took a cup of tea, said he'd been drinking the stuff all day. His father had suffered another massive coronary thrombosis; the doctors had fought like fury, injected straight into his heart, but there was no saving him. No, he hadn't seen his father's body, but they'd be able to go down to the undertaker's where he'd be laid in the chapel of rest. There'd been some form-filling, but that was done. He hadn't told Aunt Cissie, nor the school.

They sat, bound in dumbness.

'I'd better ring the headmaster,' Kathleen said in the end, 'before they go home. You'll have to go round to the Hoopers'.'

Jack squirmed.

The headmaster gradually, grudgingly, brought to the

phone, expressed shock. He had a telling phraseology, but not quite in the manner of his deputy. He stumbled through words into appropriateness, so that one felt that the man was moved. An exact contemporary had been taken away, one who had made a mark. 'When I've retired from this place,' he said, 'in a matter of two or three years it will be as if I've never been. That's the tragedy of schoolmasters.' He rambled on about Frank's verse, but quoted none. She, imagining him as a man dazed by a mugging, wondered what he did with his free hand; she eyed herself in a mirror, searching out her own grief. The teacher sighed, droned, paused, repeated himself, edged away from sense and back so that she closed the conversation with a business-like promise to keep him informed. He'd be off now to scare the secretaries, silence the staff rooms on the four o'clock bell.

She waited outside the drawing-room door. No sound.

Both men sat looking floorwards as if they had dozed off. Both jerked up as she entered, gratefully. She could not cancel their sorrow.

'You go round to Cissie's,' she ordered her husband. 'I'll ring Eric's works.'

'Straight off?' The words were strangled.

'Straight off. You'd better stay the night here,' she said to her nephew. 'Jack's plenty of pyjamas. Does your manager know? Will he still be there? At the bank?'

'I've rung him. Just after he, I, er, I rang you.'

'Is there anything else to be done?'

David stood, chewing his thumb end. He was not unlike his father.

'Some of his friends ought to be told,' he said, slowly.

'The newspapers?'

'The undertaker will see to it. I spoke to him from the hospital.' The boy's eyes swam suddenly with tears; he clutched his throat, then his lapel. 'He'll put a notice . . .'

'Do you want to talk to these people?' she asked. 'Or shall I?'

'I will.' He drew himself up, together.

'Shall I be off then?' Jack mumbled, propping himself on two arms on a table. His back bent ludicrously, misshaping the cloth on his shoulders into uneven folds.

'That's a good idea.' And I'll ring Eric, in case he ought to go home to Cissie. And Helen. She'll be upset.'

'Tell Fred,' Jack spoke. 'He'll want to know.' The intervention straightened him out. 'You stop here, Dave. It's sensible.'

She sat with David for the next hour.

At first a weight kept them quiet. The odd sentence passed, gabbled, indistinguishable from thought so that she could not say whether she had spoken until the nephew answered. He was polite, formal, belying the tie loosened from his collar. She felt it her duty to keep conversation from running dry, but could barely cope. Inside her breast a ferocity of sorrow bit.

She walked to the window, glooming over a garden lush from recent rain. A guelder rose flaunted active snowballs. Beyond, fields stretched grey over the distant nondescript Victorian church which stood once among stone cottages, but now in a regimented estate of neat brick boxes. Out there behind hawthorn hedges, small trees, hidden now, was the bungalow where Frank had lived with Louise, where David had been brought up. The fields there, the grassy mounds from the derelict colliery had an unkempt, untamed nonconformity about them; misty, blurred, sludged, they exhibited the same defiance of expectation in the brightest sun of summer. But as she turned her eyes left, she saw the white houses, row on prim row, street on street of brand-new council building. That had been wild land, beyond the cemetery, fit for the run of horses, blackberrying country where the courting couples had lain on the dry days and where sleet had pelted grass grey with winter. Her eye registered outlines of grief.

David talked.

His father hadn't suffered long. They fought, these young doctors, fisted men back to life. But they had failed. They'd asked for a post mortem because death had caught them napping; he'd agreed.

'My dad wouldn't have minded, would he? He wanted to nose things out.'

She turned; his words twisted curiously. The boy's mouth gaped; both stood, a yard or two apart, woodenly, until both wept. It was hard to know whose face broke first, who whimpered to set the other off. They sat down, did not embrace, but cried, in division, a man and a woman in separate chairs, caught by the event, blawting themselves nearer sense.

Kathleen stopped first, surprised that she could. David's head lay on his arm, face turned in to the high back of the chair. His shoulders heaved, but he was in seclusion, though the bent back, the dropped head, were eloquent. The noise he made rasped low, raw, softly savage. Soon she was able to watch him, which she did without a sound, straight-backed, dismissing interference.

In the end he became steadily silent, then glanced up as if he knew he was observed.

She caught her breath at the raising of his face. It was as if features had been erased, or melted slightly. The puffy eyes, the waxen wet cheeks, the distorted nose, sagging mouth were human but could have belonged to anyone; the rubber of this mask needed fierce straightening into individuality. He eyed her; a sigh split his chest; his face resumed its identity, a miracle.

David was recognizable; dishevelled fringe, tears, strain notwithstanding, the man was himself. He dabbed, then smiled.

The smile, unmistakeable, bruised her as she watched, and she put out her arms.

Without embarrassment he stepped across, took her hand. His were warm. They embraced, lost, inside grief, swaddled, not drowned.

'I didn't think . . .' he said, voice remarkably steady. That he loved him? That he could weep with such abandon? That he felt no shame? She did not know, mouthed soothing noises, patted him, until a moment or two later they recognized how untoward, ridiculous they must appear. To whom? They drew apart, glad of their breakdown, reciprocating care. Leaden grief blanketed back; the windows demonstrated no new urbanities, but the two had passed an hour they might wish to forget in its breaking importance.

David made his calls, and she drove him to his lodgings to collect clothes. The evening meal was subdued. Jack went out unannounced. She and David read. Just before he went to bed, at ten, he said he'd go to work, and that meant he'd need a call at eight. She commended his decision, kissed him.

Cecilia came round next morning, well dressed, balanced, even distant after the first tears. She spoke of Frank's cleverness, criticized his marriage, said he'd acted oddly of late. Kathleen, bothered by the telephone, encouraged her sister-in-law's views, though she dismissed them. They discussed funeral clothes.

'I expect you'll be in black,' Cissie said.

'No.'

'I thought you would.'

Two tears screwed out from her eyes. She did not wipe them off, left them to glisten, rain on granite.

Kathleen and her husband accompanied David to the chapel of rest. It was odd to step from an evening street, light still, clouds tinged with orange, green streaks in the sky, into this antechamber. The man on duty concentrated on David, but noticed all three. He behaved as in heaven, with unostentatious comfort, matching ceremonious clothes. Kathleen knew the reek of fear, remembering her father's taking her to a joiner's workshop. They had been sent across the yard, and there on a bench, half-made, lay a coffin. Light wood, blond shavings, gold handles and fittings still wrapped. Fear had caught her then, high in the chest, so that she could not speak. Her father chatted about the repair he wanted doing. The carpenter made his suggestions. They were busy; they did not notice her; a small girl stood terrified, without outward sign, eyes turned from the shining shape.

Now into contained, carpeted corridors, through smooth doors, to dimmed lights. The duty-man ushered them forward. In the hygienic glitter of cloth, and wood, Francis's face seemed dull, not exactly greyish, but without the redness of life, shrunken, a little puckered. His hands were white, saintly, vaguely misshapen. The savage wounds of the post mortem were hidden.

They stared. Silence, lighted silence.

Kathleen felt she should speak, throw aside the constraint, the emotional cage in which she was nailed to the floor. They did not look about. She was mastered, full of tears, of pain, threats of breaking.

David stepped forward, bent, kissed his father.

She and Jack did not move. Their heads dropped down. She needed prayer, words, a spell. None spilled.

David drew away. The usher moved with him.

'Poor old lad.' Jack's voice from the other side of the world.

The door slid; they walked, not looking back.

Once into the waiting room, the undertaker took David to one side, where they discussed next day's arrangements. The low voice, insistent but delicately concerned, filled the room though they could not catch what he said. The business-like passage settled David, for when he turned back he seemed slightly smiling, relieved, a youth again.

'Right, sir. No need for you to trouble about that.' Now the other two were included. 'A great man in his way, I understand.'

The phrase hit Kathleen like a missile. Defences crumbled round the weakness of sorrow. A great man. She wept. Husband and nephew took her arms. A chair, a glass of water were forthcoming. The official placed himself discreetly behind, away from grief, ready to hand. A great man. Puzzled brother-in-law, that dazzled and fumbling lover. She sipped. Jack dabbed her face; she allowed it. His cheek was wet. Reaching for life, she lifted her hands to the handkerchief, hid in the aroma of unsmoked tobacco, thanked them with a steadier voice. A great man. Last evening's newspaper had called him 'schoolmaster and poet'; her mind had demanded a hyphen. Foolishly.

> When between wintry trees
>   I come across that road,
> Night-light blanches, the wind bucks,
>   And I am flawed.

Thus she prepared herself for the performance in church, and the succinct sentences at the crematorium. The parson with St Paul was persuaded; the headmaster stumping through Bunyan, accompanied Mr Valiant-for-Truth to the riverside as if he were personally recalling the event; 'For all the saints' sung cockily with Vaughan Williams affected her, but within bounds. Only when she turned, to see the line of blazered, hair-brushed school children singing 'Oh enter then His gates with praise' with the wooden ferocity born of practice, was she suddenly lifted. The solemn measure of the Old Hundredth suited Francis by incongruity; he'd enter heaven, shuffling, hands in his pockets, elbows patched. He, an unbeliever, would have relished divine service, and set one or two of God's servers right.

Three days later on Sunday evening, David called in.

'I'd like to ask you something.' He refused hospitality, looked uncomfortable. 'Are you leaving this house? Helen said something about a place in Newthorpe?'

'I did consider it.'

'Did?' Something of the ironical politeness his father had sometimes affected.

'I haven't the energy. Not now. Not for a time. Why do you ask?'

'Thought of moving into my dad's. But I wouldn't if you'd gone.'

'What difference would that make?'

'Don't know. But it does. We'll have to have a sort-out of his writing. Would you do that?'

They left it there.

She contacted Judith Powis, and her tutor, a Dr Byrne. They'd scour the house for paper. David acting out of character said he'd not move in until they'd finished, however protracted the operation. A room was set aside in her own place, equipped with tables, and from Jack's office a filing cabinet. Byrne, a stout young man, given to stroking his balding head, read them a lecture on care, thoroughness, impressive in his roll-neck sweater and short coat. The exact physical placing of each manuscript was to be recorded.

'May seem outrageous to you. In most cases it will be time wasted. We're legislating for the one in a thousand.'

David had accompanied her on her first visit.

They discovered how tidy Francis was; she quizzed her nephew.

'He had bonfires every so often. Letters, mostly.'

'Dr Byrne will be disappointed.'

'I don't suppose my dad bothered about that.'

She remembered how private a man Frank could be. This excessive neatness must cover the lacerations, the loose edges he wrote about.

'I don't need notebooks,' he'd said at a lecture. 'If a thing's important enough it'll stick in my head.'

She became used to the quietness of the house, calling in most days to dust or sometimes only to moon. Her search for papers did not begin until she had conducted Byrne and Judith Powis on a tour of the place. Both had taken photographs, notes briskly, more like bailiffs than scholars.

For some days she put off her own start, telling herself that she must be sure what she was about, make no errors. This was an excuse, she knew. Soon she had to break through Francis's reticence. She said as much to Byrne, apologizing for delay.

'But he's a public figure,' the man said. 'He allowed us into his confidence in his poems.'

'On his terms. He decided what he'd say, and what he'd keep quiet about. Now we might let out something he wanted hidden.'

'But he's dead now. Who'd suffer? David? Your husband? You?' Certainly she feared that. 'Mrs Hooper?' Byrne was a platitudinous wretch. 'We are all admirers.' He'd enjoy scandal. He'd make his name and money out of dirt. 'You get a start, Mrs Weldon. David wants you to. He chose you. And I think Francis himself . . .' Ughh.

On impulse she took the first step.

Jack had been home for lunch, and very attentive. He said as he left that they'd drive out somewhere for dinner. She walked with him, unusually, beyond the door to his car. The sunshine of June, tempered by a touch of breeze, brightened the garden, warmed arms and shoulders. The sky stretched unbroken light blue.

'We'll go up to the Peacock Inn,' he said, and kissed her.

'Are we celebrating?'

'No, saving you work.'

She had gone straight in, washed her hands, collected a notebook and marched down the drive for the cottage. Inside at speed. Upstairs to his study. She made a sketch of the room on page one. It was easy. Outside the weigela matched pale shrub roses. Buddleia alternifolia swayed. The red of the smoke tree paled in sunshine. A late lilac had not yet finished.

First the desk. She catalogued the papers on top, in the drawers, put aside one or two business letters David would have to answer. The job was easy; there seemed only one manuscript of a poem amongst these bits and pieces, but she worked as she had been instructed. A noise below interrupted her. Jack called from downstairs. 'I've brought you a new photo-copier. Do you want it here or in our place?'

He stood delighted with himself. She loved him. She ordered him to take the machine to her room, and to set it up. She kissed him; they hugged. He clattered off.

'Try it out,' she called. 'So you can show me.'

The whole job she completed inside a week. They made their discoveries. An historical novel, never typed, about the Luddites. A verse play, on the trial of Charles I. A curious fragment of a chorus from the *Philoctetes* of Sophocles; Frank knew no Greek. He kept his main work in three folders; one, completed poems; there were fifty-seven of these. Two, poems he worked on, in holograph, with sometimes as many as six or seven sheets to a poem, often scribbled over, illegible. The third envelope, by far the thickest, contained notes, cuttings, haphazardly crammed in. As she carefully took one fragment out after another, and noted its position, she laughed, for she'd seen Francis now and then empty out 'his rag bag'.

'I chase inspiration,' he said. 'It's no use, otherwise. I've notes in my head and this lot. When I've nothing to write, I rummage.'

'I thought you said that if it was important enough . . .'

'It'd stick. I know, I know. But I'm not confident.'

She found the poems she'd dreaded, those written when they'd had an affair, and was disappointed. They were in a notebook headed 'K', perhaps ten complete. She recognized his voice, but he said too little.

She showed them to Jack.

'Poems to K,' she said.

'Is that you?'

'Very likely. Have a look, will you?'

He did so, spoke noncommittally, interested but puzzled. She, likewise, found Frank more inclined to hide than to expose. No passion seared; perhaps that was spent in his physical contact with her. These seemed more akin to the chess or bridge problems at the end of the weeklies.

> Here is a comfortable
> Way of making safe
> The end of days. Death
> Cannot but propose relief
> To us so charmless, harmless.

She did not think highly of this. Still, she discovered
no poems at all to Louise, except one or two apparently about
her funeral, including a humorous jingle.

> The church inside's near empty:
> The yard outside is full.
> The congregation's quicker
> But both ungodly dull.

In a thick, hard-backed exercise book she found a stretch
of prose. It had been written at different times and each
section was carefully dated. He had been working on this
over the past few years, and the last paragraph had been
scribbled then heavily revised just a few days before his heart
attack. The novella was unfinished, broke off with a pencilled
note on the ideas to be treated next. The title, too, was lightly
in pencil, *Glory begun Below*.

She read with amazement. The hero was Francis Jacob
Weldon, an inmate of Topcroft Hospital, the local lunatic
asylum. In the opening, slow pages, Francis, described
exactly as himself, walked on a summer's afternoon in the
sunshine. Behind him the dark, red buildings, the saddening
iron stairways, the black, barless windows humped ominous
as winter, but he walked, in warmth, conscious of comfort, of
the white, perfumed stars of mock-orange, of the blue sky
and unthreatening holiday crowd. Beyond that he was in-
human. He did not grudge his incarceration, had only vague
memory, did not recall the man he once was, and yet his
appearance, his health, his vigour was that of a man in his
late forties, the age of the writer.

Sometimes he spoke to other inmates, or their visitors as
they walked in the grounds, but his words made only random

sense, as though thrown up by a computer that had control of grammar, but not sense. He rested his hand on the hot roof of a car, one of two dozen parked in front of the building, and pronounced, 'Wheels trundle us out of trouble.' To the parents of a rolling, contorted young man, who flung his arms about like a clumsy swimmer as he walked he said, 'Feet are not enough at the shallow end.' These aphorisms, Kathleen decided, were not meant to provoke thought about some further plane of reality, some meaning above commonplace, elicited by madness in a world where common sense was so close to lunacy that only the purely insane could approach truth, but a series of metaphors suggested by objects, illustrating nothing but inconsequence. 'Bushes flower round the ruins of nests.'

At one stage in the narrative a doctor explained to Louise, who, alive and busybodying, demanded a report once a month. 'It's as if his poetry has escaped himself. A poet in the end puts words at the beck and call of reality, even when he seems to be doing the opposite, wildly pandering to his imagination, or working on ambiguities. Your husband is letting out sentences that as a poet he would have to tie to a sense, even if he did not completely grasp that sense. Now he ejaculates his spurts of words. "Sand buckets are complemented by cigarette ends." Any respectable literary critic could offer you an explanation, give you a context for that, but Francis speaks and is satisfied, is done. He's carried his poetic gifts into the madness that maims it, that does not allow development. "Doctors speak energy. Drugs swoop like kites." '

Her own reaction to this insane Francis was ambivalent. His pronouncements made suggestions, hinted that there one speaks with a meaning that dismissed the world of ambition, even of ideals. At another time the madman seemed quietly happy, tucked away, sounding out nothing because of his content. 'The length of a room is its importance, not the width.'

However, Francis the inmate was visited, and here the writer's skill told. Louise bustled in, snapped about laundry, housework, money, though she was, somehow, financially secure. She came in, and lived her life before her mad husband in a concentrated vigour. Small clashes with tradesmen, a tussle with some rosebud in the garden, David's open day at school she described. Kathleen could hear her voice as she read. Louise darted like a wasp against the massive calm of the dark buildings, their disinfected corridors, her husband's plenitude of quiet. She made regular, but short appearances in the book, six to ten lines, but frequently. Each small outburst, inthrust, threw up two or three sharp anecdotes.

Cecilia appeared only twice.

Francis the author had exactly hit off her mumbled inconsequentialities, but her attitude was clear. She was ashamed of her brother. He was in the 'sylum. She never said this, preferring to whine about her husband's failure to remember this errand she'd set him, or a friend's inability to understand the importance of some meeting. As she talked she squinted round, fearing someone would recognize her, report back to the Conservative Club, the Mothers' Union, the Circle of Help. Francis Madman did not object, but neither did Francis Writer, who looked on this behaviour as entirely rational if not exactly commendable. She was entitled to her shame as to her choice of Sunday hat or meat for Monday's dinner. He would have acted otherwise, but found no immorality in her.

Jack amongst the visitors was not so well sketched.

His unease was suggested, but one-sided conversation, especially if one suspects complete incomprehension, is unnerving. Jack described his work, but needed congratulatory murmurs to spur him on. He'd taken over a small factory, and now employed the former owner as a craftsman, not a manager. This sweetened his victory in a way that sickened, but no suggestion was made that the employee complained of his misfortune or seemed the happier for it. He arrived in the same little Volkswagen with his greaseproof bag of sand-wiches. His hands were oily on his pay packet. Mad Francis made no comment, but Kathleen found the description of her husband crude, lacking the suspicious peering round that characterized his selfish actions, spoilt his generous moves.

In one paragraph Jack boasted about a sexual encounter. The girl, a young married woman, was secretary to a rival business firm. They'd had sex within an hour of their first meeting. She praised him, compared him favourably with her husband, other men, touched him all the time, said that she would love to copulate with him on a stage, in public. Truth rang about that page; Kathleen thought she could identify the girl, and yet oddly she could not believe her husband would blurt out his intimacies. He'd be more likely to cobble up some fantasy around failure. This girl, with her unnatural demands, her exhibitionism, her self-indulgence, her per-versions, came from some dog-eared typescript passed round an army barracks. 'A week with her and I'd walk bow-legged for the rest of my days,' Jack told his insane brother, who stared at the wall beyond, face unlined and unmoved. Francis Madman frowned a little, groping for unhappiness, perhaps, a shattering of the calm of his state.

Kathleen herself, according to the manuscript, made two long visits.

The first described, amusingly, her arrival, her annoyance at the bad parking of other visitors, her own difficulties at getting the car in straight. She cursed mildly, but by the time she'd reached the main entrance she walked trimly, caught the eye of the porter, made an impression. She walked in fear along the corridors following explicit notices as though she owned the place; when she found the ward office, the male nurse stood, and after hesitation accompanied her.

They passed through a dining area into the television lounge. Chairs were arranged round the walls as if for a dance, but in the centre an asymmetrical group had been placed in rows in front of a set which flickered a picture, though the sound was down almost to zero. No one took advantage. Knots of patients and visitors were haphazard in the large room; one or two inmates sat doll-like in solitude. Outside the greyness of winter accentuated the darkness of the room and killed the few electric lights that had been switched on. There was no sign of Frank. Her guide smiled conspiratorially; he knew.

He led her round the corner through a gap in the fencing chairs into a sizeable alcove where stood a grand piano. Frank crouched on a cushioned window seat by the sharp end.

'There you are, Mr Weldon. A lady to see you.'

She thanked the nurse, who was loth to go, and then stood idly. Frank made no move, so she was forced to fetch a seat for herself. She inquired about his health, was answered with succinct sanity.

Next she took out of the bag the apples she had brought him, describing her call at the fruiterer's and Mr Ellis's inquiries after him. Frank had admired young Ellis, a man of nearly sixty, and his father, now retired, who with other educational advantages would have ended life as a doctor of divinity. The old chap, eighty-eight now, had come into the shop hale and straight-backed, had a word with her.

'How's the brother-in-law, Mrs Weldon?' Stiffly. Francis Weldon meant something to this man. His madness needed a wary eye. The universe might be left-handed, but not skew-whiff. The old man questioned as she answered, flatly. As she paid her bill, the younger man bashing his machine, the father said, distinctly,

' "But blasted with excess of light." '

'I beg your pardon.' She had heard, not believed, was curious.

Old Ellis ruffled his still thick hair. He had clearly spoken his thoughts out loud.

'It's Thomas Gray on Milton's blindness,' he said. His face saddened, like dough, shrank round the wrinkles. 'In its way it's appropriate.' The manuscript contrasted the lined features, doleful, heavy with care, part by part, with Frank's unmoved face, his expression of blank unconcern with the old fellow's poetry of sorrow.

There that extract broke off. Deliberately. The next line described a patient trying to borrow a cigarette.

Kathleen was moved by what she read, skipped until she found her second appearance.

This time she was changing clothes in her bedroom in preparation for the visit when her husband appeared. They made love. His advances were unexpected; he'd called in, and not finding her in the house downstairs or the garden, had come up. Seeing his wife in her underclothes, Jack exposed himself plain.

The encounter on the bed was short, utterly satisfactory.

A vignette of Jack pulling on his trousers, the hairs on his powerful legs bright in the window sunshine, accurately sketched his sexual power. Kathleen dazed, delighted, sat in front of a mirror complaining of damage to her hair, crooning she'd be late.

'In a good cause,' he said, kissing her crown, straightening his jacket. 'Our Frank won't grudge me five minutes. Not that he's capable of grudging anybody owt these days, poor bugger.' Through the glass she saw him draw his lips from his teeth, beastly. 'Still, the world's got to go on.'

On her arrival, this time she found her own way, waving to the staff, she chattered on the brightness of the day, insisted on taking him out into the gardens. He made no objection, and though his walk was described as hesitant, no explanation was offered. If he felt fear, nothing was said. The car park radiated heat; they looked down from a tree-shaded path, over a grassy bank, a beech hedge above a walk down to a road where cars decelerated, braked, hooted. Beyond, through a passage way between houses they could make out, half misty in the sun, the wide river valley below. Frank had nothing to say; in this incident he was completely dumb. Kathleen, excited by her encounter with her husband, seemed electric with energy, and determined to bring her brother-in-law somewhere near to the life in the street outside. The shouts of passing children, a high squeal of brakes, a cheerful greeting, a man hawking into the gutter represented what should be. Hospitalization, inmates' shuffling, dependence were brought face to face with the necessary implied criticism.

It made no difference.

Frank Lunatic saw the world, kept his mouth shut.

Slightly exasperated she pressed him to come out, to visit them at home for a half-day. He did not reply, not even smile; she could not tell if he heard. Withdrawn, he walked by her side, in dappled sunshine, touching his cap, a puppet.

'Can you understand what I'm saying, Frank?'

He seemed to breathe slightly more heavily.

'*Gibt es einen englischen Dolmetscher?*'

She had learnt this from a phrase book on a trip to Switzerland with Jack last year. Frank loved foreign words; he'd come round for German if not for sense. She wished she had Gaelic or Japanese on offer.

Nothing. He walked delicately on. Only the bagginess of his trouser knees suggested the poet.

Now she began to lecture him. He could hear what she said; she believed that even the most insane had some notion of the world outside. He did not make the effort. As she talked she grew angrier. If he went on like this, he soon would be incapable of coping. She was going to have a word with the authorities, and send Jack up with the car. It was disgraceful. He made no effort. Her face flushed, she nagged near tears, guilty.

At this point in the narrative, Francis Writer took over from Mad Frank. One could not tell whether he spoke as the two walked the hot paths, past the bedding plants. He wrote in the first person, explaining that his madness was a myth, an escape, a convention, allowing him, sane as the next man, however cracked that was, to indulge himself, to escape from his boredom or frustration. His tone was cool; he might have been explaining to a dull parent what 'O' level, grade E, meant. At the end of the short paragraph, the scene changed; she was allowed no answer. There followed a description, of about equal length, of a sprinkler on a cricket pitch. The whirling swish, the small rainbows, the pools disturbed by the constantly circling spray, the parched grass nearby.

She was unsure whether to read this as a metaphor, an allegory. It seemed not. It seemed like practice. She'd heard Frank quote Brahms: 'When I'm not composing, I write counterpoint.'

There were, apart from these two incidents, one or two mentions of her.

Cecilia said, 'I think Kathleen is beautiful, even when she's not dressed up.' Unexpected tribute, it rang true. David had muttered, 'I wonder what Aunt Kathleen makes of us all.' And, 'Aunt Kathleen's the only relative I can talk to. She listens, at least.' Less favourably, Eric, Cissie's husband, cross because he could not find a replacement for a broken bootlace, had snapped at his wife, 'Your Jack's Kathleen's as bad. She'd do anything for money.' But Cissie, who did not like her domestic arrangements criticized, had answered, 'Chance'd be a fine thing.' Jack had announced that he was encouraging his wife to join a tennis club. She laughed at that, felt she must make inquiries. Another of her husband's sentences: 'I tell you this, our Frank, I've never understood Kath, and I don't suppose I shall.'

She read the manuscript rapidly then with care, deciding that if it were to be published she'd change all names. Byrne or Judith Powis would object; a sound had importance to a poet. 'Jack' would resonate in a sentence as 'Tom', 'Dick', 'Harry' would not. She showed it, brashly, to her husband, pointing out his appearances. He read, pulling faces of relish, man with good cigar. On the bedroom scene he said:

'The dirty old sod. Still, it's good.' He stroked Kathleen's buttocks, laughing. She stepped away. 'Sharp, our Frank. Didn't miss much.'

On the next afternoon she decided on a third perusal, but after ten minutes put the book away, took out her car, drove up to Topcroft. Sunny still, but cool; philadelphus in creamy profusion, beginning to drop like confetti. She parked, there were very few cars, and smiled at her skill. She walked under the trees; no one questioned her. Beech hedge; river valley; raw houses. The building was hugely dark, almost purple. Presumably when it was built it stood on this crest with open fields about it. Her children had used the word 'Topcroft' in school as a synonym for mad. 'Topcroft, Topcroft, weak in the top loft' they'd chanted in the yard. Bars and strait-jackets had gone; patients went out to work; bus trips, dances, garden parties brightened their life, as the square towers, the barrack blocks, the blank fire escapes darkened the sky. When had Frank been up here? Why? He described accurately. Did the room with the grand piano exist?

She went in, explained to the uniformed porter about the poet's description. 'Could be,' the man said. 'Couple of rooms here like that. For the concerts. Lot going on for 'em now-adays. In the evenings.' Another figure in uniform was called across. The first official exactly described what 'the lady' wanted. The two argued. 'Sounds a bit like St Martha's. New place down the road.' They offered to show her the stage and entertainments room, but she refused with thanks. She'd done enough. They both stood at a kind of pleased attention for her. Frank would have noticed.

'What did you say your brother's name was?' the second asked. 'The poet?'

'Francis Weldon.'

'We did one of his at school. About feeding hens.'

All smiles broadened. The men of grace had found glory begun below.

14

Some time during August Byrne rang Kathleen to say he had completed his sorting of the material and had contacted Francis's agent. He suggested a visit to London together. She included Judith Powis, who had passed her examinations with distinction and now concentrated mainly on puddings and shirts. After the trip, when Byrne had been dictatorial, all sorted out, all material in his neat parcels, Kathleen asked the girl back for a drink.

'Make a day of it,' she pressed.

Judith's reluctance melted. Yes, Alan could get his own meals. She seemed down in the mouth, and Kathleen attributed this to the Byrne take-over, said as much.

'No. It's not that. He'll do it well.'

Kathleen did not press, waited for a confession.

'We're thinking seriously of going to New Zealand,' she said. They were washing up.

'And you don't want to.'

'There's another year before I get my B.Ed.'

'You want to do that?'

'Well, yes.'

'Doesn't your husband know?'

Judith glumly recited the facts. A relative had offered Alan a place in his business; it was a good offer; he'd be a fool not to accept.

'Let him go, then, and you join him when you've finished your course.'

'That'll be a year out of our lives.'

It sounded like tragedy. Neither of the young people had considered this seriously. If he emigrated, she went with him. Judith spoke well of her husband. Alan Powis had not had much encouragement from home; his parents had insisted on his leaving at sixteen, though the school said he was university material. He'd shaped well at the bank; but here was a chance to join a prosperous export business, near the top. His uncle had made inquiries, was nobody's fool, had interviewed the manager at the Midland, gone up higher in London, had called on Jack when he learnt he'd offered Alan a job.

'Jack knows you're going, then?'

'He knows we're considering it.'

She suspected that this girl was her husband's mistress, that Alan dragged her out of Jack's clutches. She did not say as much. Judith talked badly, in broken sentences, depressed.

Kathleen spoke to her husband.

'I hear the Powises are going to New Zealand. You didn't say anything.'

'Should I?' Stared her straight in the eyes.

'At one time you were full of her praises.'

'A smart girl.'

'She doesn't want to go. I told her to finish her course first, then join him.'

'He'd be a fool to refuse. Shrewd chap, the uncle. Young. Built his business up in a few years. Wants a steady, hard-working accountant type. Powis would do. Quick, not reckless. I'd have had him. I liked the uncle as well. Useful contact. He's a flier. Made a million already.'

'Sounds unlikely,' she said, coldish.

'Why do you say that?' He was pleased she opposed him.

'Would you give David a job, just because he's your nephew?'

'No. Nor more would Sid Street, this man. Dave's a fly-by-night. No, that's wrong. He's not mad keen on making money, or anything else. He's not even like Frank. I'd give him a clerk's job, out of sentiment. No more than that.'

As soon as she had finished with Francis's papers, David moved into the cottage, set about haphazard decorating. He seemed cheerful. His aunt spoke to him about Powis's New Zealand job, but he'd heard nothing. He'd met Judith once; bit of a blue-stocking, wasn't she? The old-fashioned term reminded her he was his father's son, but his jeans, bobbed hair, fringe of beard belied that influence.

'Call in,' he told her, 'any time. You've got a key.'

'You don't want me.'

'I do. That's why I'm inviting you. If you'd have moved, I shouldn't.'

She felt uncomfortable with him; he didn't mean what he said. He talked like a subdued market huckster, saying what suited him.

In August she had spent four days in Paris with Jack, not altogether successfully. He had to work; she tired quickly of sightseeing, of throwing money about. The weather back home was tropical; dust coated the gutters; she could not summon energy to work indoors or out. Jack suggested she take herself off for the seaside. It did not appeal; Paris again writ provincial. She'd know her way about on the coast, in the bars, the grills, the restaurants, swimming pools. She might even botch up a six-day friendship. She'd not bother.

Bored, she decided to walk down to David's place.

The garden would require attention, and she'd see whether the house needed a duster on it. Anyhow, she'd pass half an hour. Nobody walked the hot street; the public library door was shut; the church rose, squatted, duller for the sunshine; empty beer crates in the drive of the Liberal Club suggested an abandoned operation. Newspapers, ice-cream wrappings, a scatter of coloured cartons in a dead street.

She examined the garden shrubs which would need pruning. In autumn she'd smarten it. David had done nothing, not even cut the grass. Still, wildness suited the style, a botch, a crowding with big standard roses or hybrid teas in the thickness of green, of the privet, magnolia, guelder rose, cherry. Honeysuckle hung battered and exotic; she bent to sniff.

Quietly she let herself into the house.

It smelt stuffy; the morning's paper had been dropped by a chair. She refolded, tabled it. This was a dull, little room, a bachelor's hide-out, without comfort, or taste. With Frank it did not matter. There he'd eaten; there he'd watched television. Nothing out of the way happened here. He woke upstairs; he taught and lectured outside. He thought on his feet. The curtains were dull, unassertive red, faded. She rubbed her hand over the mantelshelf, grimaced at the smear of dirt on her fingers.

She opened the door into what Francis had called 'the parlour'. It seemed darker, because the curtains were drawn. Alarm thrust itself like a rod of steel into her gullet, held her petrified, reeling, dumb, nerves screaming.

On the settee, which faced the door, David sat, his head on the shoulder of a girl. They seemed sun-drunk, eyes barely open. Both were stark naked. His right arm circled her waist and their heads, one dark, one blond with hair upthrust, lolled together. Tired. Drunk. Satiated. They shifted slightly. Kathleen muttered an apology as David sat straight up. The girl buried her face into his back.

Kathleen slammed the door behind her, staggered through the first room, painfully rapping her hip on the corner of the table, took three steps out of the back door, and stood, foot-rooted, but swaying. She blushed in every inch of her skin. Blood pulsed in her temples. The trembling of her arms and legs rushed fierce but mechanical. Her mouth, throat moaned small, breathy noises. Her distress coated her body, tore it inwardly, but did not allow her to think, only to be attacked by the shock waves. If a bus had knocked her flat, her body's squeal of protest would have been no keener, madder, no less uncontrollable.

She shuffled towards and down the steps.

The street had not changed. Shadows were small, sharp.

Bushes did not stir. She watched a bee, smelt honeysuckle again, with faint nausea. For the first time her mind suggested capability, and she forced herself to walk, steadily enough, along the pavement. A passer-by wished her good afternoon, and she replied, but had no idea to whom she'd spoken. She made herself, rusty key in lock, turn her head to find out. A woman dragging a shopping trolley. Light blue dress; stockingless legs. Tartan container. A woman. No face suggested itself. A broad-bottomed woman, with white calves and brown shoes.

As soon as she was indoors, and she remembered nothing of the walk, she opened the gin, poured a dose, drank sitting. Halfway down her glass, she stood to test her legs. Though she could make out still vestiges of the trembling, she was in control, able to order her limbs. She tapped the sill, adjusted the catch of a huge sash window; all was well. A breathlessness, an apathy remained, but undominant, a trace only.

Back in her chair, sipping, she chided herself.

This was a permissive age, nobody doubted. Yet she had reacted like an old maid, or, she put it into words, like her mother. David was a man, nineteen, twenty now, and woman-struck. She'd had it from more than one source. What did she expect? Chaste hand-holding? A pecked kiss? Perhaps it had been the surprise. She'd decided David was at work; he was entitled to a day's leave here and there, wasn't he? She would have been jolted if she'd come across him on the settee fully clothed, but there would have been jokes, mock accusations of idleness or burglary, invitations to tea or sherry, a chat, a walk round the garden, advice, plans, shared trivialities. Had the girl been dressed there would have been an introduction, and now, after a shorter stay, unless the girl had been socially most adept, she'd be sitting there expecting that David would tell her, in his own time, whether or not he was serious about this particular miss.

He'd always been slightly odd, unexpected. His finding his own lodgings when he'd got a job, or, equally, his return to his father's house. He took after his mother, both un-assertive on casual inspection, but obstinate, a sticker, with narrow mind, primary will. To say Kathleen had never got on with Louise was wrong; she'd never cottoned on to her. Of course, the relationship with Frank. That, that. They'd never sat naked together. Perhaps better if they had. They'd never been caught. It was a secret between them, shabby or not. She finished the gin, helped herself to a second. She was calm now, settled, a woman of the world, able to look straight at a mirror, speak to a neighbour, answer a question.

The phone shrilled.

She jumped; her body registered again its recent pains. She spoke her number. 'Good afternoon, Mrs Weldon.' BBC formality. 'Your errant nephew.' Again the word suggested the father. David, unembarrassed, pulling your leg. 'Sorry I was in no state to receive you.' He laughed; she reached for the gin.

He sounded so clear, she could hardly believe. This boy mumbled, unemphatically, was blown about, was unimpressive. Now he spoke with a lucid candour, unashamed, putting her in her old-fashioned place.

It was his day off; they had such things in banks. A fly buzzed like a machine in her window. Would she like to come down again, try it now, and they'd have a cup of coffee or a glass of, and he'd introduce Sharon?

'Who is she, David?'

'A young lady standing at my elbow at this,' he giggled preparation, 'moment in time.'

Kathleen declined.

'We've upset you,' he said.

'I suppose so. I'm sorry, David. It's silly, isn't it? Oh, I don't know.'

He waited.

'I'll come and see you on my own some time,' he said.

'Do that.'

The young man mumbled, in uncertainty. She didn't want

to go round reeking of gin. Two devious, dubious people. He rang off abruptly.

Jack, home for dinner early, sauntered down to the kitchen. 'Young Powis on the phone just before I left. His wife wants to stay to finish her course. I told him to ask you, but he said you'd told her that's what she should do.'

'You said?'

'The New Zealand offer's too good to miss. He should be off whatever she does. Can't understand the man. He'll blame himself for the rest of his life if he packs this chance in, but here he is, doesn't know, needs advice.'

'They don't all think like you, you know.'

'What's got at you?' he asked, not staying to find out.

As soon as dinner was over, he cleared off, in short-tempered quiet. They had barely exchanged a word.

At eight Alan Powis phoned her, explained his dilemma again.

'My husband said you'd rung him up. He thinks you should go. It's too good an opportunity to miss.' He muttered objections. 'I agree with him.'

'But you told Judith . . .'

'She should finish her course. So she should. I know what you're going to say. It's a year out of your lives, you've not started a family, you'll be in a new situation where you'll need her care and attention, she mightn't like it when she does arrive. Jack's no fool. If he says this chance is a marvel, I'd guess he's right. So go. But let Judith here have her pound of flesh.'

'I don't think you quite understand, Mrs Weldon, what . . .'

'Put it in words of one syllable then.' She sounded almost violent inside her own head.

'A year, or nearly a year, is a long time. We're young.'

'You can't do without sex for twelve months?'

'It's not exactly that, but it comes into it.' He produced sentences about marriage, companionship, a developing relationship, that he might well have lifted from one of his

170

wife's college essays. Oddly, she thought, simmering down, he spoke as if he believed his propositions. She wondered how near these statements came to reality, to the couple saving money in the semi-detached, and then, how far any such words were of any use whatever. She allowed him to repeat himself, that's what he needed, and paid no attention to the earnest platitudes.

He ended, sounding unconvinced himself.

'Listen,' she said in mock patience, 'and I'll have one more try. Then you'll have to make your own minds up. If you stay, you'll end up at best as a bank manager in a place like this. Good. Substantial. A useful job. Moderately well rewarded. If you shape well in New Zealand, you'll be rich. New life-style. Big house. World travel. Influence if you want it. Businesses go bust, and banks don't. That's the risk. But you've got your feet under this table. It's not everybody has an uncle. As to Judith, she won't need her qualifications and degrees, if you're as affluent as all this, but she wants them for herself. You both sacrifice something. It might lead to tragedy, but every time you turn your gas stove on, so might that. If you don't, you'll both regret it, reproach yourselves, blame each other.'

As she spoke she sounded more like her husband. As Alan attempted to argue, she dismissed him, refusing flatly, leaving him stranded. He gasped, gave in. She turned from the telephone displeased with herself. That she could talk with such certainly took her by surprise. Frank would have havered, humming, ha-ing. 'Stay with your wife. Let her make her way.' And in five years she'd have two or three children, while the bank had offered him promotion to a place where they didn't want to live. 'Out of these quandaries,' Frank would offer diffidently, 'we become what we are. Side-step them, and equally we become ourselves.' She angrily hitched the neckline of her frock. Making up matchbox mottoes for a dead brother-in-law didn't suit. The doorbell shrilled.

'Am I in disgrace?' David, unabashed. She asked him in,

gave him a drink. 'I've come to apologize for this morning.'

'It wasn't your fault.'

'Oh, I know that.' Clothed, he was less impressive, needed this cheerful impudence. Naked, in a naked woman's arms, he'd been himself. She was away again at her thumbnail impressions of life. The boy talked, not clearly, said a word or two about the girl, Sharon Corbett, about leave arrangements. No, he was not thinking of marriage. He chattered, spoilt himself. This morning's phone call had been sufficient.

'You were upset?' he asked.

'Yes.'

'Sex hasn't just been invented,' he said.

She did not answer that, could not. She had committed adultery with this man's father, two or three times only, in his desperation, or hers. As she saw it now it seemed an impossibility. They could not have acted so. They had. Her children were young, a nuisance in spite of home help; he'd married a curious, dour, assertive, self-contained woman who seemed to herself more diamond-bright than the rest of the world. So she and Frank had come together, in this house, while Jack was out roistering in clubs and hotels with his mistress, a supervisor from the Leicester business. They'd hesitated; she'd made the running. She'd led him to that north-facing attic where on a shabby palliasse they'd committed their insignificant acts of protest. Never once had they been naked; they registered, or rather she, her snivels against boredom, her husband's flagrant breaking of his marriage vows, the children's constant demands, the everyday routine of restoring what tomorrow would spoil, the small-town, dull-silliness. So she, tired and dispirited, had dropped her knickers to a poet in a stuffy junk room, with faded curtains undrawn because the windows were too high for snoopers, the bolt in the door, rammed, jammed rustily home.

She'd had little out of it. Certainly no sense of revenge on her husband. Dust. Doubt. If this was adultery, she'd do better with lemonade or clock golf. Even at the time she'd wondered how she'd drummed up the energy. It all seemed so cursory, ill-arranged, token. She exerted herself and the result, no score. Nor was Frank any better. Hesitant, needing not temptation but baby care, he'd been no lover. Untalkative. His orgasm palely, silently achieved. But then, a poet's secrets lay in his head. Now she had seen the 'Poems to K'! second-rate secrets, wrapped up, round-the-corner, puritan dodging. She'd expected some burst of pagan thanksgiving, some paean that the schoolmaster had been let out on a half-holiday. Instead, these evasive, hollow, literary counters arranged into conventional patterns, because he was shamefaced, afraid of the consequences, unfit for love, uninspired.

Kathleen smiled to herself.

Unashamed she looked David over, advised him to put a sign up in the window next time. He slapped her bottom and cleared off. More afraid than he showed, he had not wanted to annoy her. Why? The jaunty back meant nothing.

She told her husband the story that night.

He'd been bar-room coarse, saying she had all the luck. Some anecdote from a stay in South Africa, a mother and daughter both naked, was delivered; she did not listen. But her husband had become excited, insisted that she took a second drink, made love to her, fiercely, like a young man. She lay delighted, young again in the darkness, her body eased and electrified. She had married the right man. Next morning, he was up and about early, whistling, brought her a breakfast tray upstairs.

15

Jack Weldon inquired again if Kathleen wished to move house.

'I'm too idle just now,' she answered. 'I haven't the energy.'

'Because of Frank?'

'Not that I know of. Do you want to change?'

'I don't know what the hell I do want.'

'That's a pair of us, then.'

She laughed, and he humped himself off to work. Sooner or later, he'd come back to the subject, so she made a trip or two round the house agents.

'I've been thinking.' Her husband, in a day or two, over dinner.

'Go on, then,' she said. 'Let's be hearing it. Then I'll change my dress and you can take me down to the Mansfield for a drink.'

'You don't mean it.' His face had lighted up. 'Put these things in the machine and get ready.'

'No. Tell me what you've been thinking.'

He rolled about in his chair, started sentences, fiddled with a plate, straightened his back.

'Come on.' She enjoyed this, chaffed him. 'Can't be as bad as all that.'

There was something of Dr Johnson about him, a big man, troubled, showing it.

'It's about our Frank. Can't help thinking about that lunatic asylum thing, article, whatever it was.' She waited for him. 'I mean, he had some success, didn't he? They read his poems in schools.' Again the pause as if he needed her encouragement. 'And yet, when all comes to all, he sees himself as fit for the madhouse.'

'Go on, then.'

'He must have seen his life as wasted. In his own opinion, he wasn't anybody or anything, just an inmate.'

'We look at the worst. Sometimes. And he was a writer, so he made something of it.' That sounded weak, God knows. 'That was fiction.'

'I think about my dad. Who was he? Chief clerk at a finishing company. I suppose that was something. He'd worked his way up, by his own efforts. His people were nobody. But it wasn't much, was it? Chief clerk, head cashier. And yet there was no sign about him that he had failed. Not so far as I could see. Not when he was a younger man. He'd lay down the law. He'd tick people off in the street. He'd twirl his walking stick.'

'That might just have covered his uncertainties. He blustered his way out of fright. You didn't notice because you were only a child, and in any case he was taking it out of you.'

Jack nodded, clicking his dentures.

'But look at the way he lorded it over our Cis. Treated her like a slave for years, and then when she got married, had her at his beck and call every afternoon of the week, running up to do for him what he could have done for himself, or paid somebody else to do for him. No, Kath. He seemed in a different mould. Perhaps times have changed, but people, well, people I know, haven't got that sort of confidence. Our Frank, there, a somebody, wouldn't say boo to a goose, and yet my dad's chucking his weight about.'

'You didn't get on with him, did you?'

'Not too bad. We've had rows, I'll tell you. He's ordered me out of the house more than once.'

'And don't you think,' she asked, 'these quarrels troubled him?'

'I expect they did. But by and large he'd a confidence in

what he believed, or wanted. That's the difference.'

'I think Freddie or David or young Powis would all describe you in just those terms.'

'Would you say so?' He grinned, delighted with the idea. 'It doesn't feel that way to me.'

'Aren't things going well, then?'

'It's not that. This is a slackish period, but we're shaping. No. I wish I could be dishing it out with the confidence my dad did.'

'And I'm telling you,' she said, 'that your employees are certain you are.'

He nodded, uglifying his face comically, not displeased.

'Our Frank, now.' Jack indicated his next conversational move, but she expected nothing. His serious exchanges often consisted in a name-dropping and the silence while he staggered in thought round that name. 'He was in love with you. At one time.'

'Yes.' She mystified him.

'You don't think . . . ? You didn't marry the wrong man, did you?'

'I'd be a widow now.'

'If he'd married you, he might not be dead.'

That was good, had a dull ring of truth. When her husband talked to her like this, she was impressed. There was something of his brother's quality about him, a depth, a probing, a sense of vast discovery to be made. The quick-fire business decisions, the long hours of slog, the sexual aggressiveness, the bar-bonhomie hid a thoughtful, a puzzled creature.

'He never talked about it,' Jack said. 'Not to me, any road. I tried to apologize, once, for taking you. He shut me up. "She wanted to go. Otherwise she would have stayed. That's all there is to it." But it must have rankled.'

'In view of your other escapades?' She'd not let him off.

'He talked about that?'

'Not to me.'

'It's rum. In that way we were different. I don't think

176

he ever put a foot out of place. And yet my dad, he had a fancy woman at one time. While we were kids. I didn't know about it. Our Frank was,' he leered, pleasantly, 'the fruit of reconciliation. I only heard when I was an adult. Dirty old sod. Yet our Frank stuck to Louise.'

Should she enlighten him? Dash her own adultery in his face? He could talk to her of his peccadilloes as if she weren't touched by them. The days of anguish when she paced round the house, flung herself sobbing to the carpets, walked the streets to tire herself out only to wake to a destructive welter of nightmare rocking in the small hours he'd not noticed, or ignored or considered bought off by generous presents. She believed he could barely help himself. Approve of a woman's appearance, get her to bed. Her own phrase of a few minutes back, 'escapades', would have encouraged him. 'My wife's modern, broad-minded.' He'd explained, when she kept her face straight, 'American for a woman', but she said, 'Not funny', frigid, superior. Suddenly she was depressed, taking no more pleasure in this exchange. Her life was a failure in its deepest source of good.

Her gently interested face betrayed nothing.

He talked again. He must be enjoying himself or he'd be pressing to get out to the Mansfield Club, where he cut a figure.

She compelled herself, not easy, to listen.

'. . . couldn't make head or tail of her. Funny woman. Like a little chunk of suet. But she'd got something. Must have.' No answer. No taker. 'Come on, let's get down to the Mansfield.'

He praised her dress, joked with the barmaid about being treated out by his wife, but once they sat down and he'd hailed everybody he mumbled about Louise again. Amongst these well-dressed people, in enjoyment, her sociable husband sat her in a corner to talk.

'Do you think they got on?' Business-like after his initial half-sentences, allusions.

'Not too well. But he didn't complain.' Not even when he made love.

'She'd a big opinion of herself for somebody with nothing to write home about.'

'I don't know. She could make her presence felt. I taught in the same school for a few months. The kids didn't like her. She didn't approve of herself, wasn't good enough.'

'Wasn't her dad a parson?'

'Nonconformist. The Rev. J. Clevely Armstrong. He was a loud-hailing nobody.'

'Why is it,' Jack asked, weighing his drink in his hand, 'that you and I dislike her so much?'

'She never said a good word about either of us?'

'Neither does our Ciss for that matter.'

'We don't say much in her favour.'

They laughed, friendly, clubbable, pleased. They watched a round-bellied man, baldly beaming, proposing a drunken toast at a table a few yards away. The crowded room, the obvious attention of the other drinkers encouraged the man to strengthen his voice, accentuate the rolls of fat round his jowls by smiling. 'I am not afraid to say,' there was no alcoholic slur, but a weighty firmness of diction, 'that this woman is in character the finest in the county. She's not a raving beauty. She's not an eloquent speaker. It's possible you'd pass her by in the street. But I tell you this, if she went, the world'd be a worse place, and by a long, long chalk.'

A middle-aged woman sat with downcast eyes smiling and abashed.

'Is it his wife?' Kathleen whispered.

'No. That's his wife on his left.'

'Perhaps it's his sister-in-law.'

The round man completed his oration. 'On this her birthday, we wish her many happy returns of the day. She deserves them.' His table rose, clinked glasses. The subject blushed. Then, because of the strength of the voice, people rose elsewhere, lifted drink in health, so that there were twenty-odd strangers, men mostly, up in greeting. Jack stood with them, excited, and Kathleen feared he'd reply, or shout a toast of his own. Baldy took it as his due, mopping perspiration from his face and head, bowing round the room. 'Speech,' they shouted, all round the room. 'Speech.' The woman scrambled to her feet in a welter of acclamation. 'I don't know what to say,' she said. 'But thank you all, very much.' She crumpled back to her seat, not daring to lift her eyes. The proposer now leaned back in his chair, overflowing it. He looked like a caricature, a Boz and Phiz monstrosity of pleasure, twenty stone of delight.

The bar gleamed with satisfaction. Conversation had broken out again at the tables, but there were smiles. All had been present at a happening. They had played their small part. Spirit had risen.

'That was lovely,' Kathleen said. Baldy's eyes were bright with slopping tears. 'Do you often go in for that sort of thing?'

'No. Not seen it before. Mark you, don't put anything past 'em here.'

They discussed Louise again, but without rancour. Kathleen heart-warmed, loved her husband. Jack talked freely. Baldy was a traveller in tyres, was called Pocock. Pocock was wishing guests loud good nights as his party cleared, and a group of young people, beautiful and beautifully dressed, took over. She and Jack sat silent in a violence of chattering.

'Our Frank should have seen that,' Jack said.

'A bit obvious for him.'

She wished she had not spoken. Sourness. They healed the breach in minutes, left at midnight hand in hand.

Undressing, Kathleen said, 'I often wonder if Louise made Frank the sort of poet he was.'

'He was writing before he met her.'

'Differently. Not so thorough, somehow.'

They made love, the pair then, in the lighted bedroom,

wrapped in each other, but as if overlooked by Frank, an approving voyeur.

'It's the wives make husbands do things,' he said, flat on his back, too satisfied to let the night end.

'What have I driven you to?'

'Don't you know?'

He returned to the theme again and again in the next days. She could not exactly grasp what had happened, in that he now spent longer hours at home, seemed to be courting her anew. He pressed her to be serious in the search for a big house; he wanted to hand over a gift she wanted. His care, his fussy consideration she enjoyed, especially now she had inured herself to his adulteries, could even speak about them to him, in a guarded way. Her pleasure was touched, she expected it, by suspicion; she peered for the snag, expected it huge and damning. Then she felt her guilt because she was incapable, it seemed, of freely accepting her husband's generosity. Common sense?

Jack spoke again of Louise.

'What's so interesting about her?' Kathleen. 'You kept out of her way when she was alive.'

'It's what she made of our Frank.'

'And what was that?'

'That's what I don't know, either. He married her, you know.'

She remembered the wedding.

Frank had phoned her, and Cissie, with invitations three weeks before the event. She had not connected her brother-in-law with Louise Armstrong, though she knew the woman. When she asked about presents, Kathleen learnt that the bride was well-stocked for matrimony, and that Frank had bought a bungalow, without advice. Jack had blustered about the secrecy, had poled round to hear from his brother, but had splashed out on expensive old silver for a wedding present.

Pregnant with Helen, sick, on a wet Monday of half-term,

Kathleen had been depressed by the ceremony. The Rev. Mr Armstrong and his superior had heavy charge; the bride's half of the church was filled with hatted women. Polished pews marked the Weldon sector. 'Ex-Lord-Mayor's Grand-daughter Weds'. Hearty singing and tears, teetotal toasts, speeches in the unheated schoolroom. Drab and strong. The festivities, she felt, excluded her and her sort. These people held beliefs that were unknown, unattractive to her; their principles were cold, iron-hard, cloaked with a frown, a laugh that stopped, a warning, a rebuke, symbolized by sermon and tea-urn, bare floorboards and Sankey zest. She could not join in. They would not want her to.

There was no honeymoon. On the Wednesday the couple returned to their classes. Tuesday was spent painting the bungalow. Francis Jacob Weldon at twenty-seven looked pinched and middle-aged. Louise May Armstrong, thirty, Mrs Weldon, was confident in her choice. Jack, Kathleen discovered, had not been nearly so distressed by the cere-monies as she, claiming that it reminded him of his youth, that chapels hadn't changed, and that they encouraged red nose-ends in women on weekdays. There followed an account of the clouts that had warmed him in Sunday school, and the cost of heating a great, draughty, pseudo-Gothic barn. His disdain and nostalgia merged into a kind of cheerfulness. 'They're too big. They should be more like pubs, cosier.' As she recalled the statement now, she remembered the palatial staircase to the Mansfield Club, the pillars, the great solemn leaded windows.

'Was she ever happy?' he wanted to know. 'She never looked it.'

'She didn't let on. I wonder if Frank was the first.'

'Did he start that Topcroft Asylum thing while she was alive?'

'About the time Louise began to be really ill.'

'Puts a different complexion on it. She doesn't make long appearances. Just like stabs. Perhaps he knew she'd die, and locked himself away up there as a widower. Might be. Mark you, our Frank had no idea what it's like to be mad.'

Kathleen waited for him.

'When I was a boy I used to be taken up to Topcroft to see my dad's eldest sister, Aunt Gladys. She'd been a case all her life, and they put her away about the time Frank was born. She'd be in her forties then. She lasted three years.'

'What was wrong with her?'

'No idea. She was touched. That's what we said. The case wasn't much discussed in front of us, but once every month my dad took Cis and me up there. She'd be eight, me six. There were some sights, I tell you. But Gladys, she seemed old as the hills to me, just sat there, and her mouth trembled. I can't remember her saying anything. She looked shell-shocked. Thin as a rake.'

'Was she married?'

'No. She'd always been odd, though she went out to work now and then. But she wasn't all there, literally. She wasn't there at all. There were what we thought of as proper loonies; they looked and acted daft. But Gladys sat in a chair and let her mouth tremble. She didn't seem to see us. I may have got it wrong. I was only a kid.'

'Why did they take you?'

'To get us from under my mother's feet, I should think. I wouldn't say my dad was too keen.'

'Didn't it frighten you?'

'Ummh. Yes. Suppose it did. I think I had dreams. But they took children in to see corpses and God knows what. We liked the tram rides. And he always bought us two ounces of licorice comfits, torpedoes.'

She reached back to her own childhood, but it seemed kinder than this. Frustrations and punishments rankled, but nothing of this eccentric juxtaposition with death and madness. Jack sat steady enough now, even when he talked of his history.

'That's why I say Frank had no idea. He was just there

saying incomprehensible sentences, while other people outside lived their lives.'

'Literary convention.'

'Right. But with old Gladys, the machine had stopped. She
was a zombie. As far as you could tell nothing happened in
her mind.'

'Did Frank never see her? Didn't they take him up?'
Kathleen asked.

'No. He'd only be three or so when she snuffed it. She was
delicate, somehow. Physically. Died of pneumonia. I don't
think she was fifty. But she looked like an old grandma.'

'Was it some hereditary thing?'

'She was the only one. I sometimes think our Ciss is a bit
that way.' He laughed. 'They say the First World War put
the tin hat on her, but she'd been off centre well before that.'

'Poor woman.'

'There were madmen amongst the poor, you know.'

Kathleen did not answer that. It seemed accusatory.

This new, attentive husband cheered her. One hot, August
afternoon he dawdled at table in no hurry to return to the
office.

'What's the trouble?' she asked. It was best to chase him
into answering.

'Nothing. I enjoy your company.'

'That's new,' she said, sharply sweet. 'Let's hear about it.'

'There's no bloody pleasing you, is there? I come home,
butter you up, neglect my work, and what do I get?' He
reminded her of her husband as a young man, on the grumble
when gladdened. She waited. 'I'd like to do something for
you.'

'Such as?'

'This new house you don't want. A cruise. It's since our
Frank died. I'm next, I think.'

'You don't believe that.'

'I don't physically feel like dying, true. But did he? And
while I'm here, I'm going to do something for those I . . .

bother about. Love.' The word came out like a stoppage of phlegm. 'You, you . . . wife.' He laughed. Provincial statement of importance. O, she doth teach the torches to burn bright. 'You know that Judith Powis? You should have seen the way she thought of Frank.'

'In love with him, you mean.'

'I don't know about that. Perhaps she was. But here was a man who'd written poems that were jewels to her. And she was allowed to speak to him, help him on with his overcoat, turn the light off for him, ask him questions. She said to me, and I didn't see her as a big spouter, "It was like heaven coming to earth." She actually said that. And I thought to myself if I dropped dead, who'd say a bloody word in my favour. And then I thought, "Who'd I want to?" '

'I see.'

'And it was you. If you had a word of praise. That's what I wanted. I'm not likely to write any poems. And I know I can't buy you off.'

'You're writing one now.'

'What?'

'A poem.' She smiled with her whole body.

'I'll go to our house.' He spoke it in joyful dialect, Ahl gutter ar ahse. 'I don't know sometimes what I'm missing with you. You're there, flitting about, and I see you, and belt off to work. I haven't treated you properly.'

'When you talk like this,' Kathleen answered, 'you embarrass me.'

'An' a bloody good thing.'

'In a month or two, we shall be back where we were, though. Flitting about.'

'Is that what you want?'

'You've been good to me this last month or two. In a way I didn't think you had it in you. I don't want to spoil it by talking about it. You've surprised me. I wonder what you're up to, but part of me doesn't want to know. It's lovely. I didn't expect it.'

'I'm . . .'

'Don't explain.'

'But I'm taking pleasure in hanging round the house. I shall be putting shelves up next, or painting the kitchen.'

'You used to. At one time.'

She explained, uncertainly, that she wished to visit Helen, had angled for an invitation. Her new domestic satisfaction did not demand his presence, in fact militated against it, but she felt she risked its continuation. Jack encouraged her.

16

Kathleen spent three days with her daughter.

The Kittos, brown, lean, eager-jawed had just returned from camping in France, and Harold set off early most days to the university library. Helen had not found a teaching post, but had decided she'd do a research degree on the city's river and river trade. Next week, mother out of the way, she'd join her husband to read 'the literature'. Helen showed a balanced enthusiasm; she was keen to start, but the thesis would be a nothing when it was done.

'No. It'll clear cobwebs from quite a big corner,' Harold said.

'The spiders will soon fill it up again.' Helen.

'That's the inadequacy of my metaphor rather than of your project.'

Neither of them saw anything out of the ordinary in that sentence. They were fond of each other, but not demonstrative. Harold pontificated, sometimes, as if Helen were still his pupil, but she had her own way about the house, and everywhere else, Kathleen guessed. A smart young woman.

'Are you happy, would you say?' the mother asked in a mild malice.

The young couple nodded, immediately, but then began qualifications, disclaimers.

'To be busy is better,' Helen said.

'Or the same thing.' Harold.

'Not always,' Kathleen objected. 'People often work because they're dissatisfied.'

'Not in our case,' Helen. 'Is that boasting, Haro?'

'Fairly near it, darling.'

Later, while Helen was trying to prevent her mother from helping round the rooms, the young woman, perhaps re-establishing supremacy, asked about her father. Kathleen, claiming all was as usual, queried what the question meant. She could not avoid mischief-stirring, even on dangerous subjects.

'Well, my father was, had the reputation of, a lady's man. Sidelong look.

'Did he tell you that himself?'

'He did not. He tried to give the impression of a strict, middle-class parent. I first learnt when I had a holiday job at the firm, and I overheard the others talking about him. I mean, I don't know if that made it true. Then I saw him one night, dressed up, out with some blonde charmer.'

'This shocked you?'

'Yes. It did. Still does if I let myself think about it.' Helen writhed round a flower arrangement. 'I don't know how you can put up with it.'

'That's what I thought at one time. He's shown no sign of ever wanting to leave, to divorce me.'

'Because you've let him have his way.' The clipped voice, academic like Harold's, sounded confidently. 'You could have left him, got a job. They were short of teachers then.'

'I did.'

'Did what? Left him?'

'Yes, and you and Fred. You'd just started school. Your father, well, I needn't go into . . . But I'd had enough. It wasn't the first time, by any means. I packed my bags when I'd got you two away, found digs and sent your father a letter by hand – I knew where he was that day – telling him what I'd done, with instructions to pick you both up at Holly Road at three-thirty.'

'How long were you away?'

'Six days.'

'I'd be five, but I don't remember a thing. It oughtn't

to be a blank.' Helen shook her head, fingers amongst the flowers. 'Why did you come back?'

'He found me, for a start. He can move, when he wants. He contacted the police, some private detective, people he knew in the education office. But he got it out of my father who was still alive then. I wrote to him in Surrey, put my address on it, and he phoned Jack straight off, I don't know why. He liked to have information nobody else had, and then give it away. Jack was round in no time.'

'What happened?'

'You know what he's like. He soon lost his temper and there was a blazing row. He was frightened. We shouted and screamed at each other. He ranted on about neglected children crying for their mummy.'

'Who looked after us?'

'He'd got a nurse from an agency.'

'I don't remember her, either.'

'No. There you are, then. I missed you two, and felt guilty as hell. That's one reason I went back.'

'I wonder if Fred's remembered any of this? He's never said anything.'

'He never does.' Kathleen sat straight. Under her daughter's cut-glass manner she detected nervousness, as if Helen realized that tragedy crouched by every saucepan, Mini, holiday, garden tool. Sorry for the girl, she offered what comfort she could, stressing how attentive Jack had recently been.

'On account of Uncle Frank's death?' Brusque again, back to the history books.

'That's something to do with it, I suppose. It scared him. He thinks he'll be next. He seemed to have all the time in the world for his business; now he hasn't. I can understand it. And perhaps he thinks if he treats me well, God'll be less vindictive.'

'Does he believe in God?'

'I've never heard him say otherwise.'

188

'Harold and I go to church sometimes. There's something in it, you know.'

'I'm sure.'

Helen wagged a finger at her mother's irony, but continued to talk.

'When Uncle Frank died, I wrote to David. It was just a formal note, really, but he sent a marvellous reply. I was taken aback. He always seemed a lout to me. I know he was three years younger. And I never liked him. He was a nuisance, wasn't he? Wouldn't stay on at school, left home as soon as he could? And when his mother died he didn't seem bothered. I was in the sixth form and had proper notions what he ought to have been like. He should have been deso-lated, but he just went on with his cricket, and his army pack with football clubs or pop groups daubed all over it. But this was a lovely answer. He seemed to know exactly how much his dad had done, and what it was worth. As if Frank had written it for him.

'Did you like Louise?'

'Not much. "Here's Neat Helen," she'd say. I used to be pleased at first, but then I thought she was criticizing me. You know, Goody-Two-Shoes. It was her manner more than anything. You were afraid she didn't approve. David wasn't his mother's boy. He just flagrantly disobeyed her if he felt like it.'

Kathleen listened. They hadn't confided like this since Helen was twelve. She said so. Her daughter had a beauty about her, a new manner, self-confidence and satisfaction. She picked up the accent quickly enough and with it a high gloss, as if hair, complexion, clothes had been lacquered. The merest glance dismissed this as fancy. She dressed well, but like a slim matron, childish things put away. Balance and sobriety matched zest. She had chosen rightly, got what she wanted, stood proudly by it. Harold would soon be a pro-fessor; he'd given up political ambitions; Helen hinted that vice-chancellorships were not remote; those ladies at the college who'd suggested that the laws of the universe were fractured when a senior lecturer married an undergraduate student had stopped muttering, were invited to meals, put into their place. Just for the present, this had the appearance of a home where one had control over what happened.

Helen was intelligent.

'You're worried, aren't you, Mum?' The return to the demotic diminutive spelt both affection and brains.

'One of the drawbacks of middle age.'

'You liked Uncle Frank, didn't you?'

Should she tell? But what? The rejection, the two or three furtive acts of sex, the intense puzzlement, the alienation? It bore no reasonable explanation; nothing would be achieved by further titillation of curiosity. She kept her mouth shut. She recalled a 'Poem to K'.

> When I squint over my old work
>   It exists in an energy
> Like a woman in a high wind
>   Confident, progressing.
> This image is, moreover, placed
>   In the town of my birth, by
> A shrubbery of dusty holly, lilac,
>   Laburnum, bridal wreath. . . .

She knew the spot, exactly, an area on the road, railed off from the gardens of council houses behind it. A path, also between palings, divided it, led to a covered entry through the line of buildings into a street or close beyond. He'd not named all the shrubs; laurel would have appeared, but bridal wreath was good amongst the clichés of public gardening. The spot was not quite neglected; a man in green overalls dug it, loosened the top soil once a year, and perhaps there'd been half a dozen prunings or re-plantings in the forty-odd years of its existence.

But when had Frank seen her there? He had not. His imagination worked, took the woman and put her, here only, where he wanted her. It did not bring him much comfort, it appeared, returned him back to saddened self.

> In plain, I am back where I was,
> > Wishing I could exult.
> Exultation is not in my nature.

'He was different,' Kathleen said, 'in some ways.'

'He had a sort of respect for you. I noticed it when I was quite young. Reverence.'

'I don't think so.'

'You never knew where you were with him. He could be marvellously entertaining. And always gentle. But sometimes you might not be there for all the notice he took. Daddy could be good company, and bounce us about, and tell us tales, but when he was busy he said so, showed he didn't want us, bawled at us. Not Frank. He went into his own world.' Helen smiled, brilliantly. 'I wonder if I'm making all this up.'

'That bit about "reverence", certainly. You must have got that from the sermons in church.'

'You're a clever woman.'

Then they smiled, touched hands.

As they stood on the university campus Helen mentioned *The Times* obituary notice on Francis.

'Harold thought it was just a shade grudging,' she said. A crowd of young women crossed the flagged courtyard, chattering in German. Helen rapidly explained about holiday conferences.

'Frank had a shot himself.'

'How?'

'Wrote his own obit. Fiercer than *The Times*, but just exactly like them. Provincial. Limitation of subject matter. Some flatness of language. Absence of the larger gestures. Awkwardness. But, but, but. Characterized by a deep sincerity, a single eye, an attachment to reality, a love of humanity and the townscapes of his Midland home. Oh, our Frank,' she smiled as she used her husband's phrase, 'was sharp all right. Shrewd as they come. He headed it, "Poet of the Prosaic!" ' '

'Did he show you this?'

'No, it was in a book he was writing. A prose book. He made out he was a patient in a lunatic asylum, and we all went visiting him. The obit. was on a loose leaf.'

'Will this be published?'

'We don't know. A man called Byrne is dealing with the agents. It's up to them. You make a little appearance. In the book. Or, at least, you get a mention. It's reported to Frank that you've won a scholarship to the high school. He says nothing, but Louise who's there snaps, "She'll be in the right company for the first time in her life." '

'That's unpleasant.'

'Probably. But not only about you, but about me as well.'

'She thought I was a snob, I take it.'

'Presumably.'

'And was she right?'

'What's it matter?' Kathleen shook with anger. 'When you're disturbed you take a kick at the nearest object. Louise was no exception.'

'Frank wrote it.'

'That makes it worse. As if you can't trust anybody. I don't suppose you can.'

Harold joined them for lunch in a staff dining room. Dons talked loudly about their holidays. They grumbled over money. One woman inquired about Harold's forthcoming book, seemed dashed to be given a firm date for its appearance. Kathleen enjoyed the meal in the clashing of crockery and cutlery, the smell of cooking. The atmosphere was both relaxed and noisy as these, the scholars, took to muddy coffee, then without too much enthusiasm returned to the afternoon's work. These people were thinking things out, though there was little sign of it, and how important their conclusions would be, if they reached them, she could not guess. But it was not unpleasant; she could see the attraction for her daughter. This closed society at their cheap, unpretentious meal represented a kind of stability. Break the group apart, and individuals would fret over work, ambitions, status, health, families, God knows what, but here with middle-aged waitresses who knew them, named them, doctored and professored them and were greeted by christian names in return as they served and cheered, there was an impression of progress, optimism, achievement made possible.

Kathleen belonged nowhere, except to her home, her garden, her husband. Jack was a club man: he had his peers, his dirty drinking pals, his work face, secretaries, mistresses, business associates, but she was self-dependent. Frank, like her, was cut off out of the land of the living, but in his case deliberately. His colleagues, his pupils liked him; he did not make himself unpopular, but his serious self was somewhere distanced, taking in, not giving out. Amongst the bonhomie Kathleen sat momentarily sad, chilled. Harold and Helen introduced her to friends; one dapper, grey-haired little man with a bow tie made quite a fuss of her, invited her over to his laboratories. The Kittos chaffed her afterwards on her conquest; this professor was a distinguished chemist, Fellow of the Royal Society, pro vice-chancellor, famous really. He did seem alive with his croaking voice, his frog's skin, and she had enjoyed standing by him as he pointed out buildings. He was dry, precise on costs, but she could imagine that in his office he'd make a pass, let his energy loose, run his hands up her skirt. She wondered how she'd reply, but it came to nothing, in spite of Helen's encouragement to spend an hour in 'those marvellous science blocks'. The professor said she was wise, grinned monkey-like, hoped to meet again, made off for his scarlet Audi and research.

'He's got money as well,' Helen warned.

Kathleen sat in the sunshine, well content, while her daughter looked about in the library. Nobody interrupted her. She watched workmen repairing a wall, a gardener mowing lawns, and became bored. If she could have lain flat on a lilo with fewer clothes on, she'd have managed. Now she dozed uncomfortably off to sleep, on a seat, woke with a jerk.

For a moment she did not know where she was. A seat in sunshine; lawns and vague concrete blocks, vita-glass windows, spartan stairways. Under the palest blue sky, the place stretched deserted, a landscape denuded and silenced. She widened her eyes to bring herself awake, but did not succeed. These buildings, this horizon, these gravel paths, had no connection with her. Her blankness of spirit was matched with desolation. Waste, barren lack of expectation weighed her down, prevented her from coherent thought, from determining her context. She seemed to herself miserably in a nondescript desert, without extremes of heat, but the more frightful for this moderation, a place of grey dust. She moved her legs; that was painful, but it did nothing to erase her misery. She was not shocked by her paralysis of will, but by the desolation, desiccation in herself, the knowledge of nothing accomplished in an inexplicable, dumb present, a future of dependence on the non-existent goodwill of others, without aim or achievement. Earth was pale as sky; the concrete of libraries, of lecture halls grey, unalive. The grass lacked greenness, moisture, lush growth. The walks were ruled colourlessly in an insipid landscape. Winds made no noise; no birds wheeled or swooped.

How long the period of sterility lasted or how it ended she could not say. She was locked there on the seat, capable of physical movement, but robbed of all senses but this flatness of despair. In the time she remembered words; she attributed them to her husband, but wispily, not to a figure of flesh and blood, without warmth, a faded writing on the wall. 'Who'd say a bloody word in my favour? Who'd I want to?' Pain, lasting trouble, terminal illness.

Nothing amounted to anything.

She, a prisoner, was forced to watch unhappening, displacement. Her husband had managed nothing. Neither had she.

Their total lack of ability or success was sketched in this campus with the square spareness of a Mondrian, but without his art. Art could give a flash of hope. Here in the dust, the pallor, infertility was all.

A small movement three yards away.

Two sparrows dabbed at a crust of bread. For a moment she watched without interest or grasp until she realized their firmness of outline, the strength of their drab colours, the vivacity of quarrel. She squinted, concentrating. The bread was nebbed up, dropped, pecked at.

She lifted her legs.

The sky was cheerfully blue, sunshine drenched. Buildings rose solid now, with shadows and weight, worthy of men. Trees grew in soil. All substantial. Without mist. Stone. Serene. Earth. Summer azure. People, not a few, walked about, talked, not always in English, hurrying on business and pleasure. The bricklayers persevered at their wall, though the groundsman had gone. This was a quiet afternoon in a decent place. Kathleen felt the warmth on her cheeks, her hands, through the clothes on her thighs.

Release. Relief.

She stretched her legs. The scars of desolation pained still, but bearably. Hopping sparrows were dappled, heads quick as mechanical toys. They took off together, in fright, at nothing, returned beaking the grass. When she began to stroll her legs dragged, a headache lurked behind her eyes, but she saw the world, touched, was part of it.

Somewhere behind a science block, she visited a series of hothouses, where tropical plants rampaged. Palms and screw pines. Cycas, bougainvillaea, brownea, ixora. Bamboo and banana labelled. A young woman in wellingtons sprayed the leaves, the mould, the aisles. Once she whirled her nozzle into a far corner at a young man bending over a bed. The girl grinned at Kathleen, face red with sun, eyelashes short gold. The heat and humidity overpowered, but fertility rampantly flourished. Fish slid about a tank at ground level. Exotic leaves writhed, their shapes carved into fantasies of huge, ridged, dripping overgrowth.

Kathleen let herself out.

Mild, temperate, easy. She could walk smartly now, was greeted once or twice, paused for a word with the gardener emptying his lawn-clippings. Lovely afternoon. Ay, they'd be praying for rain soon.

Helen appeared on time at their rendezvous, a neat folder under her arm. They'd just get a cup of coffee or a glass of orange before the refectory closed. Didn't want one? She eyed her mother. They sat in the foyer of the library under a bust of Aristotle, lettered in Greek, facing Plato. Harold appeared complaining smilingly.

'Don't you work together here?' Kathleen asked. They had never considered it. They showed suspicion, but that dissolved as they discussed some small errand they had both forgotten. They'd leave it.

Kathleen intervened; they were to go, do it now, the pair of them. She didn't mind sitting here with Plato and Aristotle. She might even think.

It was quiet. The one passer-by wore suede shoes.

She remembered a photograph she had taken. She and her two children, Francis and Louise with David had taken a walk in the local park, and at the side of a stream in a wintry wood she had snapped Francis, in topcoat and gum boots. He seemed alone in the darkness, looking upwards almost blindly, though the children dashed and shouted in and out of the stream, warned constantly by Louise.

This photograph, black and white, very still, humanity frozen out of the man, she had found tucked loosely into the manuscript of *Glory Begun Below*. It was not a good likeness of Francis, being too statuesque, too posed and upright. He was a hunched man, squinting at life, taking it in, drawing no attention to himself. This would have made a frontispiece for his *Collected Poems*; this was the picture of a poet, not of her brother-in-law. No children shouted near this man;

no wife nagged; no sister-in-law ordered him to stand still until she'd got the focal length right.

She'd turned it.

On the back he'd copied some music, ruling the lines carefully, the first three and a half bars of the right hand of Beethoven's A Flat Sonata, Op.110. It said so. Above and below were Beethoven's directions. *Moderato cantabile, molto espressivo. Piano, con amabilità.*

Kathleen did not know the piece, could not read the music. Francis, she remembered, played a little, listened to records, patronized recitals.

At the bottom of the card he had written firmly: 'I walked this wood with Beethoven.'

She could guess what it meant. He'd often marched here as a young man, perhaps while he was learning this sonata, or with some recording singing in his head.

I walked this wood with Beethoven.

17

Kathleen fumed at home.

She had written to Helen and now, beef in the oven, vegetable saucepans bubbling, waited for Jack's return. He had promised to be in for six; it was now twenty past and she had heard nothing. On the half-hour she rang his office, where he'd been working, got no reply. At six-forty-five she tried again, without result. Furiously she ate a spoilt meal, phoned the Leicester and Lincolnshire branches, but again went unanswered.

She washed the dishes angrily, dropped a plate. He had no right to treat her like this. The power of her anger took her aback. Her husband had recently acted with such decorum that this neglect smarted. A year ago she would have made sure he found little worth eating in the house on his return, and left it at that. He'd cut a sandwich, or change and drive to the club for a steak. Now and then he'd announce he'd already had dinner. 'Knew mine'd be on the compost heap when I got back,' he'd said.

By eight o'clock she fretted, tried two clubs, and desperately the office. No return. At eight-twenty a car she did not recognize hummed in the drive, and in the dusk a young policeman made for the door.

'Mrs Weldon?'

'Yes.'

'I'm afraid, madam, I've some rather bad news for you.' Her stomach turned. She propped herself on the door jamb as she invited the young man in. In her distress she noted the adverb 'rather'; it spoke hope. The constable stood at a stern ease, his flat cap with its check band correctly held. Her heart rioted. 'Your husband is in hospital.'

Chest emptied, throat full, she begged for details.

'He's burnt, madam. He was involved in a fire.'

'At his office? But the phone's working there. I rang . . .' Breath gave out. She leaned forward, left breast painfully on the table's edge.

'Can I get you a drink?' He'd laid down cap and gauntlets. His face was white, like a boy's, anxious, uncertain.

Her husband was burned. Even in the present horror it seemed unlikely. The policeman was not informative. Some sort of fire, in a private house, in Hollis Grove. There were two or three casualties. No, it wasn't the usual practice for the hospital to . . . They preferred a message to be brought personally. Now his expression was priggish, or comforting.

'How badly hurt is he?'

'Well, they said it was not serious. They . . . they . . . burns are nasty, but he'll be all right.'

She questioned. He did not know much. If she'd like to take things to the hospital, he'd been instructed to drive her down. Yes, he was on duty. Yes, she could go in her own car. Perhaps that was better. Things? Pyjamas, washing materials, towels, he thought. She felt sorry for him because he had been so vaguely briefed. The burns were superficial. She wondered why the devil he hadn't said this before. He looked about eighteen, with his shoulders back and his uncomfortable eyes. His boots were not large, but neither were they spotless.

'Now, madam, is there anything I can do?'

'No, thank you. I'll go straight down.'

'Are you sure you'll be . . . ?'

'Perfectly.'

He left, still stiffly. She packed a bag, saw to her face, drove fast to the hospital in the sparse, evening traffic. The light had gone; shop bulbs gleamed harshly. The porter was efficient, directed her to a ward, where a nurse waited.

Her husband lay, naked to the waist, hardly bandaged, though his bushy eyebrows were reduced, his front hair singed.

'Did they phone you?' he asked quickly.

She described the policeman's arrival. He spoke in a slurred voice, under sedation, but grinning. He'd seen this fire. Somebody was screaming. He'd walked in. His eyelids fell, his face sagged; he was barely able to keep awake. He wanted to talk to her, but could not manage it. Kathleen handed over her bag, demanded what else she should bring. The nurse rummaged, expressed satisfaction, knew nothing of the accident. He was not badly burnt, shock, asphyxiation. He'd been brought into casualty; there was one old lady seriously ill, but she was elsewhere. They talked; Jack slept. Useless to stay; he'd be asleep till morning.

This was the hospital where Frank had died. She never thought of it until she made her way out. Here was a different sector, newer; she seemed to be walking along a corridor of boards, a shed. At the main door, the waiting-room rows of chairs empty and unlighted, the man on duty did not even glance from the evening paper. His day had run down.

Outside it struck suddenly cold. She stood on her own, in the twisted yard. No parking. Ambulances only. Dr Peake-Bridges. The street glistened with damp, though it did not rain now. A wind chilled so that she was glad to reach her car. She sat, tapping her wedding ring on the steering wheel, gritting her teeth, unable to think, alive enough to dislike the rattle, not firm enough to desist. Her husband, face diminished by the damaged eyebrows, grinned sluggishly at her.

She had not been in the house five minutes before a journalist phoned. When she had offered him a sentence or two, he said,

'You don't know what happened, then?'

'No.'

'He didn't tell you?' She described his drowsiness. 'He rescued two old ladies.'

Now she pressed.

'He was walking along Hollis Grove. This house had caught fire. Somebody was screaming. He turned his rain-coat collar up, and went in. He brought one woman out.' The man read from notes. 'Then he went back, rescued the other one, wrapped up in a rug. She was bad. When he got outside the front door he keeled over, fell against the iron railings. Quite a crowd. But he just turned his collar up, they reckon, and strolled in.' The voice breathlessly cut the sense into short lengths, hardly believeing.

Jack.

'What was he doing there?' she demanded.

'No idea. Isn't it near his work? In he went, cool as an ice-cube.' The journalist sounded young and excited at the heroism. 'The others just stood there. He marched in at the front door.' He asked questions about Jack's business, but returned three times to his bravery, as if he wanted some confirmation from her, some award, or perhaps confirmation that her husband always acted thus.

She slept badly.

The local radio station was drily full of Jack's praise. One of the old ladies died in the night. A bystander had recorded his report. 'This gentleman just looked, took it all in, and got through that front door in no time. There was smoke as black as your hat, and screaming. But he went in there as steady as if he was walking to a wedding. Great flames. Smoke, you know.'

She searched the national paper, found nothing.

At nine her husband telephoned from the hospital to say he was going to discharge himself. He felt right as nine-pence, but he'd agreed to let the doctors examine him. Some-body'd bring him. He was supposed to go to bed, but he'd see.

Ten minutes later the reporter again. They were making a lead story of it. They'd eye-witness accounts, pictures. One of the two old ladies had died. Both over eighty. Sisters. He praised Jack again. She added her news. Could he interview?

At nine-thirty Judith and Alan Powis drove up.

They were breathless, gaping with admiration. They'd heard it on the Midland Home Service and then on the local. Judith said they must come straight across to see if there was anything they could do. They did a bitty cross-talk act, not sure of their sanity, expecting to be thrown out. They'd dashed here on impulse, had begun to regret it.

Kathleen sat them down, provided coffee, told them her all.

They questioned, excited as children, laughing, glad to be in on the act.

'It's marvellous to go in like that. Turning his collar up.'

She calmed them, asked about their concerns. She was glad of their company; their exuberance shrilled, but steadied her. Judith, who'd seemed so self-contained, blushed to the cheekbones with adventure. Her husband, a tall young man, would have shaken hands gladly with all the world. Yes, they'd made their minds up about New Zealand. She would stay.

'I don't know if we've done right.' Judith, the leading figure.

'But we've decided now.'

'Would you have split up with Mr Weldon?'

'I expect so. When I look back on my marriage, I don't really know what I have or haven't done. It seems such a short time. All gaps. Twenty-odd Christmases together. I doubt if I can recall ten. But you'll remember saying goodbye. And meeting.'

It sounded ridiculous, unconvincing, unappetizing even.

'He's a marvellous man.' Judith, breathless again. 'Would you have expected him to do something like this? I'm sure you would.'

Kathleen shook her head.

'Will he tell you about it?' Alan Powis asked.

'He might say something. Give me some bit of detail. I don't know. He boasts about things he hasn't . . . No, that's not fair, either.'

Kathleen realized that she looked on her husband in a new light. For how long she did not know, but this heroic action altered the relationship. It should not be so. Jack might have died. He'd collapsed; he had a constitution like iron, but he'd keeled over. A couple of minutes longer inside and he'd be in the mortuary this morning. Had he thought of that? When he turned his collar up?

Unable to sort it out, excitement swirling, she turned to the flushed young couple in relief. She plied them with coffee and sherry until they made fun of their year apart. That was as it should be, for they were serious, heart-sore and frightened of the sundering. Kathleen would have liked to question the girl about Jack, but dared not. She might let something out. This was an hour of shrieking laughter, of upraised glasses, of fortified truth.

The young couple left tipsily to do the week's shopping.

She called out to them, unwilling to let them go. Their youth suited the time; Judith's poise had been toppled by a giggling hero-worship, and it was good, acceptable. Alan drove off steadily enough.

No sooner had she reached the hall than David telephoned. She gave the news.

'He'll be pleased,' her nephew said. 'This puts him in my dad's class.'

She ought to have taken offence, could not.

'He always wanted to match old Francis,' David continued. 'He's said so. His business meant nothing in that way. And do you know why? Because he understood what making money entailed, he knew how to do it. Poetry was a mystery, which Francis had, and he hadn't. But hauling old biddies out of fires, when half the town hung about the pavement, that's put him among the angels.'

'Have you been drinking?'

'At this time on Saturday morning?'

'Might be last night's skinful.'

He tut-tutted.

'Friday night is for sex,' he announced. 'One thing at a time.'

They laughed; she felt weak standing there, dragged up a seat. Suddenly she was afraid she could not laugh without this enervation. She was not normal. She could weep easily. Carefully she composed her face, the set of her shoulders to speak into the telephone.

'Tell you one thing,' David said, 'I couldn't have done it. And I can't imagine how he could, either. It only takes about two minutes' worth of these cushion fillings burning to do you. Not like wood and feathers. And he'd know that. You're not telling me he wouldn't.'

The excitement that juvenated Judith Powis flashed in him.

'When he talked about the army,' she said, 'he boasted about skiving and dodging. He always kept his head down. "You don't argue with a bullet." He made out he was frightened, and sensible. He never mentions the Desert War now. Just says how cold it was at night; nothing about the fighting.'

He rang off, chirpy, but bustled into the house at twelve-thirty while she was waiting for Jack.

'Read all about it,' he said, splaying out the early edition of the evening paper. 'I had to go into town for this.' The headline type was huge. 'City Fire Rescue – One Dead. Director "Walks in".'

They put their heads together over the smudged picture of a front door and bow window. The text described how John James Weldon (55) had walked in without turning a hair. 'I have never seen anything like it,' said a neighbour, Mrs Evelyn Cree (38). 'It deserved the VC.' Smoke poured from windows and doors as Mr J. J. Weldon, managing director of Welcar Ltd, Weldon and Frost, Weldon Holdings, Geary Plastics (Leicester), Wakelin Transport, Lakin (Hucknall) Ltd, turned up his collar and battled his way in. He carried from the burning house Miss Letitia Smith (82) and returned for her older sister Miss Emma Smith (85). 'It was sheer heroism,' said Mrs Cree. Three in hospital, death of the elder lady. The story petered out.

'How's that?' David asked.

'All those phone calls, and then . . . that bit.'

'There's never much in the first edition. And by this evening, even that might be shifted.' They laughed together over the stilted phraseology. 'It was heroic, just like the television.' An eye-witness. Miss Smith and Mr Weldon both said to be comfortable by a spokesman at the General Hospital.

Jack arrived. They displayed their sheet.

'No photograph,' David said, staring. His uncle looked comical, with eyebrows singed flat, front hair uneven, skin mottled.

'Good job.' Jack said he was hungry, glad, by God, to be at home. David refused lunch, but chatted for a while as Kathleen concluded in the kitchen. She complained that they might join her or shout up, but the men made no move. 'I've got to go easy for a day or two, the quacks said,' he bawled as she passed through.

'What's wrong with you?'

'Shock.'

She thought he seemed strained, with his hairless face, bloodless.

'See that you do then,' she warned.

David stayed till the meal was on the table, then banged his way out of the door. His voice shouted bright, but hoarse, as if he couldn't temper it to the occasion. Jack ate heartily for a few mouthfuls, then toyed with his meal.

'Don't know what's up with me.'

'Are you under sedation?'

'Shouldn't think so. They let me drive home. They wouldn't if they'd drugged me up to the eyeballs.'

'How did you feel? In the car?'

'Normal.' But he stared at his saucy plate in dismay. 'I'm tired now.'

'You should go to bed this afternoon.'

'I will. I've got some tablets.'

His expression was as foreign as the singeing. Something went on just beyond his comprehension. He would have liked to please her, to play the trencherman, to joke, but he could not. A ghost of himself, he grinned at her, Rather slowly, lethargically, he gave an account of his contact this morning with the media; he had done his utmost, but they seemed insatiable.

'I can't understand why they need so many men just to go over the same bit of information. It's ridiculous.'

She packed him off to bed where he slept, heavily, flushed, all of a heap. Every half-hour she ran upstairs, straightened the edge of a sheet. He did not budge. In between she answered the phone. Acquaintances rang, had to be staunched. Three secretaries were breathlessly similar from three counties. The Powises tried again, making sure he was home, asking to do something, seemingly dashed to learn Jack was in bed, unfit. They needed triumph not trouble.

'Will he be all right?' Judith. The two were in a telephone box at the end of the street. It cheered Kathleen to think of them, Saturday-smart, together.

'I expect so.'

'I can't think of him as ill. Can you?' The question tailed off. 'I mean I see him as full of life.'

'It quietened him.'

'I'm not surprised.' Judith offered sentences about the danger of new materials. The girl was disturbed. She bothered that something had hurt Jack; she'd say a word, did so, in his favour, added an eloquent, tortured silence of tribute.

'He's a somebody,' Kathleen said. A bait.

'Yes, he is. There aren't many who'd do what he did. I don't think I know anybody.'

'I didn't think I did.'

Now they laughed. Cissie rang the doorbell, insisted on entry, had to hear the tale.

'He's always been a mad-head. He'd shin up trees like a monkey. I remember him high-diving into the old quarry. Terrified me. And then he borrowed a lad's bike to take some girl on the crossbar. My dad saw them up the park. "You'll kill yourself, you little hooligan. Get off." But he just shouted, "Can't. No brakes." Our dad was fuming. Always the same.'

Cecilia enjoyed herself with her brother's riotous past. How he stood drunk in the yard when he was fourteen, throwing stones at her window. 'And there was a girl called Betty Burchfield. Her dad came round to warn our Jack off. He was a big, heavy man, but Jack just hit him, right in the belly. You never heard such a goings-on. He revelled in it. Just in his eye-holes. Now our Frank was the very opposite, quiet as the dead. But I think he relished it. What our Jack was up to. I'm sure he did. Though Jack had left home when Frank was little; there were six, seven years between them.'

This excited reminiscence wasted an hour, but Jack slept on. Cecilia departed strutting, proud of her brother. As she left, she picked up the evening paper, scrabbled for her glasses to see Jack's photograph, which now held large pride of place.

'I don't know what his dad would have said.'

'He'd have been proud, wouldn't he?'

'You never knew with him. He was a bit jealous of Jack.'

Up in the bedroom the invalid roused himself sufficiently to read the newspaper account and eat a ladylike tea. Then he put his head down, willingly.

'I feel like death.'

'There's always a drawback.'

She sat downstairs and found herself dozing in front of the television set. At eight o'clock David reappeared, dressed for Saturday, but very soberly. When she complimented him, he said,

'What my dad used to call a snogging suit.'

'Your Aunt Cissie said that Grandfather Weldon would have been jealous of what your uncle's done.'

'She'd say anything, that woman. I feel sorry for her,

though, with those three. It's no wonder she married old Scotch-mist Hooper. You wouldn't know he was there if it wasn't for his indigestion.'

'I've been thinking . . .'

'Don't for Christ's sake do that, or you'll rupture yourself.' This bank clerk was a Weldon, straight-backed, ready and awkward tongued. 'Go on. Let's have it.'

She explained how this affair had beaten energy out of her.

'I don't like to see,' she pointed upstairs, 'him as he is.'

'Sedation.' Forcibly knowledgeable. 'You'll notice the difference tomorrow.'

'I suppose so. I can't help thinking back. The years we've been married. I wonder if he's done something of this sort somewhere else.'

'You'd have heard. He'd have told you.'

'He's hardly said a word.' She puckered her forehead. 'I never expected anything like it, but Cissie seemed to.'

'She would.'

'When I look back it's nothing but loose ends. Nothing ties up.'

'Come on, then,' David said, mocking her. 'Tell us what you do want.'

'Don't you think there ought to be some sort of pattern? So we can judge what somebody's likely to do?'

'Isn't there?'

'Not that I can see. It all seems haphazard. Chance and compromise. And even when you insist, stick to a principle, the whole thing's beyond your control.'

'You didn't guess, then,' David asked, 'that my father was going to be a poet? You knew him, didn't you, before you met Jack? Or so he said.'

'He wrote poems. I knew that. I saw some. But I didn't know he – whether he was any good.'

'You didn't want to influence him, affect them?'

'Not his poems. I didn't bother my head about them much, I can tell you.'

'He didn't look like a poet? Or act like one?'

'He was a teacher at the school I was at. An interesting young man. In some ways the most interesting I'd met. But, well, indecisive, made me furious.'

'You didn't want to make him a great poet? Writing for you?'

'I'd no idea. If anybody had told me that twenty-six years later Frank would be famous as a poet, I might have believed it. Just as I might have believed it if they told me he'd be dead.'

'But you didn't want to influence him?'

'I wanted to influence all my boy friends.'

'Do you think you helped make Frank what he became?'

She looked at David, grey-suited and sober-minded, wondering why he conducted this investigation.

'To some small extent. I'll give you that. But with dozens, hundreds of others.'

'That's not altogether how he saw it.'

'What's that mean?'

'He once said,' David spoke quite briskly, nearly mumbling, unostentatious, 'he was ticking me off at the time for something I wanted and couldn't have, that he'd asked you to marry him. "She wouldn't. It altered everything. But I survived." I didn't forget that, because it was very unlike him. He never let much of himself out. He just said it.'

'Oh.'

'Yes, you can "oh" now. I never questioned him. He wouldn't have answered, sent me off with a flea in my ear anyway.'

'I see.' She did not. 'Have you ever written poems?'

'Yes, I have.'

'Were they any good?'

'No.' He screwed his mouth. 'Why has Jack done so well? Those two have made their mark, considering where they started. Jack's produced business; he's got his factory, his offices, his lorries. He helps the export drive. Makes jobs.

He lives well. He's coined a bob or two.' Dad's phrase. 'Now why is it? Were they beating their father at his own games? Power, not poetry; being somebody who counted. Or did it come about through you? You ditched one, accepted the other, made the pair of them? It's interesting.'

The last, flabby sentence, for the school debating society, took the edge off his fervid questions, left him younger.

'Don't know,' she said.

'Don't care, either.'

'Yes, I do. But I can't answer. It's not as simple as you put it. This energy may be inherited. A propensity to excel.' That sounded flatulent.

'Which do you prefer? Jack's money or Dad's poetry? You couldn't live on that.' He goaded her, she thought, wondered why. Perhaps because of the naked girl on the settee? Or the thinness of his father's legacy? Or mere daily distress?

'It's not much of a choice,' she said.

'Make it.' Stern, sergeant-majoring.

'I can't, and certainly I won't just to pass an idle hour for you. I don't understand it, or myself for that matter. Frank's poetry's more important, but that may have disappeared in a few years except for the second-hand bookshops. But I couldn't have lived on it, you're right. It wouldn't have kept me in shoes.'

'So you're selfish?'

'Yes, I am. As well you know. Like everybody else. But the thing about the Weldons is this. They had a few dogmas or principles which stuck out. Like salients. They weren't even of necessity good, but the men didn't depart from them. In certain fields they wanted their own way, and they got it by hook or by crook. The old man wasn't contradicted in the office or at home. Frank wrote until he had satisfied himself. Jack wasn't to be beaten in a deal, and wouldn't stop working until he was sure he'd clinched it or lost it. They worked; they wouldn't be pushed about in those parts of their life that counted.'

'Didn't this carry over into minor matters?'

'With the old man, yes. Though I'm not sure. I kept out of his reach. But the other two, awkward as they are, will give in like lambs. It's what I like most about Jack.' She spoke as if Frank lived.

It sounded plausible enough. David looked impressed. He in no way resembled his father, especially now. Nor did he appear much like her stereotype of him, the long-haired yobbo, smoker, rake, pop addict. He was a bank clerk, with a mischievous expression who stripped off with women and did not lock the doors.

'I shall have to talk to you again,' he said, wishing her good evening. 'You come up with some not bad ideas.'

He left her the newspaper he'd brought. Who'd say a word in his favour? She would. She wondered why she'd had so little interest in him before. Did he have to flash his sex for her to see his head?

'Such as what?' she asked as he made for the door. She thought, comically.

'I told you once that I was reading *Great Expectations*. For "O" level, and you said it tied up too neatly. It upset you, it was so clever and neat. I'd never heard anybody criticize Dickens before. I told my teacher, and he said, "That's its strength." I thought about it. You were right. It did get across me. But I wouldn't have seen it if you hadn't said so.'

'Did you tell Frank?'

'I asked him. I hadn't much hope. He said, "Shouldn't be surprised." I don't think it interested him.'

'Should it?' she asked.

'He'd his own concerns, that man.'

He waved, was legging it down the drive, laughing. She wanted to question him, stood for some minutes in the coolish dark, before making her way upstairs, where her husband opted for an unlikely cup of cocoa.

18

Next day Jack was up and about.

At nine-fifteen Helen rang. She'd seen a short paragraph in the *Sunday Express* about her father's exploit. Giving up the phone, Kathleen listened to her husband, but learnt little.

'Fancy them having the *Express*,' Jack said.

At eleven he drove down to his office, but returned inside an hour. In the afternoon he helped her in the garden, wheeling and tipping compost. Not until the evening did she get information out of him, and then only by direct questions.

She came down from a bath, found him staring at the restlessly flashed faces of hymn singers on television. He sat still, whisky in hand, whistled with shrill sweetness Vaughan Williams's 'Sine Nomine', did not smoke. She waited until credits rushed up the screen.

'Aren't you going to say anything, then?' she asked.

'You've done well,' he answered. 'Bottling it up.'

'Do you want to tell me?'

'You want to hear, I know that.' But he switched the television off. 'I don't know why I went out that afternoon. Don't usually. And there was plenty to do. But it looked sunny. There was a red creeper on one of the old houses opposite, bright scarlet. So I called out to Linda to see if they'd done the mail. "I'll post it," I said. She said, "It's not everything", and that decided me. She'd contradict God. I put my raincoat on. Don't know why. Usually it's in the car. And it was sunny. I posted the letters, and walked down by Hollis Grove. There was a bit of a crowd, and some shouting.'

When he'd arrived, he'd learnt that the fire brigade was on the way. He asked about the screaming. 'Must be them as live there.' Then he'd gone in. He'd pushed through people at the gate. Smoke came out of the open front of a bow window, and the front door.

'Were you afraid?' She was, to interrupt.

'Never thought about it. Walked up the path to the door. Didn't cross my mind. If there'd been a raging inferno when I got there, I'd have stopped. There wasn't. Bit of smoke.'

He'd shoved the front door open with his shoulder, stepped into a passage way perhaps five yards long, dark and window-less, leading to straight stairs. There was smoke, but not too thick. The two old ladies shouted; one hung on to the newel post as if she tried to pull it over; the other sat on the bottom step. He'd ordered them outside. The one on the step stopped screaming to say something about a cat.

'Why was she sitting there?'

'Eh, damned if I know. She was bawling and stamping her feet. Like a kid in a tantrum.'

'Panic, perhaps.'

Neither woman had moved, so he picked the one up from the stairs and carted her outside. She weighed next to nothing, didn't struggle, seemed glad to be taken. He handed her over to a couple of young men who'd advanced up the path. On his way back he'd noticed a towel on a coat rack on the wall and had snatched it down, wrapped it round his head. He could see nothing of the other old woman. She did not scream.

'You didn't think of turning back, then?'

'No. The smoke was worse. But there weren't any flames or heat.'

'But there might have been?'

'Never crossed my mind.'

He'd moved forward to the end of the passage.

The old lady knelt in the front room, squatted on all fours. Now she made no noise. There was a waste-paper basket pothering smoke, and an armchair. The carpet smouldered, and a drawn curtain over an alcove. The woman squatted there staring, swaying. He called out. She nudged forward. He shoved the chair aside to pick her up, and fire leaped, dashed flame straight into his face.

'Did it hurt?'

'It was too quick, like when you cut yourself. It's done, you're splashed with blood before you realize what's happened. I fell over. It did my eyes and hair. The towel saved a bit.' He pointed at the singeing.

He picked up the woman by her middle, kneed her like a small doll into his arms, about-turned. At the door his lungs heaved rebellion so that he thought he'd been struck, so violent was the spasm. He turned left, catching legs on the upright, staggered. Smoke thickened. Ahead the rectangle of light contracted, buckled. His legs sagged. He lunged.

'Were you frightened?'

'I didn't think I could manage it. I was robbed. I'd no strength.'

'You mean . . . ?'

'I was too dizzy to mean anything. One side of that door I'd been right as ninepence, a bit scorched, the other I was a goner. I can hardly believe it now, that that was it.'

'What did you do?'

'I swore, cussed it.'

'What did you say?' She laughed to cover her own violence of distress. He'd sworn. Damned the fire. Nothing but in his mind.

Yer bogger, and he'd toppled on. Pace on sinking stagger, from one wall to the other side, head spinning, eyes gummy with tears, dry, dry, without breath, weakened, coffin-wood. He'd balanced on the threshold, galloped three steps. Hands relieved him of the body and thus of balance and he'd pitched forward into the two feet border, the uncut lawn, the railings, a privet bush.

'Were you unconscious?'

'Out for the count.'

'When did you come round?'

'Not long. They were rolling me over to get me on to the pavement. I felt like death. Burnt. And my lungs scraped out and my face melted. I couldn't tell what people said. They shouted enough. They stretchered me, gave me oxygen. I passed out again in the ambulance. I felt as if I'd been turned inside out, and they'd slapped my stomach on my face.'

It had been unpleasant at the hospital, and not quick, he'd thought. He still couldn't hear the talk. A fierce crackling like a tinder fire raked his head. They worked on him. He had answered questions.

'How could you if you couldn't hear?'

'God knows. I did, they tell me.'

They injected and examined, touched and settled. He'd gone beyond them, these young fellows in white coats. They'd cleared him out, scraped his lungs, dazzled him steadily into bed. And that bloody office had closed its doors at five-thirty, shut the shop and pissed off regardless.

'What do you expect? They'd thought you'd done the same.'

'They know me better than that.'

'Obviously they don't.'

As he'd lain out on the turf he'd been outside himself, hurt, maimed, but living an angel's life, beyond the humdrum, drifting like smoke, in a flame of existence, without frame, in a variable geometry that had no co-ordinates of work, responsibility, marriage, even embarrassment. Hair shortened by the one leap of fire, he stretched in the street, their hero, his own no-man.

'I suppose it was the cushions that choked you? They're made of some synthetic stuff, aren't they, that'll kill in a minute or so once it's afire?'

'Something clobbered me.'

'That frightened you?' She had to pry, to reduce.

'It finished me. It filled me with poison. I was done. My chest was chocka with venom and cement.'

The front-door bell rang.

'Who the bloody hell's that?' Jack asked, cheerfully. Kathleen went out in no hurry. Eight o'clock on Sunday.

'It's us, mummy.'

There smiling, trim as you please, seemingly tall in a light trouser suit, husband behind her shoulder bag, stood Helen.

'What on earth . . . ?'

'We came to see Daddy. How is he?'

'You rang this morning.'

The hall echoed their voices in duet. Harold murmured a comforting bass, *piano e legato*.

'It's Helen,' Kathleen called. Her daughter dashed into the room, but stopped a yard from her father, repelled perhaps by the bald comicality. Then she launched herself at him, for a cheek kiss.

'What have you been doing?' She managed the upper-class public shriek to perfection. Her father wagged a finger.

'What are you two doing reading the *Express*?' he asked.

'We don't usually . . .' Harold began.

'*Crossroads*, next,' Jack said, a naked ape.

They sat together.

'I could not keep her quiet,' Harold said. 'There was nothing for it, but to get in the car and come.'

'Have you got to go back tonight?'

'Yes. Harold has a lecture at ten tomorrow.'

'Stop the night, then, and get up at the crack of dawn.'

'That would mean Mummy would have to.'

'She'd love it.'

'She would not.'

Kathleen went out for sandwiches, drinks. She did not try to listen, but Helen's emphases were paramount. But this smart authoritarian could not sit at home, had made her husband drive for three hours up the motorway because . . . Because?

When she sat down she learnt that Harold was pleased with his wife for this daughterly concern. Helen, as usual, was more enigmatic, giving little clue whether she'd come to check her father's health and safety or because he'd become extraordinary, a hero. She talked, she banged questions about, but her plangency was stained with irony; she cheered with reservations.

'You should let us know,' she said, 'when you're going in for things like this.'

'I will, next time.'

'We were stunned,' Harold. 'In our mild way. Car accidents happen now to people we know, but not anything of this order.'

'It's not murder,' Kathleen protested.

'No, but it has that sort of rarity. Statistically, in our milieu.'

'We approve,' Helen said.

'I wouldn't have done it otherwise.'

It was difficult to make them out, but they talked and sipped and ate and laughed and kept an eye on the clock. Helen described eccentric neighbours, half-day outings to consult local historians, her husband's progress on the academic ladder. An American university had made tentative, encouraging sounds; there'd be real advantages.

'To go for good?' Kathleen asked.

'Why not?'

This girl would push her husband somewhere, and soon. She had the Weldon fire. Dr Kitto would not be allowed to settle for a readership and one good book. He'd make his mark, or else. Else what? What were Helen's sanctions, her blackmail? One could not guess from his restrained, balanced periods or the girl's more violent, almost hectoring determination expressed in middle-class vowels and jargon. Grandpa would have approved once he'd accustomed himself to the surface style.

'You rescued somebody before.' Helen spoke suddenly after a silence when all had seemed content with the lifting of glasses, the stretching of satisfied limbs.

Jack grimaced.

'Where did you get that from?' he asked.

'Uncle Frank. He said to me once, "Your dad has done two things most of us haven't. One's find a murder; the other's saving a life." We were walking down Bannerman Road. I was coming from the bus; I'd been at the school play. It was *Macbeth*, and awful. Played by girls, you can imagine. But I said to him, "I don't know what it's like to plan a murder. I'd like to kill some people sometimes, but that's momentary. I couldn't prepare it." I talked like that to him. I always did. I felt I had to say something. Speaking to him was like writing an essay. You had to try to be out of the ordinary.'

'Haydn put on his best suit to compose,' Harold said, very calm, very far off.

'And you know that slow, breathy way, nasal, that Frank had. He said that about Dad.'

'What was the point?' Harold again, pained.

'I think he agreed with me. Most of us don't have that experience, or even the imagination to cope with it. But daddy had trespassed outside, into the abnormal. He knew something we didn't, something parallel to planning a murder. And I think that's right and important.'

'How "important"?' Harold.

'It's not often one has the chance to examine, or even talk about, extremes of human behaviour. When one does one should first recognize what's been at stake.'

'Do you think that most human beings once or twice in their life experience these extremes?'

'I wouldn't like to say. It would depend on your definition. But first-hand acquaintance with murder, or saving life, must be fairly rare?'

'I was thinking of soldiers,' Harold said. 'Killing could become almost commonplace. And there are quite a number of men we know who served in fighting units.'

Jack showed no interest, sat back, froggily.

'Who did you save, Jack?' Kathleen demanded. Helen

looked offended, not pleased to have the parenthetical dialogue shortened, when she had that question ready, unforgotten until its time ripened, matured by an unhurried, academic approval.

'Ahhr,' Jack said.

'He snatched a boy off a railway line.' Helen, in a cold voice. 'On Basford station.'

'When was that?' Kathleen.

'The child fell off the platform just when a train was coming in.' Helen again, and then they sat in silence, each concerned for the self. The lack of speech seemed like an orchestral climax, every instrument at violence and the searing blaze a unity.

'Come on, then.' Kathleen was first to recover. Helen waved her father on.

'He tumbled off. And he just knelt there, didn't get up.'

'And you?'

'I scrambled down, pulled him over to the other track.'

'How near was the train?'

'It was up to the platform. Not too far.'

Again the silence, while they considered. Kathleen, bruised, wondered what was in Jack's head this minute. He looked crumpled in his chair, fat, unstiffened.

'Would he have been killed?' Harold put the question for them, mildly, without offence, a necessity.

'If he'd gone down flat between the rails the train might have gone over him. Wouldn't have been pleasant. Wouldn't like a fire-box going over me, or a length of coupling chain. He wasn't very big. Don't know why he didn't up himself.'

'The surprise perhaps. Suddenly finding oneself on the track,' Harold said. 'How did he fall?'

'He could only have been a yard away, but I couldn't tell you. First I saw he was there, on his hands and knees, not moving.'

'And you jumped?' Helen.

'Must have.'

'Without thinking?'

'I seem to remember considering it. There wasn't much time. I might be wrong? But when I think about it now I seem to be asking myself, judging it, you know.'

'Then you went?' Kathleen.

There was no answer; they had it already. He'd snatched the lad up, and stood as the train squealed at their turned backs.

'God. How did you feel?' Helen asked.

'Pleased. Dizzy.'

'And the boy?' Harold.

'A cut knee. It bled. Gave his mother something to do.'

'Well, I've never heard this before.' Kathleen spoke tartly, if not denying, nor doubting.

'Before we were married. Before I went in the army.'

'You never told me.'

'You never asked.'

'Nor did Frank, or you, Helen, or anybody else. Did they reward you, or anything?'

'I got a certificate.'

'Where is it?'

'No idea.'

'And is that all you think of it, then?' Kathleen the fish-wife. The guests laughed awkwardly, fell silent, studied glasses, shoes, carpets. 'How did Frank know about this, then? Was he there?'

Jack did not answer. He smiled at his daughter mischievously, would have put thumbs under his lapels to waggle his fingers. In spite of his weight, he seemed a youth now, ready for a bust-up anywhere with anybody. The two young people did their social best with sentences on bravery, modesty, neatly dovetailed, relevant but pointed elsewhere. Jack interrupted and the youthful image disappeared. He spoke hoarsely, clearing phlegm.

'I'm sorry our Frank's gone. There was nobody like him in the world.'

They looked askance. This man would revert to seriousness, would not be saved. Harold began on the uniqueness of every human being. As he spoke, and the drift seemed sensible, the level voice emphasized the triviality of intention, as if one lectured on first-aid in a city devastated by nuclear bombs. Yet it was Jack who nodded agreement. Perhaps he felt embarrassment at his own statement, its exaggerated nature, or his earlier confessions.

'Why was Frank so good?' Helen asked Harold and silenced him.

Jack's face was grey; his hand shook. Harold stood by the mantelpiece eyeing a ridiculous, bulbous paperweight. Helen swooped alongside her father.

'Don't you think Daddy should go to bed?'

The girl stood fiercely, fighting fit. Her father, feet out, reached up and took her hand. Caught like that, she blushed, face, neck, arms down to the held fingers.

The women fetched biscuits, oatcakes, scones, made mugs of chocolate, milky and unsweetened.

'It's like Christmas,' Harold said.

'That remark's not like you,' his wife chaffed.

'We are all unique.' Jack stumbled on his last word.

While the others feasted, Kathleen switched on the electric blanket on her husband's bed. Harold insisted on washing the dishes before he and Helen left at ten.

'We'd like to stay,' he said, 'but it'll be the small hours as it is.'

'We like to see you.' Jack made the effort.

'We like to come.'

Jack leaned on the door post, but waited outside until the tail lamps turned from the drive. He moved heavily, sighing.

'Does you good,' he told Kathleen.

'I think she improves. She's still got some way to go. Off to bed, hero.' He turned round and saluted, did a step or two upwards. 'And I might have died without knowing.'

'That she improves?'

'No. That you went about snatching children off railway lines.'

'Surprised our Frank didn't say anything.' He stumped upwards.

'Why?'

'Couldn't keep anything to himself, except about himself. That's what a bloody poet does.'

'And that's nice,' she stopped.

He turned round on the landing.

'I feel rotten.'

'I know that,' she answered. 'Get yourself into bed.'

'Are you coming?'

'Soon. Are you scared, then?'

He grinned, shook his fist, went on, slapping the banister with a flat hand at each change of tread.

Downstairs she turned out lights, decided against sitting down to television, invented small chores to keep her on her feet before she went to see her husband.

He sat upright, pyjama collar awry.

'I didn't take my teeth out,' he said. She returned from the bathroom with a glass of water. He dropped his dentures.

'Husbands,' she said with affection. 'How do you feel?'

'Not so bad now I'm in.'

'Have you taken your sleeping tablets?'

'No.'

Again she made for the bathroom and a second glass. He swallowed the capsule, raising his water in a toast.

'Anything else, my lord?'

Closing the bedroom door, she went downstairs again and locked up. For some minutes she stood at a small window. In the garden was a blue spruce perhaps two and a half feet high, very solid, very regular. Frank had one almost its twin in his garden, hidden from the house so that one needed to descend to the street to see it. Without interference, given time both would be huge.

> Give me a tree's growth when
>   Mine sags or twists.
> Dead, it survives, sturdily then
>   Crucifies its Christs.

She could see the lamps in the street, undisturbed. When first they had lived here, the street lights were suspended on wires and swung in the wind so that night brought the shift of shadow patches in intermittent brightness. Now concrete posts shone efficiently, drying the pools of darkness. It was safer for drivers, but she preferred the light whanging through foliage or reflected uneasily on the wet branches of trees in winter.

Upstairs, the house safely locked, she made for a top-floor window.

Again the sodium lights, the garden trees, and beyond all the fields that symbolized her husband and brother. Soon they'd be gone, built over into council estates without amenities so that at night the vandals would burn down the schools, trample the few planted gardens, break ornamental trees to a yard's ruined height. Where Jack had run wild with the rabbits and the girls, where Frank had walked with his stunting dreams, the new generation of dissidents were mindless, demonstrating conformity of graffiti with their aerosol sprays, mugging and slugging because they could not bear dad's breathing as he slumped over the television set.

She could not see.

Houses already erected traced pretty lines of light. The fields were blots of darkness, black holes. She remembered her own childhood in the Home Counties and for the moment felt glacially lonely, exiled, out of it in a world of strange languages, beliefs, customs. She wished she could see David's cottage, to check on the natives there, but it was impossible. Francis could now only repeat himself. She tried to fetch back some lines of his:

> We touch, not see the blackening ghosts
> Dark in our darkness.

It was not hell, not Hades, but himself he tried to reach. Clouds covered the sky, unevenly; in one ragged gap a star dimly blinked. Her father had a monkey puzzle in his front garden, neat and ugly. It died inconveniently from the bottom, but it represented his marriage for he'd planted it in the first year. He kept his privet trimmed to right angles and his un-walked grass was never less than dark green.

She smiled. He and her mother had died unobtrusively within three months of each other, just before Fred was born. The Burtons. Frederick James Burton Weldon. Awkward as the monkey puzzle. He'd not rung. He'd not known. David was more of a son, now. Helen would be in Northamptonshire staring down the motorway, as Harold efficiently, brilliantly exceeded the speed limit. David would be at, in, love. Fred, there was no telling. She pressed her cheek to the cold pane. She stood alone, stood for the solitary. Her eyes strained into the black vacuum of fields. What mark had Jack left there? Or Frank? He had not mentioned them in his book; they were hidden by the town buildings from his own windows. She would go there, with a lying camera, before the county council sprawled its civilization further across, and take Judith Powis so that in New Zealand the girl would remember grass-tumps, a cold wind, dullness.

Kathleen liked the modesty of the conceit.

She descended a storey in darkness. Jack was asleep, snoring, turning once heavily.

Tired, she made for her own room. An aeroplane crossed the sky as an ambulance signalled rescue. Men were about, if only just.

She shut her door.